"WHAT IS YOUR ORIGIN, AND WHAT IS YOUR OCCUPATION?"

I think this over. "I'm a teacher. Others came this way, and I'd like to join them."

"ARE YOUR PART OF SHIP CONTROL?"

I don't think so. "No," I say.

"YOU'RE IN THE OUTER REGIONS OF HULL ZERO ONE. IT IS NOT SAFE HERE."

Praise for

HULL ZERO THREE

"Not for those who prefer their space opera simple-minded, this beautifully written tale where nothing is as it seems will please readers with a well-developed sense of wonder."
—*Publishers Weekly* (Starred Review)

"One of Bear's most thought-provoking and well-crafted novels to date."   —*Booklist*

"Bear's a pro who knows his way around a starship's bulkhead and keeps the narrative taut and suspenseful. Importantly, he leavens his hero's grim steel-and-space ordeal with flashes of lyrical language and imagery to evoke the world that he has lost—and that he hopes to find again."   —NPR

"Greg Bear is one contemporary master of the old ways, and in HULL ZERO THREE he gives the generation starship theme—crystallized beautifully by Robert Heinlein in 1941's *Universe*—a vigorous makeover."   —bn.com

"I loved HULL ZERO THREE—this book reminds me of why I fell in love with science fiction in the first place. Searing questions of humanity, a good old-fashioned riddle of a plot, and excellent conceptualization make HULL ZERO THREE more than worth the effort."   —thebooksmugglers.com

"A menacing wonderland of a ship."   —Marc Laidlaw

"HULL ZERO THREE is a lean, mean, supercharged sense-of-wonder engine."   —Alastair Reynolds

"HULL ZERO THREE is a grand adventure of scientific discovery in the tradition of *Orphans of the Sky* and *Rendezvous with Rama*—by turns chilling and touching, it poses challenging questions about what it means to be human."

—Charlie Stross

"Greg Bear's voice is a resonant, clear chord of quality binding some of the best SF of the twentieth century to the short list of science-savvy, sophisticated, top-notch speculative fiction of the twenty-first. More than a grace note, HULL ZERO THREE is a compelling allegro in the growing symphony of Greg Bear's finest work."

—Dan Simmons

By GREG BEAR

Hegira
Beyond Heaven's River
Psychlone
Strength of Stones
The Wind from a Burning Woman (collection)
Corona
Songs of Earth and Power
Blood Music
Eon
The Forge of God
Tangents (collection)
Sleepside Story
Queen of Angels
Eternity
Anvil of Stars
Bear's Fantasies
Heads
Moving Mars
New Legends (anthology)
Dinosaur Summer
Foundation and Chaos
Slant
Darwin's Radio
Collected Stories of Greg Bear
Vitals
Rogue Planet
Darwin's Children
Dead Lines
Quantico
City at the End of Time
Mariposa
Hull Zero Three

HULL ZERO THREE

GREG BEAR

orbit

www.orbitbooks.net

Copyright © 2010 by Greg Bear
Excerpt from *Leviathan Wakes* Copyright © 2011 by
James S.A. Corey

Orbit
Hachette Book Group
237 Park Avenue, New York, NY 10017
www.HachetteBookGroup.com

Originally published in hardcover by Orbit.

First Trade Edition: October 2011

Orbit is an imprint of Hachette Book Group, Inc.
The Orbit name and logo are trademarks of Little, Brown
Book Group Limited.

The publisher is not responsible for websites (or their content)
that are not owned by the publisher.

The Library of Congress has cataloged the hardcover
edition as follows:
Bear, Greg.
  Hull zero three / Greg Bear.
    p. cm.
  ISBN 978-0-316-07281-6
  1. Deep space—Fiction.   I. Title.
  PS3552.E157H85 2010
  813'.54—dc22

                    2010016421

      10 9 8 7 6 5 4 3 2 1

Printed in the United States of America

ISBN 978-0-316-07280-9 (pbk)

FOR VINCE GERARDIS,
Master of the Big Idea

HULL
ZERO
THREE

PART ONE
- - - - - -
THE FLESH

- - -

Cloud modest, the planet covers herself.

Our chosen is perfect—more than we could have hoped for. Rolling beneath, she slips aside her creamy white veil to reveal the sensuous richness of blue water, brown and tan prairies, yellow desert, a wrinkled youth of gray mountains hemmed by forest so green it is almost black—and the brilliant emerald sward of spring pastures.

Impossibly rich.

My flesh is partner to the long journey. Like a hovering angel, I look down upon the dazzling surface and yearn. All the springs of my youth flow toward this new Earth. A long limb of dawn in the east—how lovely! Our world turns wisely widdershins—the best of luck. There are two moons, one close in, the second much farther out and large enough for icy mountains under a thin atmosphere. We will explore that other promise once we are established *here*.

We—dozens of us, so many gathering in the observation

blister, finally bathing in real light! There is sweet joy in voices from real lungs and tongues and lips—and such language! Ship language and Dreamtime-speak all musically mixed. So many friends and more to come. Our laughter is giddy.

We want to spread and lock limbs. We want to couple. We are eager to meet children as yet unconceived—eager to hurry them along so they can share this beauty with proud parents.

We!

Kinetic, no longer pent up or potential...The long centuries are over.

We!

We are *here*!

Planters and seedships have descended before we came awake. They have analyzed and returned with the facts. Our chemistry now matches this world's.

Fons et origo.

Fountainhead.

I don't remember the name we've chosen, it's on the tip of my tongue—not that it matters. I'm sure it is a beautiful name.

We form teams, holding hands in waving, weightless lines in the blister, calling to each other using our Dreamtime names and smiling until our cheeks sting. We make awful, funny faces, like clowns, to smooth and relax the muscles of our joy. Soon we will choose new names: land names, sea names, air names, poetically spun from the old.

My new name is on the tip of my tongue—

Hers is on the tip of my tongue. She is nearby, and I find myself strangely embarrassed to meet in person for the first time, because I have known her for all the sleepy ages. We played and learned together in the Dreamtime and resolved our earliest disputes. Making up, we realized we were incapable of being angry with each other for long. She is a master of Ship's biology—myself, training, and culture. Long, lazy times of instruction and play and exploration shot through with intense training, keeping our muscles fit. There is no experience like it, except for coming awake and meeting in the flesh.

The world, the flesh.

Our lines move toward the chrome-silver gate in the translucent white bulkhead. We are moving into the staging area. Landers await us there, sleek shadows ghostly gray.

Our beautiful Ship is too large to land—twelve kilometers long, huge and lonely. Once she embraced an irregular ball of rocky ice over a hundred kilometers in diameter—the shield and yolk of our interstellar journey. She still clutches a wasted chunk of the Oort moonlet—just a few billion tons. We decelerated with fuel to spare and now orbit the prime candidate.

How long?

The years are spread out cold and quiet behind us, the long tail of our journey. We do not remember those years intimately, there were so many.

How many?

It doesn't matter. I will look at the log when there is time, after the teams are chosen to make our first journey to the planet's surface.

Our new names are called, and we arrange ourselves in the loading bay, ceremonial outfits like so many brilliant daubs of paint, the better to see and be seen.

She is here! Comely in blue and beige and green, her look is bold, confident. Large, deep eyes and wide cheeks, brownish hair cut short—her look my way is a loving, thrilling challenge. She sits away from the others in the lander, by a spare seat, hoping that I will join her. She and I will be on the first team!

We.

I recognize so many from the Dreamtime. Friendly, joyous,

hugging, shaking hands, congratulating. Words spill. Our tongues are still clumsy but our passions are ancient. *We* are more than any family could be. We fought and argued and loved and learned through the long, cold voyage. We chose teams, disbanded, re-formed, chose again, and now the fit is perfection within diversity. Nothing can stand between us and the joy of planetfall.

A smooth jolt of perfectly designed machinery—

Severing connections with Ship. The lander is less than a hundred meters long, a tiny thing, really, yet sleek and fresh.

Time is moving so fast.

I unhitch and push off my harness to be closer to *her*. She scolds but she wraps her arms around me, and the web accommodates, the net stretches. We laugh to see so many others have done the same.

Viewing Ship from outside, along her great length, we marvel at her condition, weathered yet intact. Noble, protecting.

Ship, combined from an early formation of three hulls, now resembles two ancient stupas joined at their bases. Designed to protect against the hard wind between the stars, streamers of plasma convection once flowed and glowed ahead of and around the hulls like foggy gold rivers, ferrying interstellar dust—icy, glassy, metallic—aft, where it was processed into fuel or forged to replace Ship's ablated outer layers.

Now, the last of the plasma feebly glows around the pinched middle, a vestigial beacon. The view distracts us for only a moment. We are lost in simple wonder. One out of a hundred ships, we were told, would survive. And yet we have made the longest journey in the history of humanity, we are alive, and

WE!

ARE!

HERE!

LIFE START

A jerk and an awful sound, like water rushing or blood spurting. Everything's dark and muddled. A little redness creeps into my vision. I'm surrounded by thick liquid. My legs and arms thrash out against a smoothness.

Have we crashed? Did we break up in space before we landed? I'm already losing bits and pieces of what all that means. My memory is becoming like a puzzle picked up and shaken apart.

Puzzle. Jigsaw puzzle.

All wrong!

My entire body hurts. This is not the way it should be—not the way anything I know should be. But then I can feel what little I do know slipping away, including my name and why I'm here.

Alone in a shrinking tightness, like being squeezed out of a tube, legs still trapped, fingers ripping through the rubbery membrane, opening holes through which

I *breathe.*

I'm kicking my way out of a smothering sac. My chest aches and burns. The air hurts. Then the noise hits again and pounds my head, my ears, metal on metal. Doors closing. Walls moving, scraping, squealing.

My lungs seize. Hands and arms grow stiff. Naked flesh sticks to the deck. Skin comes away. I'm *freezing*.

A little one pulls on my exposed arm. She's thin and wiry and strong. She tears at the sac until all of my upper body is cold. She makes sounds. I think I understand but my head isn't locked in yet.

There was something wonderful before this.

What was it?

CHASING HEAT

Don't just lie there—get up."

The little one's still tugging and pushing, dancing on the frozen deck. I try to move but I'm uncoordinated. I'm losing skin all over. I try to fight. Maybe she's the reason I'm in so much trouble.

"Hurry! The air's going to freeze!"

All I can do is grunt and cry out. I hate this skinny creature. Who is she? What is she to me? She's pulled me out of the Dreamtime, and it's no good.

I turn to look at where I came from. Bodies are pushing out of a gray wall. They're enclosed in reddish sacs. They're trying to move, trying to punch and tear their way out, but the bags crystallize and shatter. The room is long and low. Carts wait on the floor. Bodies flop down on the carts and squirm but they're moving slowly, slower still.

They're all going to freeze.

I lash out, pushing her away.

She encourages me. "That's it," she says. "Breathe deep. Fight. Hurry. The heat's going fast."

Standing makes my head spin. "Help…them!" I cry out. "Go bother *them*!"

"They're already dead," she says. "You came out first."

So that's why I'm special. This time, when she takes my arm, I don't resist—I'm in too much pain, and I don't want to freeze. She drags me through a tall oval door into a long hall, curving *up* far away where there's brightness, to my *left*. The brightness is moving on, going away.

Receding. Strange word, that one.

The little one leaves me behind, running, dancing. Her feet never linger on the cold surface. Either I make it or I don't. It hurts too much to stay. I stumble after her. My legs are getting a little stronger, but the cold sucks my strength away as fast as it returns. It's going to be a close thing.

It gets worse. I see black stripes and thousands of tiny lights wrapped around the long, curved hall. The lights are going out. Walls fall in place behind me. They make the horrible clanging sound I heard at first. They're called *bulkheads* or maybe *hatches*. I blink and look up and down and see notches, indentations. That's where the bulkheads will rise or fall and close me off, trap me.

Where I am is bad. All wrong. The only place to go is in the light ahead, *receding*, getting smaller, soon to vanish unless I run faster and keep up with the little one, a faraway, tiny figure, all thrashing legs and arms.

I start to really run. My legs catch on, my arms pump in rhythm. The air is warming a little. I can breathe without pain, then I breathe deep, as instructed. Swirls of fog drape off the walls and split as I pass through them. Other oval doors fly by. All are dark and cold, like little rat holes.

Rats. Whatever they are.

No time for questions.

"Come on!" the little one shouts over her shoulder.

No need for encouragement. I've almost caught up with her. My legs are longer. I'm taller. I can run faster if I put my mind to it. But then I realize she's deliberately lagging, and with a burst she's way ahead, pink in the full blaze of light. She turns and waves her hand, beckoning.

"Hurry! I've got clothes!"

A bulkhead slides down, and I jump forward just before it slams shut. It would have smashed me or cut me in half. The long, curved hall doesn't care. That violates everything I think I know, everything I think I remember. The next notch is a few steps ahead. The floor rumbles and shivers. I pass the notch. The bulkhead puffs cold air on my back as it slams down. I'm gaining on them.

The little one jumps for joy. "Almost there!" she shouts.

What a way to wake up from the long nap, but I'm almost in the light. The warmth is delicious, the air is sweet. Maybe there's hope.

I look back. Another bulkhead drops. So far, my life—away from the Dreamtime—is filled with simple shapes and volumes. Striped halls, hatches, oval and circular openings, gray and dark brown except for the lights. Then there's the little one, like me, legs and arms and running and shouting.

I look ahead. The little one holds one arm up, head turned sideways, mouth open in surprise, staring at something I can't see.

She suddenly flinches and covers her face with her arm.

Something new and terrible enters the picture. I see it in the square of light, where the little one is, where I want to be. A thick, furry blackness fills that square, blocks it with a huge, unfurled rug of a hand that swoops behind the little one and wraps her and lifts her. She screams a short scream and then throws something as far as she can—something small. It lands in the hall, bounces, slides to a stop.

Something moves in the blackness, and three gleaming beads focus on me—*looking* at me. Then it's gone. She's gone. The light opens up. Warmth pulses down the hall like a temptation, a lure. I stop and stand, shivering, under a spatter of condensation from the roof.

A wall flies up between me and the horror waiting in the light. I don't mind. I slump and lean against the wall, a bulkhead five or six paces behind me and now one in front, nine or ten paces. The little one is gone. The light is gone.

I guess it all started badly, so I close my eyes and hope maybe it will stop. It's quiet. The walls aren't freezing but they are still cold. I think if I lie flat, they'll suck out what's left of my heat. That's what I need. A reset. Time to start over. I'll be painlessly absorbed and wait for a better start, more like what the Dreamtime promised. I hardly remember any of what came before the sac, the tugging, the cold. It's gone but leaves a beautiful, troubling impression.

Things could have been so much better. What went wrong? I lie back and stare up at the dripping brownness. The coolness is pleasant after the exertion.

Who *was* the little one? I think past tense because I'm sure whatever it was that got her ate her or recycled her or something like that. Obvious and inevitable. First lesson learned: Don't go where it's comfortable. Something bad will be waiting.

I don't remember any swear words yet, so under my breath I just repeat formless murmurs. Like grunting, only they would be words if I could remember. There was no swearing in the

Dreamtime. How wrong was that? What could they possibly...

"I want it to stop," I croak. "Stop it NOW." I begin to rant. I'm special, I have needs, I have a job to do—once I get my act together. I'm going to be important. I get so angry I start to feel weak. My voice goes up a couple of notches and I hit myself. Blubbering, incoherent. Strangely, I can feel myself smile as I shout out my frustration. I *know* how ridiculous I look, a grown man, having his first tantrum.

That's what it is, of course. This body hasn't learned self-control. I don't know how to get mad without hurting myself.

That absolutely scares me and I stop. My sobbing drops back into hiccups. I don't want to think that way. I'm a grown man. I have memories—I know I do.

I just can't find them.

Slowly, my anger rebuilds, but I don't shout, I don't hit myself, I hold it in—by main force of will. I don't blame myself for anything I've done, but I see no reason to act like a fool.

Still, it should never have started this way.

They should all welcome me, celebrate me.

Hell, I'm *new*.

Hell. Fantastic! My first swear word. I wonder what it means. Maybe it's the name of this bad place. But it's a mild word, *an empty glass word*, not nearly shocking enough to convey the awfulness. And yet now the awfulness has been replaced by simple misery. Half of that misery comes out of foiled *expectations*.

More words, longer, richer words, implying a process—a surrounding world with its own *expectations*. The words are like doors that open. They hold their own promise. Soon I'm shouting big new words into the brownness, the not-quite darkness. Some of them mean nothing. Others provide strength and relief.

There's a pain in my middle. It's called hunger. If it gets worse, the misery will turn into agony. I'd better do something other than just shout words. I can see that. No luxury to sit shouting and bemoaning my fate.

More words rise up and I shout them, shout around them. Monster. Fate. Death and duty.

But worst of all, *hunger*. Better to be frozen with the others in their sacs, way back behind the bulkheads.

The little one threw something. It's still there, probably. I'm not dying. I had hoped my end would be quick, but obviously I've come too far just to turn to ice on the floor. I roll and crawl forward. Walking and running got me nowhere good.

But that sentiment is fading. I learn that hungry people wish for only one thing, and it isn't death.

Death. Fate. Which word is the name of this new world?

Hunger.

And the solution is *food*. The little one became food because something else big and dark was hungry. My hand closes over the thing she tossed—a little square thing. I can feel it but not see it clearly. I wonder what it is. I think it's made of light metal or maybe plastic. More memories return with these words: My world is made of things, and the things have properties. Funny how it all fills in unevenly.

The square thing flops in my hand and I realize it has a hinge, opens on one side. It's a *book*. I can feel pages, thin and tough. If there was enough light, I think I might be able to look at them, read them—if they're not blank.

If I can still read.

My fingers feel out scratches on the flat part, a *cover*. There are seven scratches—I count carefully, since there's nothing else to do, and I'm not going to die, and there's no hope of finding something to make the hunger go away.

The walls are getting warmer. That temporarily takes my mind off my hunger. I'm sealed in this section of hall like a piece of meat in a can. Meat. Can. If it keeps getting warmer, maybe I'll be cooked.

Nobody eats meat out of a can anymore. Nobody eats *meat*. Except maybe the dark armored furry thing.

My stomach gurgles. I'd smell pretty good, cooked. I think over the words for the various parts of my body, internal and external. I apparently know a lot of useless things, but maybe not how to avoid being eaten. I know what I am, how big I am, I know how to move, I know useless things and simple things, but I don't know what's going on, I don't know where to find food, I don't know what's inside the book or why it has seven shallow scratches on one side.

I'm dozing in and out. I can see myself—imagine myself— talking to young humans, young versions of me. They mostly pay attention, as if they don't know what I know, and I'm saying things that are useful to them. I imagine turning my head and seeing that some of the young humans—many, actually— are female.

The little one—she was a young female human.

A *girl*. That's what you call a young human female. A *child*. *You're a teacher, dummy. Teachers talk to children.*

"Are there still children?" I ask. Plural of "child."

It's time for sleep. Maybe I'll be eaten. Maybe I'll fall asleep in front of the children, and they will laugh at me for being silly.

The little girl with the curly hair will be in the front row, laughing the hardest.

WAKE UP

My body takes a while to come up out of a cozy hole. The floor and the walls are warm. The warmth has made me sleep so deep and hard I feel stiff. I want to keep my eyes closed. Sleeping hurts less.

Then I realize there's more light. The wall that sealed me off has pulled back into its notch. My head casts a fuzzy shadow. Instantly, my body tenses and thrills. I get to my hands and knees. The light is so bright I blink, but nothing's waiting for me, and there's no sound except for my breathing. Heavy, scared breathing.

I stop breathing for a moment. Silence. Almost. There's a light purring noise, more of a vibration in the floor than a real noise in the air.

I stand up. Step forward. Step again. Walk for a few paces, over the notch, hesitating in case the bulkhead wants to drop and squash me. The notch remains just a notch. The lips of the notch are smooth, no gaps.

But there is blood. A few drops of dark red on the brown surface. I step over the blood. All that's left of the little one. I wonder what she was like. Teacher doesn't have all the answers, children. Monsters are supposed to hide in the darkness, but here, they wait in the brightness. At least, one did—once. Even so, I prefer the light.

Nothing to do but walk away from the darkness and into the brightness. I'm on my own, following my own internal instructions. This is the real beginning of my journey.

But someone opened the bulkhead. Someone's helping me.

You're on a Ship, remember?

Not really, but that's a good hypothesis. It fits what few impressions remain from my Dreamtime. But what the hell kind of *Ship?* Apparently it's a big one. I've been walking for a while. Some parts cold, some warmer. Some bright, some dark. A Ship that wants to stay asleep but has to keep turning over, restless, to avoid getting stiff.

Wow. That's a lot of stuff for one thought. Ship is a *metaphor.* That's a true teacher word, and I'm embarrassed how weak it makes me feel.

The hall is getting wider, taller, and the corners are going away. The hall is turning into a wider tube. I crouch down close to the floor—keeping an eye on whatever lies ahead—and see lots of little spots of glowing stuff set randomly but evenly into the surface. That's where the light comes from, and maybe the warmth as well.

The lights are called *glim lights.*

All the time I've been walking, I've felt a little *dizzy.* If I had food in my stomach, it might not stay there. Everything starts to feel really strange. I lean forward, then back, then sideways. My feet start to lift up from the surface. One foot stretches down and accidently kicks off and I start spinning. Up and down are going away. I'm moving along the tube, faster and faster, and I bump along like a ball, then start spinning, bounce off and hit the opposite side.... And after a few more bumps, I've caught up with the corridor, or the corridor with me, and I'm just floating, barely moving at all.

The dizziness is impossible to deal with, because dizzy makes you want to fall down—and without a down, just forward and back, dizzy means I might spin completely around and start walking—I mean, floating—back where I came from.

Necessary to pay attention to the little random patterns of lights. Fortunately I seem to have sharp eyesight and can tell if I'm turning around. I'm not.

But there won't be any more sleeping, not until up and down come back.

Now, how to move! I push away from one side to the other, using my hands. I can wave my arms, but they weren't made for flying. I'm naked, so I can't take off my *shirt* or my *pants* or my *jumper* or whatever the hell and flap them like a sail. That probably wouldn't work anyway.

But there is *friction*—the first teacher word that turns out to be useful. It hurts to push against the tunnel with my bare feet and hands—they're still raw from the cold—but with some practice, I manage to control both orientation and direction. I learn the trick of drifting and echoing along the lazy curve.

My stomach has settled—no food helps.

The quality of the light ahead changes—it's pinker, then bluer. There's something ahead, an opening in the side of the tube. Getting to it takes me about fifty hops and pushes. Then I am there. The opening leads to a larger space, a chamber or void filled with drifting objects, large and small. Some are irregular, others geometric, smoothly curved, or angular, like pieces of structure or machinery. I recklessly kick into the space.

Something wide and black and massive wobbles out of nowhere and nearly squashes me against the outer wall. I scramble around and out from under large flopping limbs, plates and matted fur. Out of the fur seeps a glob of dark fluid that bobs against my face. With a slight suck the blob surrounds my head and I can neither see nor breathe. It's heavy and thick like syrup and smells cloying, poison-sweet, stinging my face, and if it gets in my eyes—

Frantic swipes and wipes of my hands and arms get most of it off, but a film still clings. I fling my arms out to clear my fingers, and thick drops fly to the far walls or spatter against other masses, other shapes.

Blinking, I try to see through a blur. I'm half-blind. All I can hear—once I clear my ears—is faint sounds of bumping, knocking, sucking. One hand still clings to a hank of fur on one side of the dead creature that nearly smashed me.

More dark blobs extrude from some other nearby dead things. I can't make out their shapes clearly. The blobs collide and merge. I dodge one about the size of my head. It wobbles and shimmers in the breezy current of my motion, then spatters against a long, hard chunk, part of a broken machine, I assume: edges irregular and hard. It's big, three times my height. The blob wraps around one end and decides to travel up its length like paint on a stick.

In my head, I've been putting together some sort of diagram or map from both memory—such as it is—and logic. The hall/tube seems to run around the perimeter of something—Ship, presumably. I vaguely picture Ship spinning, pressing me down against the outer tube. When Ship spins, the hall or tube seems to curve *up*. Up would be *inboard*; down, *outboard*.

I take note of the fact that this void, filled with broken or dead stuff, extends from the inner circumference of the hall's curve—what used to be the top, before everything began to float and fly.

That means the void is inboard. I'm in a floating pile of junk. Useless as I am, maybe I belong here. What original use the junk may have had is not obvious. Some of it seems to have been alive—animals of a sort, leaking life blood—but nothing I see is familiar.

An odd feeling comes back to me, however. I've done this *before*. I know from weightless. For every action, there is an equal and opposite reaction. I've practiced this sort of maneuver before, often—in Dreamtime.

Large masses remain dangerous even when weightless—they can crush. They can also provide good points of vantage, good sport—kickoff, flight, stopping. Big masses will move only a little if I hit them, little masses I can use to propel myself if I fling them away.

After a little practice, I will move around in the void and take an inventory of its contents, may be useful later on. Maybe I'll find something to eat. The leaked blobs, however, did not taste at all good.

"You're a mess."

The high, sweet voice, is practically in my ear. I can almost feel the breath on my neck. Frantic, I try to twist about, but I'm between two objects, kicking away from one and hoping to bound off another, to get back to the opening and the tube. I can turn only by pulling my arms in, and then I rotate around an axis that runs through my left shoulder through my right hip.

Only then can I catch sight of the little one, floating about three body lengths away. She's drawn herself up in a graceful knot, legs crossed as if squatting in a *lotus*—another teacher word. Her arms are folded. She follows me with large gray eyes.

She looks disappointed.

"You're not dead," I say.

"No. But *it* is." She unfolds an arm and points at the big thing that had nearly crushed me.

I manage to kick off from another jagged white mass, heavy as a boulder. The mass slowly moves in the opposite direction, knocking aside other chunks and shapes. One of those shapes, I see, is part of a human body. The head is half chewed away, the legs are missing, and one arm is gone below the elbow. My shock nearly causes me to go off course, but I correct by pushing at a blackish, rubbery shape half my size, then correct, rather skillfully, to drift slowly in front of the girl.

"He's dead, too," she says, indicating the mangled corpse. Her arm is wrapped in a piece of dirty gray fabric. Blood shows through.

"The big thing tried to eat both of you?" I ask.

"No," she answers. "It doesn't eat—it cleans things up. It's a cleaner. Sorry about your clothes. This body has already been stripped. We can find another, with pants."

"You rob the dead?"

"Or anyone else who isn't paying attention."

"This is a trash heap? We're in a junkyard?"

She nods. "Cleaners bring stuff here. Even dead cleaners." She looks at the square book in my left hand. I've managed to hold on to it for all this time, unwilling to lose my one possession, but too busy to actually open it up and look inside.

"That's mine," she says, her eyes bright and sad. "I earned it."

"Is it?" I bring it close to my eyes, reluctant to give it up. Up close, I see that what I took to be seven grooves on the back cover were in fact seven groups of seven scratches.

"It is. I earned it."

I slowly reach out and place it in her outstretched hand.

"Where do you come from?" I ask.

"I don't know," she says, clutching the book to her chest. She's wearing a loose red tunic and shorts and looks like a dab of paint in a void otherwise filled with duns and blacks, grays and muddled whites.

"How long have you been here?" I manage to wipe my eyes clear enough to focus on the farthest wall.

"We need to get you to water. You should know better than to get that stuff in your eyes. Don't rub."

Water. I realize how thirsty I am and think back on the dripping condensation—how I should have caught it on my tongue, lapped it up.

"Is there water nearby?"

"There might be."

"Where? Here?"

"No." A sour expression. "This is just a good place to hide."

"Why did you pull me out of the cold?"

"I get lonely," she says with a sniff. Somehow, I doubt that's the whole truth.

"What happened to the thing that grabbed you?"

"*They* killed it when it tried to clean them."

"Who killed it?"

"Others, not like you and me. Well, maybe a little. There's a lot of variety, most of it bad."

This expands my thinking to a painful degree. I'm drifting away from her again on air currents, bumping up against small stuff. So many questions, and this girl has reversed roles, making herself a teacher and me a student.

"How long have you been here?" I ask.

She shrugs. "I stopped counting after forty-nine."

Seven groups of seven.

"Forty-nine what?"

"You're ugly without clothes," she says. "Let's get out of here and find you some." She uncrosses her legs and extends her arms, then unexpectedly uses my stomach to kick off. I whoof and drift back, and she shoots away toward the tube, though how she knows where it is in all this floating stuff is beyond comprehension.

But so is everything else.

I rebound and clumsily follow. The girl keeps her legs together, toes pointed, arms at her sides, spinning like a little bird or fish, and swiftly reaches out to push or kick, to echo or deflect.

"Wait!" I shout.

"Quiet," she says. "If you're noisy, I'll leave you behind. Lots of things don't want us here."

The girl flies well ahead of me. Her trail is a kind of vortex of objects she has used to maneuver, most of which get in my way. I wonder what will happen if the heaviness returns while we're caught in all this debris. This thought forces a rapid learning curve—much better than the alternative, panic—and soon I'm kicking, spinning, and fending with an alacrity I hope is skill, until the half-armored furry thing looms, a wall of leaking fluid and tufty darkness, and there's nothing I can do to avoid it. I curl into a ball and crunch up against the shiny carapace. This halts my flight abruptly and sets the dead thing spinning. Dark drops and spheroids, some trailing little tails of fluid, radiate outward in a thin, clumpy cloud.

I'm now truly adrift, nothing to kick against, and thus in a position to study the black thing more closely. It's been severely damaged; *wounded* might be the right word. One whole furry side is heavily lacerated. This is the source of most of the leakage, though some fluid has also seeped from what might be a mouth, gaping beneath a trio of tiny, shiny eyes. The head, where the eyes and mouth are, is tiny, underslung, on a thick, short neck.

The sectioned carapace covers what might have been a huge hump of back, while on the sides—now spinning into view— there are six thick, equally spaced legs, culminating in flat, bristle-edged feet with central pits or holes. The legs have drawn inward in death.

As it spins, I realize that the thing has *three* heads, really, like the points of a rounded triangle. Two legs flank each head. To one side of a head is what might have been the ruglike appendage that scooped up the girl, now rolled tight and almost withdrawn into a sheath.

I can't connect this creature to anything I've experienced, and what little I can draw out of the Dreamtime is also no help.

Another chunk of debris—flat and gray and, I am thankful, not leaking—rotates slowly into position. I pull up my legs, tuck in my arms, and wait for it to connect with my feet— flat, dense, perfect. I kick away and straighten, then draw in my legs, hold out my arms, and make wide stroking motions with my hands. I think I'm swimming.

The void's great curving wall draws closer. I see now that its surface is spattered with carbonized, crusty stains, like the inside of an immense oven. I look for the opening that leads back to the tube. I see it, and there, just inside, waits the girl, floating in lotus again—the position named after a flower.

A flower from old Earth.

Pleased with myself—I got the words, I got the moves—I bounce and claw and push toward her. But she's not paying me a bit of attention. Instead, hovering near the fistula that joins the tube and the junk-filled void, she's alerted on something just out of sight, outside the void, still inside the tube. Whatever it is makes scrabbling noises—and then speaks. I hear several voices, using words I don't understand. I stop my forward motion by setting a block of white ceramic whirling away. The block hits other objects with resonant clunks, like caroming billiard balls.

"Billiard. Billiards." I say these words aloud. Brilliant! All my right words are returning in a rush—just in time for something to come out of the tube and kill us both.

The girl looks my way, one eyebrow lowered in disapproval, holds a finger to her slightly twisted lip, and nods, as if we understand perfectly well what we need to do next.

I shake my head, clueless. But I'm all she has.

The voices inside the tube grow louder, insistent. Maybe they're calling to us. The girl isn't about to risk revealing herself, so I keep quiet as well. I have to trust her, though if worse comes, I suspect she'll not hesitate to sacrifice me, use me as a shield or a decoy.

The whole situation falls into a profound quiet—all but the shuffle and clunk of slowly moving, colliding objects behind and around us.

Perversely, I again notice my hunger. I wonder if the furry armored thing has any parts that are edible. My mouth starts to water with what little spit I can muster. Maybe that's why it was killed and lacerated—to liberate chunks of food. The blood may taste bad but the rest of it good. If that's so, then why isn't the void swarming with hunters, diners? A Ship this size—if it is a Ship—should carry thousands like the girl and me. Hungry thousands, trying to survive in pointless chaos.

The girl points to the fistula—the opening. She jabs her finger and opens her mouth, but nothing comes out. Then I see what she means.

The fistula is shrinking. All the debris is shifting in one direction—to our left. We're moving as well. We're going back to being heavy. The girl unfolds her arms and legs, looks for an opportunity to push off. I follow her motions and try to calculate the vectors of tons of broken objects. More bodies come into view, one or two human, most not, some much larger, unfolding long chains of armor plates—carapaces, I think.

All dead, not moving.

Except for one.

Until now, it must have been at the far side of the void, listening for movement. I glimpse it in the gaps. The gaps are closing as the debris is compressed to one side of the void, with me in it—along with what I've just seen, a sinuous, eel-like creature, many times my size. Thick bands of limbs spaced along its length flex in unison. A huge circular maw at one end pushes out a cone-shaped rasp, studded with glistening, silvery teeth.

The dead black cleaner comes between us. I'm on one side, the long eel on the other.

The girl is flying toward the fistula, which is now less than two body lengths wide.

I see my opportunity and kick against a curved beam, but the beam rotates under my foot. Its mass is less than I calculated—very light, in fact. My opposite motion is barely a crawl. I windmill my arms and legs. The fistula is six or seven body lengths away.

The long thing with the big mouth has tried taking a gobbet out of the six-legged beast, but shivers violently, undulating in the collapsing cloud—

It all tastes bad, I guess.

A big flat sheet of something with broken, melted edges comes into view, angled just right if I kick off the leading edge—but I have to swim, push air, grab a small soggy chunk and throw it, increase my speed any way I can....

The chunk is a severed hand. No matter.

The long eel has wrapped part of its length around a big gray object and suddenly stabs at me with its toothy rasp, and from the end of the rasp thrusts out a snapping beak. The sheet is almost within reach. I hope it's massive. It wobbles on a rolling, complex axis. Then, mercifully, it hides the raspy, beaky eel from my view.

Last chance. I stretch my legs, connect solidly with the edge of the sheet, kick as hard as I can, and arrow toward the fistula.

The sheet spins and moves off in the general direction of a new heaviness. The fistula is just wide enough to drop through....

I glide toward it, arguably toward the safer option, hungry, scared out of my wits. I see it behind me again, the toothy snout and beak so close!

I can smell its acid, sour-sweet breath—

I'm through! I slam into the far surface of the tube, then scramble for purchase with my raw knees and feet and hands to get out of the way of what I know is coming—

The rasp and head thrusts through the fistula, beak snapping, teeth gnashing, meshing, gnashing in reverse, then withdrawing behind thick lips, the whole apparatus sphinctering shut. The top of the long thing's body whips in my direction. I see the little girl and behind her, other figures—but I have to get out of the way.

Then an awful noise—the fistula tightens around the thing's neck. Cartilage crunches, flesh is squeezed to bursting. The long snout shivers, and the lips pull back again, spasmodic, uncovering the beak and teeth. It squeals, then jerks and twists, and explodes a gassy breath just a hand-span from my kicking foot....

The fistula has closed.

The snout and a length of carcass writhe free inside the tube.

The beak snaps off the tip of my little toe. I cry out at the pain. My feet slip in a spray of more black fluid. I'm drenched in the stuff. I finally give up and just fall to the floor, gasping.

Weight is returning. We're sliding, pushing back along the tube. The severed toothy head seems to follow me. I kick it as hard as I can, again and again.

Then the writhing and snapping stops. It's over. Heaviness is back. I'm alive, the little girl stands a few meters away...and behind her, gripping her arm and shoulders, three adults. At first, I think they're like me. But they're not. They're not like either of us. Everyone seems frozen, as if this monster might come back to life—but the tooth-snout is decapitated. It's dead.

Good name, that. Tooth-snout.

No end of surprises.

COLD FOLLOWS HEAVINESS

The girl looks at me with her big gray eyes. In a line behind her stand three tall figures dressed in ribbons and rags. They're different colors, one Blue-Black with a flat, broad face; the second is brown, thin-headed, with reddish markings. The third, the tallest and skinniest, has pale pink mottled skin and a flat, knobby crest of bone reaching from where its nose might be to the other side of its head. The nose appears to be in the middle of its forehead.

It snorts.

All are damp, dripping. All smell sweaty, bitter. The girl seems to think they're beneath her notice, even as they grip her shoulders.

Together, they seem to be waiting for someone to take a family portrait.

The girl turns her eyes away, resigned, and wipes her nose. "It's going to get cold soon," she says.

The three don't hesitate. They grab her up and run along the length of the tube, away from me and the dead tooth-snout, with its exposed radula. I watch their backs for a moment, the flapping of their rags, not sure whether I have any astonishment left in me.

Radula. Where the hell does that word come from? I'd look it up if I were you....

"I guess this means you're not worth eating," I say to the tooth-snout. Then I get up. I can hear heavy slams. The bulkheads are going up. Best not to get left behind. Unless, of course, the three have snatched the little girl to make a meal of her. In any case, I have to follow, if only to save her—though I'm almost hungry enough to join in.

This is where madness begins. No water, no food, skin snatched away by freezing cold from my back, feet, knees, elbows—heavy exertion—nonstop terror. Missing tip of toe. Everything hurts.

I manage to run. I look back only once. Sure enough, the bulkheads aren't far behind. The tooth-snout carcass is slammed to the top of the tube, split again, and hidden from view.

I seem to run forever. Second wind is nothing to third and fourth wind. Eventually, I expect, I'll just fall over and die and not even notice the difference, because my seeing, my hearing, all that's left of *me*, is totally isolated from what my body is doing.

It's pretty monotonous. Makes being alive seem more of a boring burden than a promise of better things. Curved tube— hundreds of meters of it. Then more curved tube. And finally— still more curved tube!

And no sign of the three and the little girl. I can see pretty far ahead—maybe another hundred meters.

I begin to notice other variations. Glim lights in the wall form brighter broken lines. Occasional circular patches twenty centimeters or so wide, hard to make out, radiate striped designs.

Maybe these are road signs: stop, go, turn, *die*.

Behind me, the lights dim. Cold air is chapping my flying heels and pumping calves. Then, to my right, I see a door actually open—grow from a dark dot to a dimly lit oval. Smaller than the fistula but big enough to admit someone my size. There's a room beyond, with corners and edges. I glimpse shapes inside, nothing moving....

My lungs let out a moan in the midst of the constant gasping.

No need to stop and investigate. Didn't need to see that. Nothing but bodies scattered under a low ceiling. Maybe I've come full circle and this is where I started. Maybe this is all there is.

But I don't think so.

This thing is *big*.

Meters, kilometers—length and measure are coming back to me. I've run at least three kilometers since being snatched out of my sleep sac. (I must have been sleeping, otherwise, why the Dreamtime?) Three kilometers, but I doubt I've made anything like a complete circuit, judging from the curvature of the tube. It could be a gigantic squirrel cage.

Something's waiting for me to fall over, something that likes lean, tired, smelly meat—meat still scared shitless.

No shit. No pee.

No reason for either.

I see all four of them now. They're far away—the length of a *football field*. Small but clear. They're standing just as they were before, the girl held between them, and all watch me run. Everything behind is painfully cold, scary dark. The tiny surface lights under my pounding feet are dimming to that dead umber that will no doubt be the end of me, and before I can even remember my name.

If I have a name.

Not much strength left. I stumble, fall, get up, try to run again, then just fall over and lie there. Bulkheads slam. My skin is freezing to the surface. I almost don't care, but with the last of my energy, I roll, a futile gesture....

Then hands grab me and tug me the rest of the necessary distance. More food for everybody, I guess—but might as well let the food carry itself as far as possible.

My head bobs from my neck.

Then...it doesn't hang anymore. I feel the odd forward and backward wobble, the upward tug—the release of tensions in back and shoulders, followed by drifting—bumping. The three big ones release my legs and arms and resort to pushing me along, floating me into the new warmth.

"Football," I say to them. *"Hell. Radula. Receding.* Remember your new words, students—there's going to be a quiz."

The little girl shoves her face close to mine. She looks angry. "Shut up," she says. "You don't know *anything* yet."

"We're on a Ship," I murmur, lips loose, head lolling. I point with both hands. "That's *fore.* That's *aft.*"

She slaps my face—hard.

TEACHER LEARNS

Teacher is being a pain," she says to the man with the bony ridge.

His voice in reply is a deep honk followed by a whistle. I'm floating between the four, waiting for them to try something. Wondering if I have enough strength left to defend myself.

"Who are *they*?" I ask.

The girl wipes her nose again. "They came to the heap and took me from the cleaner. Then they killed the cleaner. The cleaner isn't very dangerous—it's a nuisance. It just wanted to collect me and leave me in the heap. I could have escaped."

"Maybe they wanted to eat it."

The girl makes a face. "Cleaners taste awful."

The three pay little attention as we resume moving along. They leave me to push and kick in the weightlessness to keep up. Amazingly, I still have some strength, but my skin hurts like fury, and I keep shuddering with painful dry heaves.

They're looking ahead, looking for something—something they lost, perhaps.

"Is this all of them?" I ask the girl between heaves.

"All I've met," she says. "I've already given them names."

"You haven't given me a name."

"You're always Teacher."

Of course, I think. My curiosity as to this point is nil. My throat is sore, my eyes feel like they're on fire, and the black fluid crusted all over me is starting to raise little blisters. "I need to wash this stuff off," I croak.

"It's factor blood. Don't worry about it," the girl says. "You'll probably be dead soon."

"Factor?"

She gives me a pained look. "Factors. The cleaner, the swim-worm."

"Oh. What about water, food?"

"Nothing so far," the girl says. "We're probably *all* going to be dead soon."

"So it's over," I say.

She shakes her head. "It's never over. We keep looking." She holds out her book. "Maybe we'll find one of these for you."

"A book?"

"It's how we know anything at all," the girl says. "They have books, too. Except for *him*." She points to the pink one with the bony crest, the only one who's tried to talk. "That's Picker. He can't find his. Whatever he's learned will be lost." She gives me a squint.

"Cleaners…" I can barely talk, so my question or whatever I thought I was going to say goes unsaid. I move and think and keep it all to myself, which is just as well, because I'm becoming delusional.

Becoming. I manage a raw chuckle.

Then the Blue-Black fellow with the flat face performs a sort of quivering wiggle and makes an extraordinary series of whistles—really pretty. The pink, crested fellow acts excited, too, and emits his own warble-honk.

They see something.

I twist my head. At the very end of what I can see of the curving tube is a large opening, another fistula—and this time it's on the left side.

"That might go forward," the girl says. "We have to get there before it closes. Keep up with us. And watch out for a big wind."

"Terrific," I say. A breeze creeps up from behind. It doesn't cool me—I have no sweat to evaporate. If there was heaviness, I wouldn't make it this time. But weightless, I'm just barely able to stay about four body lengths behind the others.

The closer I get to the opening, the stronger the breeze, until it becomes a wind. The three big fellows reach the hole first. They form up like an acrobatic team, gripping arms and shoulders and spanning the tube with their feet to brace themselves.

The girl bumps into their arms and hangs on. Her hair lufts. "Good," she says. They hold her out by one spindly arm—and let her go. She pushes her feet together and vanishes into the hole as if diving into a pool.

Bouncing along the tube, I try to hold back, skidding hands and feet, but I'm alone and it's not enough. I arrive at the barrier of arms and legs. I have no idea what's causing the suction or where the opening is taking us—but I'm almost equally concerned that something will reach out and snatch me from behind.

I reach out. "Do it quick!" I shout. But I don't really mean it.

The brown fellow with scarlet markings—*scarlet!* lovely

word—takes hold of my arm. The team rearranges, and together, despite my clinging, desperate hands, they drop me into a roaring tunnel.

I fly through. The tunnel opens like the bell of a trumpet to a bigger space. A moist, lateral wind has taken hold of me. I'm flying. I look back and see the team of three flow one by one into the chasm. I can't see the girl, but the three are about fifty meters behind me. We move along at the same speed. The opening vanishes behind us in the murk. The bigger space is dimly illuminated. I can finally see that it's a conduit—another curved, circumnavigating tube, but broader, deeper.

Circumnavigating. Going all the way around...Ship.

There's darkness inboard, something slick and glistening outboard. The air is wet on my face and lips. We fly through a kind of rising mist that feels wonderful on my skin. I try to get a drink by sucking, but it doesn't work. I just cough. I guess that's progress, but where's the real water—where's the food? Then in the general roar I hear a sound more beautiful than anything I've heard before—a slurping, gurgling rush. It has to be water, a lot of water. The sound comes from outboard—from the glistening surface.

The curved walls channel an entire rushing river, perhaps ten or twelve meters wide.

The girl reappears down the line, through the mist. She's grinning and doing spins. Looking at her makes me shut my eyes. I'm terrified, but the smell of water makes me crazy. My whole body wants to dive into the glistening surface. A river can't hang weightless in a trough, can it? Yet the water keeps to the channel. It has weight—

But we don't. We're blowing along like fluff in a breeze, suspended above the rushing water. The air currents are faster at the center, slower near the walls. The girl "swims" outward with vigorous motions of her arms and feet, slow but effective progress that she reverses once I have passed.

Knob-Crest—Picker—gives a hoot of appreciation.

Behind me now, the girl reaches out to the three, still joined hand to arm, and uses the Blue-Black fellow to pull herself in. He makes more musical whistles. The brown fellow with scarlet markings—Scarlet-Brown—and Picker draw in their legs, catch him up, and they all spin together.

It's comical and wonderful, but I'm so thirsty I can't stop myself from making little shrieking noises and grabbing wherever and whatever I can, just to reach the water. I kick and flail against the wind, the center of the spinning pair.

Just right. Now it's like I'm diving toward the water.

"No!" the girl shouts. They grab my ankle at the end of a kick and pull me toward them. All of us move outward and slow.

The girl is performing a kind of twirling handstand a few centimeters above the angled side of the channel, lifting slowly toward the center. I've never seen anything so wonderful and mysterious—and I still don't care. I kick against the passing wall, aiming for the channel, change direction and spin about…

Again I'm heading straight for the water at about a meter per second. The girl does this amazing maneuver, tucks in her legs and arms, spins about to present her legs, and kicks against the angle of the channel wall. This shoots her toward where I'll be in a couple of seconds—which might mean I won't reach the water, so I wave her off. But she collides with me and grabs my foot and uses her momentum to knock me off course. Now we're both moving down, but also passing over the water to the opposite channel wall.

Only now do I see how fast the water is moving. It's a weird taffy-streaming blur. I can make out currents, mostly parallel to the channel walls, but also whirlpools that rush past, relative to the girl and me, at about a hundred kilometers an hour.

I'll die, but I don't care. I'll die wet. I'm philosophical about the entire gambit. It's going to be a close thing either way. The girl knows more about this sort of flying than I do but seems to actually be risking her life for me.

Maybe it's a game.

I start laughing. "We're going swimming!" I shout.

The girl looks along the length of my leg and body—she's still hanging on to my foot—in a kind of anxious pity. Her face seems so mature, so experienced—maybe I'm the child and she's the grown-up.

The wind has pulled us toward the center. The water is right below us. I stretch out my hand. I'm totally insane—the smell of it is like a promise of heaven. My hand touches the stream, and instantly I'm in intense pain, hand wrenched, whole body spinning head over heels, the girl at my foot also swinging, scared—

But the dynamics of our new, combined shape pushes us outward. We strike the opposite sloping wall of the channel and carom back in a tangle, but farther from the channel, lifting over the water—and still, of course, moving briskly along the tube.

My hand feels like it's broken, but I suck at the moisture left on my fingers—very little of it, actually. Hardly worth the effort.

"That isn't how it's done," the girl says when she's caught her breath.

"I could have made it," I insist, and kick against the breeze, hoping to return to the channel.

"The water's in a trough," she says. "The trough is spinning free of the walls. That's why the water stays in the trough. It's going really, really fast. Look."

She points across the channel to the three fellows on the other side. Picker is holding out a stick and honking above the roar and hiss as if relaying instructions. Blue-Black responds in high whistles.

He's going to thrust the stick into the spinning stream.

"That's Pushingar," the girl says.

I have no idea where she's getting her names, but they stick.

The others grab hold of Pushingar's feet. The stick goes in and they all spin like tops but remain above the channel. And a few splashes are liberated by the stick, forming quivering, shimmering globules.

Where's the third fellow, Scarlet-Brown?

He comes out of the shadows behind us, arms out, hooting in ecstasy. He's kicked out over the channel, off the opposite wall, and is now rather expertly arrowing toward a fist-sized pearl of water pushing along through the air. He opens his mouth—it's an impressive mouth, filled with broad yellow teeth, big canines, and even bigger incisors—and grabs a great big drink. He scoops the rest of the broken globule into his outstretched tunic.

"What's his name?" I shout above the roar.

"Satmonk," the girl says.

The other two intercept Satmonk, and they rebound, join hands, and float together, scooping and aiming drops and globules with hands and feet, moving their heads to Pushingar's midriff, where he's busy wringing out the tunic.

All drink greedily.

"That's how it's done," the girl says. "But unless they give us a little shove, it's going to take a few minutes to cross to where we can join them."

"My fault," I say, my lips and tongue just moist enough now to manage a few words.

"Can't be helped," the girl says. "Everything here is about waiting and seeing and being patient. Otherwise, someone else fills in your book. Or worse—the book gets lost."

She points to the channel, the rushing taffy-silver currents, the swirling whirlpools.

"*Scarlet*," I say. "It means 'red.'"

She ignores me, floating just an arm's length away. For a moment, her eyes become heavy-lidded and she's lost in her own kind of self-induced calm.

Patient.

I'm really starting to like this child.

It turns out the three fellows—Picker, Pushingar, Satmonk—are happy to bound around some more over the spinning channel. In a few minutes, they've done the stick thing again—it's fine sport, they're hooting and whistling and honking—and more big beads of water wiggle past. I open my mouth and get wet—my whole head—but by some miracle, I also manage to drink deep without filling my lungs and drowning.

The water tastes funny—my lips and cheeks tingle. But it's wet, it's very cold, and after a few more collisions, my thirst is gone. I rub my face with my hands, trying to scrub away the filth—the factor blood that still clings to me. It's no good. I'll need a cloth.

And, of course, some clothes would be good. I'm still naked and even I don't like it. Everyone else has clothes.

Knob-Crest, Picker, drifts beside me, hands behind his head, lounging in the middle of the stream of air. We still have to be careful. The currents can be unpredictable, especially where the surface of the stream whips up turbulence.

It's the stream's undulations that are grabbing at the air

above the channel, dragging it along and creating the suction that pulled us into the tube and the wind that now rushes us along. The center can be tricky. The turbulence sometimes tries to knock us toward the rushing stream. But the three fellows and the girl are experienced, so here we are, close to the relative safety of the sloping channel wall.

Scarlet-Brown, Satmonk, pokes the girl. She opens her eyes. We've made something like progress. We can push against the flowing air, using the shapes of our bodies, the motions of our arms, to adjust and maintain position.

Picker looks me over with an expression I can't even begin to read. He reaches up, covers his forehead-nose, and manages to say, in a nasal tenor, "How about food?"

I give him a big smile and hold up my thumb.

"No show teeth," he says. "It's rude."

I draw my lips tight. "Hell, yes," I say.

"Not hell. Ship. Big, sick Ship. Food soon."

There's another opening coming up. It might be on the opposite side of the conduit from where we dropped in. A chance to exit, and also to continue moving forward.

The look on the girl's face tells me that getting out of the spinning channel is the hard part. She points to her two eyes, then to me, then to the others.

"Watch and learn—quick! Or you'll go around again and again—and you'll drown."

Together, they start to carom along the channel walls, at angles to the slipstream...slowing, slowing, the exit is coming up, with its inviting trumpet mouth. I try to learn from watching them, manage to keep up, and then we all grab and leap in a great big tangle.

There's one final maneuver I still don't understand, a kind of whirl around the bell of the trumpet, and then we're scrambling like children climbing a sandhill, against the breeze flowing from that side—

And we emerge into an even bigger space, away from the trumpet mouth, away from the channel and the rushing, wonderful, terrifying water.

"Great!" the girl shouts. "Sometimes it takes three or four tries."

"How long have you been doing this?" I ask.

"Don't know," she says. "Across four rivers. But this is the farthest forward I've gone—and managed to take my book with me."

I don't know what she means about the book. I don't know much of anything, really. I'm ignorant, useless, and I have no idea why this makeshift team is still pulling me along.

Suddenly, I'm scared again. I'm literally a fifth wheel.

Maybe I'm still food.

BIG IDEAS

The chamber we're in is huge. I can't see a "top" inboard, and I can't see across to the opposite side. It isn't spinning. Once we're away from the air currents around the trumpet leading to the channel, we can move only by "swimming," which takes a long time and a lot of effort.

I'm hungry enough to consider gnawing on my hands, my arms. Seriously.

"We wait," Picker says, finger over his high nose. "Soon we walk. Then cold comes and we chase heat."

The girl nods.

I've learned this much. Two of us at least think we're on a Ship. That word, to us, implies something very big. Maybe it is *sick*, whatever that means—I know too little to judge. My memories from the Dreamtime seem to sync up with some of these propositions. But the memories are woefully incomplete.

As to where we are in the Ship, we seem to still be more or less "outboard," moving slowly forward, jumping from one circumnavigating conduit to another—different sorts of channels and tubes, with different functions. One of them carries water in a spinning trough. I have no idea where the water comes from or why the trough is spinning. I remember the water's tingling taste, however, and am already thirsty again.

There are five of us. Three look different, two of us look much the same—though one is smaller and apparently younger. (Why "apparently"? Because she knows a lot more than I do. I seem to be the young one in everything but size.)

And I now think that the three different-looking fellows have been together for some time, are perhaps even more knowledgeable than the girl, and can manage with effort to speak a little of the lingo the girl and I share. In turn, the girl knows some of Picker and Pushingar's whistle-hoot-speak.

The space inboard—"up," or above us, when weight returns—is so deep and dark as to be unfathomable. After a long while, I think I can make out big curving struts arranged in interlocking, slender, three-pointed stars. But I can't be sure. It might be my eyes playing tricks.

Nothing around us is moving.

The rest period is quickly over. The girl has been floating in her lotus. Now she uncurls. I notice we're moving again, with reference to the outboard surface—the "floor." Air currents are increasing in the large space.

"Weight's coming," the girl says, and whistles something to Pushingar.

"We feel it," Picker says.

"I think there's going to be a big wind," the girl says. "All the air in here will catch up with the spin. We should lie flat until it passes."

And that's just the way it is. As we fall the short distance outboard, "down," the air around us not only gets colder, but also begins moving even more violently than the breeze over the channeled river. Soon it's gale force—*gale!*—and we're being dragged over the floor, no matter how we try to hold on. Not strong enough yet to lift us up and flip us over.

The real danger is freezing. My skin grows numb. I see Satmonk and Picker crawling ahead of me. The girl is behind Pushingar to my left.

"How far?" I shout. The girl shakes her head. Either she can't hear me or she doesn't know. Finally, despite the bitter cold, we all just lie flat on the smooth floor, our weight increasing, giving us better purchase. Besides, the floor is warmer than the wind.

I'm almost at eye level with the omnipresent little glowing beads that faintly illuminate everything. Glims. Glim lights. The whole chamber is spinning up—or the entire Ship. I don't know which or why in either case.

I'm sick of it. All of it. If this is the way life is going to be, then I'm ready to chuck it all and freeze. But my body disagrees. I start cursing my biological stubbornness. Upon this provocation, new words enter my vocabulary—words a teacher should not pass along.

The wind subsides. There's a fluting sound from high above, the structure inboard making its own noises, now audible in the slackening of the cold rush. The air above seems to still be pretty turbulent and even colder. Little beige flakes have been blowing around us for the last few minutes. I realize it's *snow.* Snow is swirling.

We stand. We walk. One by one, beginning with Pushingar, we run forward—I think, I hope. I have no idea where we're going and suspect neither does the little girl. Maybe Pushingar or the other two know something, but they're not talking—just running.

The floor is getting very cold. It's starting all over again, variations on a nasty theme. Chasing heat, staying alive, seeking food—seeking answers really low on the list of my frustrated basic drives.

Minutes of running. Maybe only seconds. But something visible ahead—a wall. A wall curving off in huge sweeps with the floor to either side, *circumnavigating*, like the tube and the channel but with actual hatches that have real doors—oblong, about my height.

One of the doors stands open.

The girl sings out her joy. "Forward!" she cries.

We all climb through the hatch, into a rectangular hallway—as at the beginning. The wall opposite is blank, no hatches. Sat-monk points to the right. We resume running. I'm mostly stumbling. My head is swimming, my heart thumping. I'm close to the end of my tether.

This time, there are no bulkheads slamming shut to close us off from going back. After a time, I notice rags on the floor—scraps of clothing, bits of other things I can't identify. I stop. Maybe it's food. I bend over and pick up something small and brownish, a smashed cube.

The others move on without me.

I sniff the cube. No odor. Squeeze it. Feel it. It's hard as a rock. I try to take a bite.

The girl has doubled back. She knocks it from my hands. "Not food," she says. "Not for *you* to eat, anyway. But there's probably food somewhere near. This is a place that's made for people."

Looking in angry frustration at the cube on the floor, at the girl, I realize I'm weeping, but my eyes are dry.

"Keep going," she says, and tugs at my arm. "We need to get to a warm place. Come on."

As we walk—she seems to know I'm too worn down to run

anymore—she stoops and picks up a larger rag, shakes it out, hands it back to me. "Not too filthy," she says. "Might fit."

I look at the scrap in the dimness. It's a pair of flexible shorts made of thin fabric. There's a big blood stain on one leg—dark, dry.

"No, thank you," I say. But I don't drop it.

"Suit yourself. Nearly everything we're wearing comes from somebody dead. Just enough to go around."

If that's meant to be encouraging, it doesn't work. Again I feel like lying down, but I know the girl would kick me. We join the others. They're sitting on the floor, lying against the walls. Satmonk and Pushingar appear to be sleeping. Picker is keeping an eye out ahead. The girl steps over them.

Picker covers his nose. "Been here?" he asks, and then sneezes and shakes his head. Its tough for him to talk this way.

"No," the girl says. "Never this far forward."

"Maybe add to book," Picker says.

The girl makes a face. The others get up and we follow, but we're not running. It's not getting as cold here, though the air is chill. Maybe the girl is right.

Then we see the light up ahead is changing. Still dim, but bluer. The blue cast reaches back down the hall.

"Is that a bubble?" the girl asks.

"What's 'bubble'?" Picker asks.

Pushingar seems to understand, and a whistling, honking dialogue follows. If I wasn't dying, I'd have laughed at the comical sounds.

But Picker concludes by saying, "They know of bubbles. Someone made it told." He almost sneezes, looks sidewise at me, then adds, tapping his nose, "Learn honk!"

"Sure," I say. I hold my own nose and sort of snort, then warble a horn note or two.

The others laugh—different kinds of laughter. And I thought

I was dying. I'm not. I'm still capable of making a joke. Either that, or they're making the noises their kinds make before they attack and eat you.

I'd sympathize if that was their plan.

But I know it isn't.

These guys are *human*. Different kinds of my people. How I know this, I can't say, but before I can catch up with the girl, we're closer to the bluish light, and I see that the hallway no longer curves up but opens out on each side—expands. The floor ends, but a kind of bridge goes on, surrounded by a cage of rails. The rail on our left supports a ladder at shoulder level.

But none of that is important. The part of the bridge we're currently walking on—let's call it a floor, though it's different from the floor of the hall—is not solid, but made of grating over crossbars and connected to the cage and the long rails.

We can see to either side, and down.

We have to stop and look. Below the bridge is an intense darkness, filled with little tiny lights—not at all like the glim lights. These are pointlike and bright, and there are so many of them I could spend a long lifetime just counting.

"What is that?" the girl asks, her voice a tiny squeak. She hasn't seen any of this before. Her face expresses resistance to revealing either ignorance or curiosity. She doesn't like new, large things or ideas—or perceptions.

"It's *sky*," I say. "It's the universe. Those are stars."

"This *is* Ship," Picker says. "Big, sick Ship."

"Where are we?" the girl asks, her voice tremulous.

"A viewing chamber," I say. "I remember them from Dreamtime."

And I do, vaguely. All of us would gather in a place like this to look down on a new world. Except I don't see anything like a new world. But there's something ahead and below, mostly obscured by the curve in the bridge and the rails. As we walk farther, the object comes into view. We're moving—it's moving, and rather rapidly. Soon it will pass right underneath us. I'm confused for a moment, so I stop walking and grip the railing.

"Is that our world?" the girl asks. She seems to remember something out of Dreamtime as well.

The object is passing right underneath—outboard, far down. It's big, all right—big and mottled white, cracked, cratered, covered with thin, confining bands and stripes. It's like a huge caged snowball. A very dirty snowball. The cage wraps around the snowball and reaches up in a gigantic strut—curved, graceful, big.

And that strut or support or brace climbs all the way up from the dirty snowball to where we are.

It connects the big snowball to Ship.

The snowball and the strut move clockwise to the other side and pass out of sight. Compared to the size of that lump of dirty ice, Ship is tiny. Ship rotates in some sort of cradle suspended above the snowball—or the snowball flies around us. But that doesn't make as much sense.

We're inside a spinning something, probably a cylinder. The spin causes the acceleration and the feeling of weight.

Ship is spinning.

"It's not our world," I say.

Satmonk seems to agree, shaking his head, holding out flat hands as if to reject all of it. I *might* know what the dirty snowball is, but I don't want to make that particular guess. Because if my guess is correct, then Ship is very sick indeed.

The snowball is *much too large.*

It comes around again. I make out a sinuous rill along one side, where ice has apparently been dug out, perhaps mined. *Rill.* That's good. *Rill* actually means a small river, but this is all ice. It reminds me of a *snake,* a *serpent.*

For the time being, what we're seeing is impressive, it's frightening, and it's informative in a stunning, useless sort of way—but it isn't food.

The bridge isn't a comfortable place to rest and try to remember, so we continue across until we reach the middle. There, the bridge reaches and then apparently passes through a glassy sphere about forty meters in diameter. The sphere lies suspended on the bridge, over the *blister* that reveals the stars and the serpent-marked ice ball. This is a place where people are meant to stop, look, and marvel. A resting place.

The dirty snowball again rotates into view and passes beneath, but more slowly. We all feel the now-familiar sensation of Ship reducing its spin—the push forward, making us grip the rungs of the ladder, the bars, each other. As the forward shove lessens, so does our downward tug.

We're weightless again.

A wind sighs through the larger bubble, swirling around the bridge rails and decking. Without thinking, I realize that I had put on the shorts before crossing the bridge. I didn't want to die naked and exposed.

The girl lets go of the ladder and floats in front of me. The last of the wind shoves her forward toward the glassy sphere. I let go of the ladder and follow.

The three other humans—Picker, Pushingar, Satmonk—not exactly like me or the girl but capable of laughter and kindness and solidarity, the best human traits of all, follow close behind.

REST AND DIE

The first thing I see in the sphere is a floating body—fully clothed, slowly rotating on an axis through its shoulders. It's an adult female, I think, but badly decayed or eaten away. There's no way of knowing what type of human she once was.

"The cleaners aren't very active here," the girl says, her lips prim in disapproval. She shoves away from the end of the bridge and intersects the body, then, as the others move toward the opposite side of the sphere, clambers around it and shows us that it's wearing a kind of backpack. Thrusting her hand into the pack, she pulls part of it inside out—it's empty.

"No book," she says with a chuff. She kicks violently away from the body, and both go in opposite directions, just as Newton intended—

Newton.

The first name I've recovered—a name apparently more important than my own.

That big outboard mass of gray and brown and white very

slowly comes back into view, then stops, parking itself "below" us at about two o'clock as I look outboard and forward. Clockwise. Clock hands. Rotation. Degrees and radians. That starts to make visual and other kinds of sense.

I shake my head in mixed wonder and sorrow, and precess until my hand clenches the end of the railing and stops me. I'm looking inboard now, away from the spectacular view, "up" toward a dark, shadowy section of the sphere. There's stuff way up there—smaller clumped spheres, like magnified foam, each filled with one or more couches, chairs—and dark boxes. Places to rest. Places to explore.

The girl grabs hold of my shoulder. We wobble together until my wrist tightens and damps our motion.

"That woman was coming here for a reason," she says. "Something didn't want her here."

"What?" I ask.

"Not a friend."

Already Picker and Satmonk have kicked away from the end of the bridge to ascend toward the glimmering cluster. The girl joins them. With my usual finesse, I follow and arrive after a couple of clumsy rebounds.

The cluster's curved, pushed-together surfaces are fogged by a layer of staticky dust. The cluster looks more and more like a bunch of soap bubbles pushed together—but with an access hole cut between each bubble. More scraps of clothing float in their quiet confines.

The girl is working on opening one of the boxes. She succeeds, but it's empty. Satmonk is in another bubble, his leg wrapped around a couch as he breaks a box loose of some sort of stringy glue. The lid comes open, and he gives a bird warble and shows it to the rest. I'm at a bad angle, but the others instantly move into his sphere of influence and generosity.

Once again, I'm the last to join them. The girl has managed

to save me a large gray bag. Other bags, liberated from the box, have been apportioned, first come, first served.

"Just say thanks," she tells me, and pulls her own bag close.

The bags are all tied shut with a drawstring. I watch the others, then pull the bow knot—

And out comes a loaf of heavy brownish cake ten or so centimeters long and half as wide and deep—a really big chunk of something that smells fruity and fishy. Fruit I get. The clusters around us are like grapes, in a weird way. I can taste a grape in memory. We eat fruit in Dreamtime.

Fishy is more difficult. I'm not sure what that really means, though I see *oceans* and silvery creatures in the water. But this is just a distraction. I'm eating the loaf before I give a damn what it smells like.

Also in the bag is a head-sized, squishy oval ball filled with—I hope—water. The cake is dry, and my mouth starts to fill with crumbs I can't swallow without gagging. The girl shows me how to hold the ball up to my mouth and squeeze. Wherever my mouth is, liquid shoots out. It's water, all right— about two liters of it, almost without taste.

"Don't drink it all at once, and don't eat all of the cake," the girl tells me.

"Thanks," I say.

Picker agrees with a nod. His cheeks are packed.

"He looks like a *squirrel*," I say, laughing, spraying soggy crumbs.

"What is squirrel?" Picker honks. He can eat and talk at the same time. I tap my own full cheeks. Again, we're laughing— laughing, eating, drinking. The cake tastes brown and dry and a little sweet. I can *feel* the food and water in my blood. Wonderful and strange, like I'm a husk filling out with both liquid and energy.

We strap ourselves into the couches within the dusty bubbles. I look through the hazy surface at the decayed body floating near the center of the big sphere.

"Somebody brought all this stuff here before they died," the girl says. "We should take the clothes. Even her clothes. They'll fit in one of these bags."

"Where does this stuff come from?" I ask. "I mean, where do you go to find it and bring it back?"

"Don't worry about that," the girl says. "Nothing makes sense until you find your book. Let's sleep."

Satmonk is already asleep. Nobody seems inclined to stay awake and keep watch. I really don't want to sleep. But I don't have much choice. My eyelids are the only thing about me that has weight.

Too bad.

It turns out to be a big mistake.

REASON IN SLEEP

Parts of my brain have time now to ask impossible questions. The body has time to assess its damage and register complaints to the incompetent management. Sleeping becomes a dark reservoir of itching, plus real pain—both sensations I can't wake up from—and then, those questions.

Part of me thinks it should be easy to return to Dreamtime and gets peevish when that doesn't happen—not the way I want it to happen. Dreamtime is the reality, obviously, and what I've just experienced is a nightmare, but struggle as hard as I can, there's no way to invert the relationship.

I remember joy and joining. I remember a tremendous sense of accomplishment and of camaraderie. Everyone cooperates. Everyone is anxious to get on with some exciting, monumental task.

Everyone looks like me, more or less.

It would be so wonderful to go back and rejoin my real friends—familiar and filled with unbridled hope. What's holding me back? Clearly, I've done something wrong. Maybe I've been winnowed out, or maybe I've been *cleaned* and put in the Ship's trash bin with the other rejects.

Maybe I'm in hell.

Not hell. Sick Ship.

What could I have done to deserve such judgment?

I can feel my body writhing on the couch, my slack mouth making embarrassing, primal sounds, but I still can't wake up. Instead, I drop into a different dream.

I'm trekking on the surface of that gigantic dirty snowball, naked again, lacking even tight, bloodstained shorts. As I stand on the crusty, frozen surface, not far from one of the sweeping, rising bands of that gigantic enveloping cage, I try to breathe—and realize I can't.

There's no air.

I'm in space. Isn't that obvious?

But not being able to breathe doesn't seem to matter. I'm compelled to learn by exploring, so I walk—and then try to *look up*. But no matter how hard I try, I can't raise my head. My sight lines stay level with the horizon.

I know the Ship is above me, but I have no idea what it looks like. This dirty snowball I've seen from above—I'm familiar with it. I can fill in the details, or at least make them up, make them convincing and self-consistent. The snowball is huge. I could walk for hours and not go all the way around it. The snowball is—

Water.

Mostly water and rock.

I begin to see how to play the game. Somewhere inside me there's knowledge, but it isn't integrated. It can only be unleashed by a combination of experience, observation, and... guilt. Trauma. I will learn by screwing up. Following that reasoning, I might learn a lot by dying.

Somehow, I've walked partway around the snowball, and I think maybe now I can look up and see *something*.... But I can't. I know something new, different, is above me. It's another *Ship* at the end of another broad spar, attached to the snowball on the opposite side. Not quite opposite, actually.

I don't know what that part looks like, either.

The Ships are big, but they are dwarfed by the snowball, of course—any schoolchild knows that. The snowball is like a gigantic yolk. It contains all the stuff necessary to get us to where we're going....

But I dreamed we had already arrived. The Dreamtime told me

WE!

ARE!

HERE!

Obviously we are not. The size of the snowball proves that fact. It should be smaller, a lot smaller, almost used up.

I'm still walking. Now and then, I *can* look up and see that incredible spray of pinpoints, the universe. Stars. Wisps with ghostly thin color. The galaxy. Then I'm walking over a third spot on the snowball where I can't look up—again, because I know what's there but I don't know what it looks like, either...yet.

A third Ship. A third part of Ship, actually. A trio strapped to a big snowball moon, under clouds and stars.

No. *Between* the stars. A serpent-marked moon lost and wandering between the stars.

I hate this hallucinogenic guesswork. The mind shouldn't be a game. Knowledge is who we are—memory and knowledge should be organized and easily available. After all, I'm a teacher.

I have to pee, but I'm also very thirsty.

I open my eyes. Really. I'm waking up. Heavy sleep still

murks my thoughts. Something important came to me in the sleep—three Ships. Three parts. Not where we should be. Nothing the way it should be.

My bag floats in front of my couch, attached by its drawstring to my wrist. I undo the couch straps and float free, wondering how one pees in weightless conditions, and rummage in the bag for the bottle of water.

Then I hear shouts and screams.

The shock makes me wet my shorts. Pee dribbles out and floats. I can't see through the smaller bubble where I've been sleeping. I focus on the translucent surface. It had been fogged with dust. Now it's spattered and smeared reddish brown. There's a handprint at the end of one smear, and streaks from trailing fingers.

Shadows move outside, forming silhouettes on the spatters and dust. From the light, I can see the ice ball is below us, reflecting up through the large blister. The shadows move fast, and hollow thumps echo through the domiciles.

The honking and warbling is awful. Then the honking stops. I can't hear screams now—the girl is silent. Maybe she got away—maybe she's hiding.

I look at the bubble's entrance. The opening is beyond the end of the couch.

Something big and red reaches through the hole and waves inside my bubble. I think it's an arm—it's covered with thick bristles or spikes and the end is like a spiky club. The club splits into a claw. I try to hide behind the couch, grabbing a strap and pulling myself down, then embracing the cushions and climbing under. I stop, wedged between the couch and the bubble, trying not to make a sound.

Trying not to scream.

The red spiky arm thumps against the couch, grabs it, tries

to yank it out to get hold of me. It knows where I am. It wants me.

As if things aren't complicated enough, I feel another push. The Ship is spinning up. Weight is returning. I'm shoved by invisible forces away from the couch, can't grab hold soon enough or tightly enough, and hang from the strap, muscles straining as the outboard acceleration grows stronger.

The spiky arm pulls back—I can see it swinging outside in wide, nasty arcs. More blood flicks against the bubble. I smell blood in the air—human blood—nasty, sweet. I still the whimpers that rise from inside my chest. If I let them out, they'll turn into screams, and the red jointed arm will come back for me—I just know that whatever is at the other end of the arm loves for living things to *scream*.

Then I hear a whimper. It's not the girl, not Knob-Crest—not Picker. Picker was the one hooting and honking earlier, and it might be *his* blood I see on my bubble.

There's a fight going on. The brownish red arm swings back with someone dark gripped in the spikes and slams him into the bubble, making the cluster vibrate and wobble.

I slip from behind the couch, grab the strap again, and drop-angle away from the center. The entrance to the bubble is near my head. I look down—the weight puts it below me, facing outboard—and consider just reaching out and pulling myself through, dropping away, hoping the spiky arm will be too busy to grab me, hoping there's not another of them, a whole nest of them....

Before I can make another move, shadows completely cover and obscure the light from outside. With a crunch, something dark is wedged into the hole—doubled up, feet toward me, arm toward me, hand curled into a fist—so close it almost touches my nose.

I shove myself sideways, feet bracing against the couch, and for a terrible moment, I'm face-to-face with Blue-Black, Pushingar, jammed in like a cork. He looks right at me, but in his agony he can't see me or doesn't care. His eyes shiver, then close. His mouth hangs open.

The arm drops back. The shadows outside pull or fall away. The weight is acting on all of us, pulling us counterclockwise and outboard. I'm stuck in the bubble. For the moment, this seems a good place to be—with Pushingar blocking the entrance. I look inboard and to my left—the smaller hole into the other bubbles is clear, just wide enough for someone my size or the girl, too small, I hope, for the creature with the spiky arm.

Spin-up gets more aggressive.

The body starts to tug free. The arm swings loose, and suddenly the whole corpse falls out. Through the spatters and smears, I see Pushingar drop away. His belly has been ripped open. Entrails precede him.

He lands with a ringing *thump* on the bridge.

I'm far from fear. Death doesn't matter—it's been certain from the beginning. I'm just a pair of eyes on the end of a stalk of neck with a brain and some hands and legs attached.

Before the acceleration reaches maximum, I crawl up toward the hole, cross through into another bubble—the one formerly occupied by the girl, now empty and no blood—and find another gray bag. Hers. Quickly, I empty the bag into my own—water bottle half filled, a mostly eaten chunk of loaf. Then back to my bubble and out through the exit formerly plugged by Blue-Black, where I hang for a moment by my hands, bag trailing by my hips, and let go.

I fall. It's the only thing I can do. My fall takes on an angle—a curve. The Ship reaches maximum spin before I land, and I realize I've miscalculated. I almost miss the bridge and land heavily on my legs, then topple over and lie there, sick, dizzy, and in pain.

Looking up at the cluster of domiciles. Around to the broken body of Pushingar, hanging over the rail a few meters away.

No sign of the others.

I get to my feet and take a quick look at the dirty snowball rolling once more beneath the Ship, seemingly around the Ship. Above the far limb of the snowball, I can see another part of the Ship—a part I couldn't see in my dream. What I can see, what is not hidden behind the crusty surface, looks like part of a long spindle, thick in the middle, drawing to a point forward. The sleeping vision was correct. There are other parts of Ship. Maybe those parts are better off, better organized than this one. Maybe I can escape and cross over.

But that thought is of no use now.

I walk the last hundred meters to the end of the bridge, across the blister. I pause and look back "up," inboard at the cluster of bubbles, translucent structures turned into homes by others before us—or traps baited with food and water.

Traps laid by something that waits until you sleep.

Despite the shock and the fall, rest and sustenance have made me stronger. My brain is working through a long list of clues and puzzles and problems—until it comes up with something obvious. Something unpleasant but necessary.

I stop, turn around, and walk back along the bridge to where Pushingar hangs lifeless and broken. He doesn't need his clothing. My lips form conciliatory words as I lug him off the rail and lay him out as straight as I can and strip him.

Soft, meaningless words of apology. I wonder if he knew the name the girl had given him. There's remarkably little blood

staining the fabric, given he was practically *disemboweled*.
That's a word I don't like—not at all.

The clothes hang on me, but I tuck up the pant legs, roll up
the sleeves, and then resume my walk.

Soon the cold will come.

Time once more to chase heat.

TRICKS OF THE TRADE

I've got some water—two bottles, each half full—and enough food to last maybe a day or two. Though without clocks, time is a shapeless thing. Each spin-up lasts for perhaps four or five hours—no way of being certain. Already I'm hungry. It seems I'll never stop being hungry.

I'm back in a corridor, but this one is wide and rectangular in cross section. There's a walkway and a rail on the right side, and to the left, on the other side of a double rail with rungs that can also serve as a ladder, two curved channels extend from the blister to wherever the corridor ends. Giant balls could roll in these channels. Maybe they are tracks for some sort of train or conveyance. I wonder at the size and obvious design and the equally obvious lack of occupants, passengers—colonists.

How many colonists could this ship—perhaps one of three—support, if it were functioning properly? The awful thought occurs to me that perhaps it *is* functioning properly. Perhaps we've all done something wrong and have been transported to this painfully difficult environment as punishment. It could be a prison for useless people, misbegotten servants, filled with things that lay traps and kill.

But things that don't always eat what they kill—the decayed corpse in the blister.

Only now do I wonder what became of that corpse while we slept. Did something come back and finally finish it off—consume what was left, after waiting a decent interval for it to "ripen"?

I see spots of blood and other tissues and fluids on the floor and on the walls. I stop and examine smears, handprints, and find the tips of a few broken spikes, sharp and orange. Another struggle. Maybe Picker and Satmonk injured whatever it was that killed Pushingar. Why would anything want to carry them this far? Where would it be taking them?

Someplace to eat them in private. Chasing heat, just like you.

The illumination in the corridor dims. Cold is coming. Ahead, I see something large, dark, and broken-looking sprawled across the walkway, draped over the railing. It's another dead cleaner, like the one in the trash chamber. As I get close, I see that the body has been cut or pulled into several large pieces. The shell has been split. Dark fluid everywhere, leaving an oily sheen.

I see no other bodies, unless they're stuck underneath the cleaner. I bend over and lift up a flat, limp "paw," and there's no sign of human remains. I squeeze past the broken shell and lifeless limbs, the somehow pitiful heads—three of them, as before—with their shiny, blind eyes.

Easy prey. Everyone kills cleaners—except the girl, who could not fight back.

I've been walking for some time now, and the wide corridor

finally reaches its end. A wall with two hemispheric bumps forms the terminus of the twin grooves, and at the conclusion of the walkway is a circular indentation about two meters wide, carved or molded into the wall's grayish surface.

I look back. The faintest breath of cold air washes over me. Soon the corridor will be unlivable. Likely the observation blister and the corpse of Blue-Black are already frozen. No going back without dying, and, apparently, no going forward.

I put down the bags. I haven't touched the girl's bottle or her piece of loaf. In gratitude for rescuing me, for not letting me die, for poking me along on a course to survival—up to this point—I hope to present her with these remnants if we meet again.

I lean against the wall at the end of the walkway. "Is there anybody else on this ship?" I wonder out loud.

"Whom are you addressing?" a voice asks. For a moment, it seems to be many voices, but then, I think, no, it's just one.

I jump back from the wall and spin to face it. I can't even begin to hope the voice is real. I don't want to test it by speaking again, much less asking another question. Perhaps there are only a few possible answers remaining—or silence. Perhaps I've used up my last question, made my last request for information—my one and only wish.

The cold is getting intense.

"How do I get through? Is there a door?"

I'm surprised by my audacity. I can't remember even formulating these questions.

"What is your origin, and what is your occupation?"

I think this over. "I'm a teacher. Others came this way, and I'd like to join them."

"Are you part of Ship Control?"

I don't think so. "No," I say.

"Then I made you. You're in the outer regions of Hull Zero One. It is not safe here. Move inboard, to the core."

Before I can react, the indentation deepens and the circle spins outward, leaving an opening. Beyond the opening is more darkness and only a little warmth. I step halfway through, then pause, waiting to be grabbed after being lured into a trap.

"Has anyone else come this way?" I ask.

"This opening will close in five seconds."

"Who are you?"

The circle starts to close. I jump through at the last second and roll on the other side, coming to rest against a sloping surface—a low, broad mound, smooth and, of course, gray. Little lights everywhere twinkle faintly in the gloom. Above me, the lights grow brighter.

I see I'm at the bottom of a wide, deep shaft. There's a tiny circle at the top of the shaft. The walls of the shaft join the floor in a curve, the mound in the center about three meters wide and a meter high.

The surface behind me shows no sign of the circular door. Up the shaft—inboard—is the only way out.

My left hand reaches out and encounters another bag—almost empty. Inside I feel only one thing, small and square.

A book.

I undo the knot in the drawstring and remove the book. It has a silver cover and forty-nine fine notches in seven rows of seven. The girl was brought this way. Knob-Crest and Scarlet-Brown might still be with her. Perhaps they escaped during the struggle with the cleaner—they certainly weren't strong enough to pull the cleaner to pieces. Cutting is more their style. The cleaner might have distracted the thing with the reddish spiky claw—that might explain the broken spikes on the floor.

They might have gotten away.

I can climb the rungs, or I can wait for spin-down and weightlessness. Examining the shaft, I see the best option—in the time remaining—is to climb.

I sling the bags over my shoulder, then adjust Blue-Black's loose overalls, trying to cinch the waist tighter. No use. After a bite of my loaf and a gulp of water, I piss against a wall—*Marking my trail*, I think, and grimace.

I start climbing. My mind is racing, stumbling over ideas and rough schematics, based on what I saw from the blister, the observation chamber, and remembering my walk in the drowsing dream.

The spindle—Hull Zero One, as the voice called it—rotates like a long, tapering axle within some sort of wheel fixed on the end of a strut. There are probably three parallel hulls at the ends of three struts, spaced equilaterally around the big chunk of dirty ice. The struts connect each hull to rails attached to the ice ball's wiry, confining cage. The hulls can move forward and aft along those rails.

I think I'm heading forward within Hull Zero One. I could also be in the rear half, moving aft. Orientation is difficult to judge with what little I know.

My best guess as to the size of this hull is that it's about ten kilometers long and perhaps three kilometers wide at the widest. As to the size of the ice ball, it's not really a ball. From what I saw, it's more like a *football*, oblong and at least a hundred kilometers long. The ice chunk dwarfs the hulls.

Too big. Should be much smaller by now.

Something has to push the hulls and the lump of dirty ice through space. Where are the motors? The engines? It seems likely that the engines are pretty powerful and not pleasant to be around. I have to conclude that the two halves of each spindly hull serve very different purposes.

I'm almost certainly heading forward.

What about the sinuous rill, the serpent shape carved into the ice?

Now my head *really* hurts.

I keep climbing. The outward tug grows weaker. Moving inboard reduces my centrifugal acceleration. The farther I go, the less the spin-up affects me. The effect is gradual but for some reason makes me feel even woozier than the intervals of spin-up and spin-down.

At least the climb gets a little easier.

I can't think of any reason for spin-up, spin-down. None of what we've experienced in the way of weight or lack of weight makes any sense, though I wonder if I might understand the theory behind cooling and heating. The hulls are huge and mostly hollow, with lots of spaces and volumes requiring lots of energy to maintain—assuming they're uniformly and constantly maintained. If we're not at the conclusion of whatever voyage we're making, and the passengers haven't been awakened...

"Then I made you."

The voice at the door. This derails my thought process but makes no more sense than anything else, so I rejoin the track I'd been following:

If most of the passengers haven't been awakened, then the spaces might be heated and allowed to cool at regular intervals, to keep the hull from warping. Or to save energy.

The passengers, the colonists, are all frozen, anyway—perhaps stored near the core, away from the outer hull, where there might be more radiation on a long, long journey.

So who woke up the monsters?

Not enough facts, not enough experience, far too much trauma, yet still not enough to complete my integration.

Climbing toward the core. I look down—and that's a mistake. My stomach almost spits back the loaf I've eaten. I concentrate on where I'm going. My feet are no longer necessary for the climb, so I just pull myself hand over hand.

"Where do these loaves come from? And the voice at the door?" The reverberation of my voice in the huge shaft is hollow but comforting. "Who or what is Ship Control?" The echo is too muddled to use as any sort of indicator as to how far I've come.

Spin-down catches me by surprise. My fingers are cramping. I've gotten used to reducing the strength of my grip on the rungs, so the gentle lurch and the resulting breeze in the shaft breaks one of my hands loose. I dangle for a moment, pulled more toward my left and the near wall of the shaft than down. I grab hold of the rungs with hands and toes and cling until the last little sensation of weight is gone.

Then, feet pointed toward the center of the shaft, perpendicular to the line of rungs, I continue on. It's almost like walking on my hands.

It's almost like being a spider.

Spider.

That word—and the image it conveys, of something traveling along a sticky strand, part of a web—sends a shiver through me. I don't know what spiders are, how big they are, or where they're from. A *spider* could have snatched my companions. But the more I search the shreds of my knowledge, the more I think spiders are too small—though still creepy.

Of course, it's always possible that in this life I'm very small as well.

I hate the uncertainty. Whoever woke me up, woke *us* up, was doing none of us any favors. What use are we? Maybe our only purpose is to be swept up, smashed around, destroyed— swatted like *flies.*

Spiders eat flies.

Ugh.

But so far, I've outclimbed and survived the cold. This part of the shaft seems to maintain a more constant temperature. Perhaps the core is more stable. The little lights in the walls of the shaft are dimming. Then brightening again. The intervals seem to be random. So much for stability. Things don't make sense here, either.

I've been focusing on my climb for so long that only when I reach down to scratch my hip and hitch up my pants do I look at a nearby patch of wall, a meter or so to my left. Some sort of scratch there. Then I see a lot of little abrasions—more scratches, lots of them, in an irregular circle all the way around the shaft, sweeping up and down—along with a few deep gouges.

Something strong, with strong claws, paused here and scrabbled against a spin-up. Something big enough to span the shaft—maybe five meters wide, limbs and all. Maybe it fell and was cleaned up.

Above the circle of scratch marks, there's something smaller, different, a patch of irregular lines. I reverse and overhand to where I might be able to identify it.

It's a drawing. A drawing in dark, dried paint—or something else. The smell has lingered faint in the air since I arrived in the shaft, but I've been trying very hard to ignore it—more human blood.

Use what you came with.

The sketch is crude, simple. Maybe it's not just a sketch, but an identifying mark. My eyes hurt trying to focus—the lights are dimming again. Finally I dangle and stretch out with one foot looped under a rung. My calf and ankle muscles bring me right up to the wall.

The sketch shows a plump, almost round figure. It could be

human, though the head is small and round and has no features except a kind of line where the eyes should be. The legs are squat and come together to form a point, with no discernible feet. I see a separate blotch, less than a centimeter broad—a fingerprint. I hold up my forefinger and compare. The lines were painted by a much smaller finger. A finger dipped in blood.

It seems likely the little girl drew this figure in the shaft—but why?

Below the rounded head, protruding like little sacs from the round body, are breasts—twelve of them. Twelve breasts, three rows of four. Only a few of the breasts have nipples. No time to dab them all in, I guess.

I swing slowly around. Fifty or sixty centimeters away, almost too faint to see—as if the supply of blood was running low—there's a handprint, the signature of the artist, just about the size of the girl's hand.

For a moment, whatever took her from the observation blister paused here, leaving scratches and gouges, while she made her own marks. In her own blood.

No time for wonder or fear or despair. I'm hungry and I'm thirsty. I move on. Try not to think. Try to keep breathing steadily. Then, before I know it, I'm at the top of the shaft, where I almost bump my head. There's a kind of big lid. On one side it's been raised enough to allow me through.

I've climbed perhaps two hundred meters inboard. If the hull is as thick as I think it might be, I'm not much nearer the core than when I began—but the shaft has reached an end, I'm tired, and I want to just drift for a moment.

Somewhere inboard I hear a deep, rhythmic sound, pervasive and faint—very distant. Like breathing. The entire ship, breathing. With the accompanying low thump of a calm, steady heartbeat.

I squeeze up through the gap between the lid and the shaft, then reach out and tap the lip with one hand, rotating to inspect the surroundings. I'm in a space that for the first time looks human scale, suited for habitation by my kind of human, with my kind of memory. A kind of room.

I catch my breath and hold out my hand to stop. The space at the top of the shaft is long, low, narrow. Lumpy shapes rise from the outboard "floor." In the shadows, I wonder if they might be furniture. As elsewhere in this hull, the walls glow with tiny spots of light, but here the illumination flows from place to place like waves on a pond, a kind of shimmer of light that somehow conveys the Ship is alive, watching—

Not that I can remember ever visiting a *pond*. A lot of things in my memory have no hooks in my real life.

Like smells. I smell a faint hint of char. My eyes are already adjusted, but it takes a physical inspection, moving slowly from ceiling to floor, approaching the lumpy objects on the floor, to learn that this space is designed to have an up and a down— designed for a sense of weight. I reach out to feel the objects that might be furniture and realize they're lumpy because they've melted, or perhaps never finished forming. Couches, chairs, tables...stunted like burned young bushes or trees. My fingers come away covered with oily soot. A blaze swept through the chamber some time ago. Floating close to the wall, squinting, I make out large, sweeping smudges from swirling flames. Many of the glim lights could have been burned, over-heated. Getting closer, feeling around gently, as if dealing with singed flesh, I study the resulting tiny pits.

Dead glims.

I move freely away from the lid and the long shaft, through the acrid air and toward the far wall, and observe another circular indentation, this one partway open but heated and warped—burned or jammed in place.

Going through the opening could help lead me around this inner circumference, a ring of rooms within the Ship.

Right now, however, I don't want to do anything but rest. Take a sip of water. Finish my loaf and consider whether I should drink the girl's water, eat her loaf, or try to read her book.

I don't actually know if I *can* read.

I hang in the air, bottle in hand, swishing the drink around my mouth. I'm near a charred wall. I hook my foot under what might have become a chair, next to an angled, agonized surface that might have tried to be a table.

I can kick away if something comes for me. I can sense a spin-up, when that happens.

My eyes begin to close.

I'm not really in charge anymore.

Oh, hello. Here you are.

It's a silvery smooth, sculptured face, more female than male but almost without feature, hovering before my darkened field of vision. I think I'm dreaming. Then I realize my eyes are halfway open. I'm not yet fully asleep. It's going to take some time to rouse up out of this exhausted torpor. The shock of seeing this face makes my muscles tingle, but it's still going to be another few seconds....

A silvery-smooth hand reaches out. Cool fingers lightly caress my cheeks, my forehead, poke under my hair to make combing motions. The face angles and gets closer, nose to nose, as if in affectionate curiosity.

Its eyes are blue, empty, and infinitely deep.

With a strangled yell, I regain control of my body and thrash. The face and questing fingers back off into shadow. I think my fist briefly connects with a semisolid, rubbery object—a shoulder or arm. I scream and thrash some more. My foot is still hooked under the half-formed table, and the pain of wrenching my ankle brings me back to self-control.

The chamber is empty but for me.

I take a deep breath, look around with several jerking motions, and confirm I am alone...now.

The room's illumination comes and goes in slow waves, as before.

I reach for the bottle of water and squeeze it into my mouth, draining it dry. Then I reach down for the bags. They're both strung around my leg, as I left them before trying to sleep.

But what I assume was—is—the girl's bag is now empty. No book. The remains of her loaf and bottle of water, still in my bag, have not been touched.

RULES AND DECORUM

I don't know how long I actually slept, but my mind feels sharper, more able to observe and cope with what I might find. This chamber is a mess. Maybe the fire scarred it so badly it just died—a funny concept, that parts of this hull are active and alive but can be injured and even die.

If I look at something long enough, I begin to put it into place, arrange it in some loosely defined perspective. But I did not dream the silvery face, because the girl's book is gone.

I've decided to drink her water and eat her loaf. With the book gone, I will have nothing to offer her should we find each other again. I don't want to think about it.

I move through the half-melted door into the next chamber. It's cooler here, but not dangerously so—not below freezing. As I enter, the walls brighten, and for the first time I see everything all at once, clearly, almost too bright to bear. My eyes take a while to adjust, and I feel exposed, but the moment passes, and

I see what these rooms must be like when they're healthy—when they're not burned.

The chamber is about thirty meters long, twenty wide, and five high—larger. Rectangular cubbies line the aft wall. The floor has many soft, square pads, arranged in parallel rows. I dimple one with my foot. Rods at the end of each pad support cocoons made of some sort of netlike fabric, bunched up and tied. They can be pulled out and crawled into so that one can sleep during spin-down. When there's weight, there are the pads. No blankets, except maybe the gray bags. Many gray bags hang from the forward wall, their drawstrings slung on loops.

I think, *People live here. Maybe they use this as a base camp while they go exploring. People retrieve bags and supplies and drop them off here. Someone should be watching over them.*

But this room is as deserted as the first. One thing seems obvious—the thing that grabbed the girl and the two others, the thing that jammed Blue-Black into the hole in the domicile bubble, couldn't fit through the gap in the jammed and half-melted door. I barely made it through myself.

Here comes the familiar push and outward tug. I grab hold of a cocoon and its rod and hang on while the spin-up brings back weight—less than I experienced in the outer reaches of the hull, but enough to allow me to walk without difficulty.

The temperature remains cool but gets no colder.

I let go of the rod and lick my lips at the thought of what might be in those bags. I'm distracted by a humming sound. The half-melted door has managed to open some more—a lot more. It's jammed at about two-thirds of its full width, a lunate remnant stuck in place. It's now about three meters wide, almost floor to ceiling.

My hope that it might block monsters is crushed.

Another door—undamaged—has opened as well, this one on the far side wall. My path is clear. Too clear, I think.

I walk to the wall of hanging bags and feel them. Most are empty, no loaves, no water bottles, no books. One contains soft goods. I pull it from its loop and pour its contents on the floor. Clothing. Blue and red, bright colors—as in the Dreamtime. Clean, no blood. I lift the overalls and hold them up to my body, then the jacket. They fit better than Blue-Black's outfit, so I strip down and put them on. They're more than a close fit—they might have been tailored for me. I reach into the overall pockets and find something in the right one—a thin, crinkly leaf. I pull it out. It's a flat square made of plastic, like a thick sheet of paper. It's been roughly erased on one side; there are still grayish marks that might once have been words. On the other side there's a red stripe.

I replace it in the pocket. *My* pocket. There's something in the other pocket as well—also small, flat, square, and flexible. I take that out. It's a reflective foil. It lies flat in my hand. I see my face in it. The image confirms what I was sure I knew already.

Mostly.

I have a nose, two eyes, a fuzz of black hair on my crown. There are raw patches on my cheeks where I fell to the freezing floor after being rescued from the storage sac—it seems months ago.

But there's something else as well. I have a ridge of low bony knobs under my skin, across the upper forehead. I feel it—it's real, solid beneath the hair and scalp. My nose is unchanged, my skin is the right color, but the bumps shake me.

It is one thing to wake up with a weird, half-functioning memory—quite another to wake up looking *different*.

I make a face, stick out my tongue, then put the mirror back in my pocket and examine the other gray bags. There are forty-three of them. Most are empty. A few contain clothing—too large, too small—but three carry bottles and loaves. Six bottles, six loaves—two of each per bag, like a ration.

The water in the bottles is not fresh but it's drinkable. I half drain one, then squat on a pad to eat one of the loaves. I finish it in a few minutes. Not luxury, certainly not the promised joy of Dreamtime (I still can't catch more than colored glimpses), but better than anything I've experienced until now.

I have strength. A stirring of curiosity.

I feel almost human.

I walk between the pads to the next door.

AN UNEXPECTED PLEASURE

The little girl is waiting beyond. The room is dark. She's half in shadow. She quirks her face, turns, walks away.

I pinch my arm to make sure I'm awake.

The room beyond lights up and shows her silhouette a third of the way across. She's wearing green overalls. She looks back at me through those piercing gray eyes.

"Go away," she says. "You're useless. You always die."

I can't think of any response except, "Where are the others?"

Two different people step into view—not our previous companions. They stand beside the girl. One's an adult female, the other a half-grown boy. The adult female is haggard. The half-grown boy has a face that seems ready to smile. They might be related—same color hair, brown, same shape and color of eyes, brown. Their skin is pale, and they have long noses and long fingers. Otherwise, they're like me.

I try to smile, act friendly. I lift my bag. "I've got food and water," I say. The woman and the boy stare.

I point at the girl. "I thought you were dead."

Finally, the woman deepens her look of resignation and says, "It's starting over."

"You didn't survive," the boy says to me.

"This one isn't *him*, idiot," the woman says.

The little girl just stands with her back to me, but her shoulders slump.

"Where'd you come from?" the boy asks.

I gesture behind.

"There are lots of doors and they open different ways," the woman says. "Did something let you in here?"

"There was a hatch, and a voice in the wall," I say. "It asked me if I was from Ship Control."

"Are you?" the woman asked.

A twinge of caution. "I don't remember."

"He's Teacher," the girl says. "He'll die, too."

"Show him," the boy says. That hint of a smile is starting to bother me.

"Not yet," the woman says. "It's nice to be innocent—for a while."

I address the girl's back. "Something snatched you. Maybe the others. There was a fight, back near the transit tube...with the grooves. Something brought you here...."

I have the strangest feeling none of them knows what I'm talking about. "There was a fellow with a knobby crest and a fellow with brown skin and scarlet markings. You called them Picker and Satmonk. A Blue-Black man—you called him Pushingar—was killed and stuffed in a hole...which is how I survived, I think."

The boy snorts. "Not too bright."

"There are doors, lots of doors," the woman tells me again. "Destination Guidance wants us all dead—wants us cleaned out."

This is the first I've heard of *Destination Guidance*.

"But something else wants us alive," the woman continues. "That's all I know. My head is full of useless crap."

"You don't know me?" I ask the girl softly.

"No," the girl says without looking back.

"Did you make that drawing in the shaft?" I ask, lifting a finger and sketching in the air.

"No."

"Let's *show* him!" the boy cries with an anxiousness not entirely for my benefit. He sounds as if he's been bored for a long time. Showing me would be exciting.

I don't like that at all. But I ask, "Show me what?"

"There's lots of food," the woman says, "and water this far in toward the core, so you're not going to be a problem—or much of a help, unless you know something you haven't told us. Where's your book?"

I shake my head. "I used to have *your* book," I tell the girl. "Someone came while I was asleep and took it."

The girl turns. "You lost it?" she asks with a flash of anger.

"Yes. Something silvery—"

"There isn't *anything* silvery," the boy says, his smile gone. "No robots. No metal men. Teacher said that—but he's gone and you're *not* him."

"How many marks on that book?" the girl asks.

"Seven big ones, seven scratches each—forty-nine," I say, suddenly lonely and knowing that if they don't accept me, I might as well just die.

"She was worth more than *all* of you," the little girl says. "But you lost her, too."

"We sleep too much, that's our problem," the woman says, then smiles in a half-friendly way, as if she's warming to me— or at least to the concept of having another join this odd little group.

"There are other books," the boy says to the girl. "Show him."

The woman waves me forward, and I step through the door. As soon as I'm in the next room, the door closes behind me. The room is empty—no cots, no bags, just brightness. The room is so evenly illuminated that I have a hard time deciding how big it really is.

"I guess this place thinks you might be useful," the woman says. "Let's go. There's another place not far from here. You'll need to see it eventually."

"You won't like it," the boy says, smiling yet again. It's not a nice smile. I decide I don't like him.

"I didn't make any drawing," the girl says.

"All right."

Nobody offers to shake hands or touch, and nobody exchanges names. Funny I should wonder about that—I still don't know my own name. I suppose that's a common condition here. Maybe this girl will name me like she did the others.

But then, the ones she named all died.

"You remember the Dreamtime?" the woman asks as she turns and heads to her left. The others follow, so I keep step.

"Not very clearly," I say.

"You know where we are?"

"A Ship," I say. "We're in space somewhere."

"Do you know that for sure?" the boy asks.

"I was near the outside. The outer hull. I saw stars."

"We've never been there," the woman says.

They do not seem curious to hear any more about the stars. A door slides open on the wall in front of us, and we step through—and the next space is amazing. It's like a jungle, only the plants are hanging in the air. Wires crisscross everywhere, shaping a three-dimensional grid. A bridge like the last bridge—with a grating and a ladder over one rail—passes through. I suppose it connects to the other side, but I can't see that far; it's obscured by plants hanging, clinging, blooming. The space is at least as big as the junk-collection void. The foliage is so thick we have a hard time crossing, and I'm almost giddy with the smell and the colors—green leaves, blue stems and trunks, red flowers, pink pods.

"You can't eat those," the boy says. "Don't even try."

"He tried a long time ago and got sick," the woman says. "Came out of a sac dumb, like all of us. The girl finds some like you and takes them elsewhere, but she won't tell us where."

"She's lost," the boy says.

"Am not lost," the girl insists. "Just waiting."

Now I know for sure this isn't the same girl. Same size, same face, same eyes, same hair, the same personality—just a different girl, less energetic, fading like a bee away too long from the hive. I don't know what makes me think of that, except we're surrounded by flowers.

The woman pushes aside branches and red petals break away and twist down. Above us, I see something moving slowly, hanging from the wires. From what I can make out through the growth, it's orange and blue and round, four or five meters wide, plenty big enough to be scary. I think again of spiders and flies.

"Don't worry about that one," the woman says. "It stays in this space. Doesn't bother us. It cleans up the garden."

We make it halfway across the bridge. Another bridge intersects, forming an X. We go left again. "There are rooms that make food," the woman continues. "They give us water and a place to live and sleep. We usually stick close to them, but there's something you have to see."

The orange and blue doughnut clambers by, passing over the bridge. Lots of thin legs with tiny sharp hooks and snipping claws. It pauses, looks us over through a fringe of shining kitten-blue eyes, then drops along the wires, swinging and hooking around the plants. It's not really like a spider, because the body is shaped like a circle, a torus, a *doughnut*.

A taste comes into my mouth, sweet and crumbly, and there's something hot and bitter along with it—*coffee*.

"Makes you think of coffee, doesn't it?" the woman asks. "I don't know what coffee is. Do you?"

"Not yet." I'm mostly glad to be with them, glad to be traveling in company again, but I'm also scared. I don't think I'm going to like what they're about to show me, because the woman is looking more downhearted and the boy more excited, with a nervous, trick-or-treat aspect.

"How long you been awake?" the boy asks.

"Days. Not long."

We reach the other side. A door is open.

"This one *never* closes. That lets the smells from the garden into our rooms," the boy says.

"It's sweet," the woman says, "but I'm getting tired of it. I think I'll move on." She puts her arm around the girl. The girl doesn't like her touch but is too tired to shrug it off.

"You *do* that," the boy says. It sounds like an old dispute.

The woman goes first and crooks her finger, urging me to follow.

TEACHER LEARNS TOO MUCH

We've crossed the garden, gone through the open door, and walk down a short corridor that intersects another corridor, where the boy sweeps his arms in welcome. "This is home," he says.

The glim lights are bright enough to see clearly but are dim compared to the garden. A long line of doors stretches hundreds of meters to either side. The curve here is more distinct. Chambers open on both sides. The ceiling or inboard wall may be transparent, but looking up doesn't solve any mysteries, because the inner spaces of the hull are dark. A few small fogged lights, vague shapes, are all I can make out. I wonder if these rooms are where the colonists will stay when they all awaken and get ready for the landing.

The boy leads the way. The girl hangs back five or six paces. The woman is right behind me, too close. We walk perhaps forty meters, passing six chambers on both sides, and the air suddenly chills. It's freezing again—but it feels like this place is *always* cold.

One of the doors is bigger, an opening into another corridor—a long one, bluish at the far end.

The woman pauses, straightens one arm, flicks her hand, then turns left again. *Wisely widdershins.* Maybe I don't remember that part correctly, about widdershins being lucky.

"Anyone have a map?" I ask.

"We don't need one," the boy says. "We mostly stay here."

I ask the woman, "Where do all these creatures come from? The one in the garden, the tooth-snout, the cleaners?"

"Some are factors," the woman says. "That's all I know."

"She thinks she should remember that stuff," the boy says. "But she just can't cough it up." He mimics throwing up, finger in his mouth, then applies the damp finger to his head and grimaces. "Messes her up."

"It should be different," I agree.

"I don't remember anything from Dreamtime," the boy says. "I'm happier without it, I guess. You say this is a ship—I've never seen it that way. It just goes on forever, with people stuck inside. That's all."

He guides me left into another hall. The hall expands into a wide tube. The floor goes on, but we're walking through a long cylinder lined with rectangular glass cases. The cold here is different. It has purpose. The light has gradually shaded into deep *sapphire*, like the inside of a *glacier*. I don't know what a glacier is, except that some existed once where we came from. Mountains of ice sliding like rivers…

I see in my thoughts a wall of blue ice and white snow and maybe somebody climbing—a poke of memory so muddled I don't feel right sharing it. Glacier. The spill of sense and imagery that fans out from this word is fascinating enough that if I were alone, I'd stop and close my eyes and just savor the visual and even tactile memories about snow and ice and sliding around on long boards, about polar caps and cubes bobbing in frosted glasses of sweet tea and lemonade—another lifetime of things icy, nothing like this bitter frigidity.

"Don't look until she says," the boy says.

I can't help it. I look. The cases are coated with rime. We walk by a dozen, two dozen—all the same.

"Stop," the woman says.

The boy watches me with that awful grin.

Blue light everywhere. More cases covered with frost. My feet are freezing. The girl hasn't kept up. I don't see her. I start to say something, but the boy pushes me forward. The woman guides me.

"It's like a meat locker in here," I say. I remember the tastes of steak and lamb and pork, all *meats* you want to keep cold so they won't spoil. But nobody eats meat anymore. There's something else—that word again, *fish*. Frozen fish, stacked like *cordwood*, whatever *that* is.

"We're all meat waiting to happen," the woman says, pleased at my expression, pleased that once again our thoughts seem to be in sync.

"We don't belong here," I say. Cases on all sides, above and below…

"Not when we're alive, we don't," the boy agrees.

"Okay," the woman says. "This one. Look close." She leans over and rubs away some frost. Behind the clear surface, the case is stuffed with the same sort of sleeping cocoons I saw earlier, drawn out full length and stacked three or more to a case.

Inside each cocoon is a body. Some are badly damaged—gaping wounds, limbs missing, heads gone. Not much in the way of color except for that glacial blue. "Are they all dead?" I ask.

The boy says, "Look *close*." He grabs my neck and shoves my head forward. I want to resist, to strike out and smash him…but I don't. My nose almost touches the case. It's so very cold. My skin would stick, just as it did before.

A few centimeters away, on the other side of the transparency, a head sticks out. It's a man. The cocoons are too short to serve as shrouds. The face's expression is hard, eyes blank, jaw frozen open. The cocoon is slack below the waist. The lower half of the body is missing.

It takes a moment to register what I'm looking at.

Who I'm looking at.

The features are the same, the shade of hair is probably the same. I bend and swipe my own hand, risking the cold. The body below shows another face in profile. I reach up and wipe frantically. The body above has no head. The body above that one has its back to me.

I shove the boy away and cross to the opposite side. There, I bob up and down in front of more stacks. Bodies above, beneath, all around. I run to the next row, the edge of my palm burning with cold, but it's the same—and the next, using my other hand—

Dozens of cases, hundreds of frozen bodies, stretching off into a deep sapphire distance. I've inspected twenty or more of the cases on both sides. The faces I can see are all like mine. All the same. Just like mine.

"Get it?" the boy asks, fairly vibrating with excitement. The woman has crossed her arms and is trimming her fingernails with her teeth. She spits out a bit of nail.

The new memories and new words mean nothing. I don't want to think, I don't want to understand. I want to be empty.

"We shouldn't be caught here when the weight goes," the woman says. "Hard not to hurt yourself."

She takes me by the arm, gently, and leads me up the long corridor and to the right, out of the blueness and toward the warmer rooms, where people are given food, where living people go and are welcome.

They push me through a door into cloying warmth. I stumble into the flowery sweetness of jungle air and the boy and the woman just stand there while I kneel and then fall over on a pad.

I'm weeping—weeping like a child.

The boy watches with satisfaction. The woman watches with wonder. "It's not so bad," she says soothingly. "You always come back."

I've been here before. I can't deny what I've seen. I've been here hundreds, maybe thousands of times, trying to do whatever it is I'm meant to do.... And every time I've failed.

Every time I've died.

PART TWO

- - - - - -

THE DEVIL

— — —

You saw another one like me?" the little girl asks.

I come up out of a deep, hot stupor and turn over on the pad. I'm feverish. Someone's slipped me into a cocoon, I've slept hard, I can feel it in my muscles, slept through a spin-down, and now there's weight again.

With a groan, I push myself out of the cocoon and lie panting and sweating on the pad. The edges of my palms hurt like hell—frostbite.

The girl holds out a bottle of water. I sit up and drink.

"You saw another one like me?" she asks again, hopeful.

"Like you." I drink more. The lights brighten.

"She had a book?"

"Yes."

"Did you read it?"

"No time. I wanted to return it…when I saw her again. I saved her food and water for a while, too, but…"

The girl nods. "Where was she going?"

"She wanted to go forward."

The woman comes through a round doorway between the linked domiciles and stands for a moment, biting another fingernail. She must put each finger through rationed rotation, ten little luxuries. "Now you're really back," she says.

I don't know how to respond.

"What do you know?" the girl asks. "What have you learned from where you've been?"

This is a reasonable question, though why she waits until now to ask it…Maybe she thinks I've learned something essential and now I'm ready to talk sensibly. I think about what I know. It isn't much.

"How many of me have you met?" I ask.

"Ten," the woman says. "They went forward. The cleaners brought some of them back and put them in the freezers. When the girl came here, she was alone. She says there are others like her…but she won't tell me more than that. Maybe you can persuade her." They exchange a look. The girl's face is rigid. She has a steel will.

"Tell us your story," the girl says.

I tell them what I know. After a few minutes, the boy joins us and listens skeptically.

"We're on a Ship," I conclude. "A Ship in space, between the stars. I thought we were supposed to sleep, to be awakened when we near our planet. That's what I remember from Dreamtime. A little girl just like you pulled me out of a room full of new bodies. She said we have to chase heat or die. Doors closed behind us.… "

I go on. The highlights for the girl and the woman seem to be that there are three parts to the Ship—three hulls—and that we're connected to a giant piece of dirty ice. I add something new: that the ice might provide fuel and reaction mass for the Ship.

I tell them again about the voice from the wall. The spin-up and spin-down they've figured out. The boy doesn't want to hear about the silvery figure. He doesn't seem interested in most of my story, but this bit really upsets him.

They don't know much about the cycling heat and cold. Here, places that are warm stay warm, and places that are cold stay cold.

"Tell us again about the voice," the woman says.

"It asked me if I was part of Ship Control. It says it made me. I didn't understand."

"You weren't asleep. You weren't awakened. You were *grown*," the girl says. "*She* pulled you out. *She* thought you were important. You keep trying to go forward."

I think this through as carefully as I can, given my thudding heart and the urge to just sit and scream. My hand reaches into my overalls pocket and pulls out the square piece of plastic with the stripe on one side and the scrub marks on the other. I hold it up. "What's this for?" I ask.

"For remembering stuff," the girl says. "You get them and make them into books." She reaches into her own pocket, feels something there, and makes a bitter face.

"Do I always tell you what I know before I go forward?" I ask.

The woman puts her hand on the girl's shoulder. The girl shrugs it off.

"Give it to him. By rights it's his," she says.

"He didn't bring *mine*," the girl says. "He lost it. Maybe the next one will have it."

I stare at the square of thin plastic.

"I don't have one," the woman says, turning away. "I've never had one. But that doesn't mean you shouldn't have yours."

"Give it to him," the boy says. "There'll be others."

"But it's been so long, and I need to find my mother," the girl says, her voice cracking. "I need *Mother*."

I look between the three of them.

"It's pretty comfortable here," the boy says. "I close the door when the cleaners come. We hide. I tell the rooms to make food. The rooms listen to me. I say, give him his book."

The boy seems to want to be in charge. This might be his version of a threat. The girl puts on a stubborn face, then simply looks tired. She pulls a black-covered rectangle out of her pocket. "It doesn't say anything about Mother. Most of it's just stupid."

I reach to take it from her quivering fingers. "Thank you," I say.

Then she pulls out a short, thin stick with a blackened, sharpened tip, a kind of *pencil*. "You can use this if you want."

I hold it. My fingers are sweaty. My eyes lose focus. We are born in ignorance, we die in ignorance, but maybe sometimes we learn something important and pass it along to others before we die. Or we write it down in a little book.

"The hallways going forward are full of freezers," the boy says. "As far as I care to go, which isn't very far, they're full of bodies. Must be thousands of them."

"They're waiting to be born again," the girl says. "Mother will make them all better. I think then they turn into girls like me."

The boy makes a face. "Let's get some food," he suggests.

THE MAN OF THE BOOK

The boy's inner residence has the usual pad and accordion cocoon, as well as a weird nest of bars and springs that might be exercise equipment. Long cables hang from the walls and the ceiling—good for grabbing when the weight goes. Most important, a thick tube rises from the middle of the floor. It has a rounded top with a square hole. The hole produces loaves, and if you put a bottle in the hole, it fills with water from a spigot that folds up out of sight when it's done.

If Ship recognizes you, you get all you really need, and not one thing more—like a *hamster.*

After we eat, everyone is quiet, and I somehow get that they expect me to go into another room—there are several open doors down the corridor—and read my book in private. That's the last thing I want. But it's a ritual, apparently. It's happened before.

Maybe I'm the only entertainment around here.

That thought almost makes me puke. I leave them to their

imaginings. I'm thinking and feeling so hard that the spin-down catches me by surprise and I stumble and have to scramble back against the push, to get into my smaller, emptier room before all the weight is gone.

I float there—echoing slowly from wall to ceiling to floor, refusing to grab the cables—and pretend to lie back. Relax.

I can't gather up the courage to open the damn thing. I am who I am. All those others…well, there's every reason to deny them their place, their reality, because it leaves me with an insoluble problem. Identity.

What lies in my memory, waiting to be accessed, might just duplicate what's already written in the book. Someone might have explored all of my knowledge, made all of my possible choices, run me completely out of fresh options. Someone might have lived my life all the way through.

I look closely at the book. Somehow, it feels like *my* book. It has little hallmarks of the character I might yet find inside my head. But I won't believe that—not yet. I am who I am, and there's no one else like me in the universe—right? That is a fact. It will remain a fact.

Until I open the book.

I've rolled it around in my hands for an hour. It's made up of leaves of plastic, thinner than the one in my pocket. A thick brittle glue holds the leaves, the pages, between the black boards. The boards have a frayed, stained look, as if they were ripped or bent from a bigger sheet—something found in a garbage void. The stains might be blood. There are also dark marks on the page edges.

Not opening the book could be suicidal. How many times have I had access to a book like this and refused to open it—echoing through mistake after mistake, without the heavy assurance of past experience to guide me? But I *know* I've lived for years, decades, that I wasn't just squirted into a sac and shaken into existence a couple of dozen spin-ups before. This conviction is necessary for my sanity. This conviction is going to kill me. Now of course it's time to curse my maker, whoever that is—the hull or Ship Control or *God*...

The first time I've thought of *that* name, that concept. It should open so many new doors...but I don't feel it. The word is curiously empty. I have a stronger connection to whatever Ship Control is, or even Destination Guidance.

I'm more miserable now than I've been during my short existence, including the physical pain and the blind, newborn fear. It's the freshness of my fear that convinces me, finally. Pain is forgotten, but fear builds and leaves tracks, and I don't feel those tracks—not in my thoughts, not in my flesh. All my fears are new and short. I don't have enough of them to help me survive. Not enough experience.

I'm an idiot not to open the book.

I pull back the front cover. The glue makes a cracking sound. I hold it up and look at the spine—wouldn't want to damage it, after all. The glue has little bubbles, might come from something organic. Maybe it's dried factor blood. Maybe the stains on the cover aren't human blood but something else. I pull the book away, focus, squint.

I will literally lose my self in its pages.

First page begins with a thick black line.

———————————

I've been alive one hundred cycles of spin-up and spin-down. Funny, the people I meet all use those words—they're part of the patois of survivors in the hull. You're a teacher. You know what patois is. The book I was given—from my previous incarnation—had that word in it, but not much else. Books get lost. I've pulled apart this book and combined it with pages from others, adding blank pages when I can to record what happens next.

The other pages come from earlier. I mark them clearly.

Good luck.

P.S. If you're me, you'll figure out how to read the rest. If you're not me...Well, we do like to trade information, and I wouldn't want to give the others an advantage.

Someone seems to really hate me.

Hate you.

The rest of the book is written in what reads at first like gibberish—random letters, scrawled slowly and carefully, or in real haste, but always gibberish. I close the book and grip it tight. I'm not even quite sure what patois is—some sort of meat paste? Or a way of speaking. I think it's the latter.

Maybe I'm not me—or him. Maybe something's been lost. Certainly I don't have all of my memories, even all of my knowledge. But of course I don't have any memories, really...if I was made just a short while back. Pulled out of a sac. Then anything I remember from before I was made, finished, whatever, is just imprinting.

Instinct.

TIME RUNS OUT QUICKLY HERE

After a while, I'm settled in, about one good kick away from the ceiling, drifting and dozing. Best not to get caught away from shoving distance of a surface, in case something comes by—something that wants to clean me up and put me in the freezer.

One hundred cycles, the first page says.

I'm just a *youngster*, then.

Youngsters play games with words. I sort of see sunlight on a bedcover, a notebook, and a game. I see a row of white pickets on a fence. Switch the pickets: fence rail code. The game has to do with letters in the alphabet, exchanging one letter for another. To make this simple code harder, I convert everything I write into pig Latin before transposing the letters. Then I show it to my kids in school to see if they can read it. (I can almost smell the schoolroom: chalk, pencil shavings, steam heat from old radiators, gym socks, ham sandwiches in paper bags waiting for lunch.)

Some of the kids can unravel the code. They become my friends. Most can't. We call them…

Losers.

That's it, then. I'm not a loser. I know how to play the game.

I come out of my doze and open the book. After a while, I'm reading pretty quickly. I might even be able to write in code quickly, with a little practice. I'm good at that sort of thing.

PAGE 2

I'm making my way forward. My cold-burns are healing. The girl is dead. She was killed by a tooth-worm. It tore her to pieces.

I wonder if the little girl always dies, too.

Some of the things here are alive but act like machines. There aren't any robots—though I did see a silver woman or thin figure of some sort, but only for an instant.

Let me describe the things that are here and can be dangerous.

FACTORS: Cleaners most important. Cleaners try to keep everything spick-and-span. They have three heads/faces and six legs. Most of the factors do very well without weight. They also do OK when there's weight. They take us away when we die—and sometimes even before we die, if you can't avoid them. Other factors: fixers and processors. Cleaners or scouts call fixers if the Ship has been damaged. They're pretty single-minded, but they're only dangerous if you get between them and something that needs fixing.

Processors look scary and can be very dangerous, but they tend to stick around junk balls. The toothy eel is a processor. It converts dead organic material to simpler slush. Ugh.

Fixers and processors are getting rare, I hear. I've seen only two.

Scouts: smaller, thinner. Rare now as well.

Gardeners: They're the only factors that have real color. The others are dark brown or dark gray or black.

Factors see heat and are generally inactive during cooldown.

And there are killers. That's what I call them. Knob-heads call them Xhh-Shaitan. Hard to pronounce, even if I hold my nose. It seems to mean "Maker of Pain."

Killers.

Only a few of us have seen a killer and survived. No one I've met can give a clear description. Killers destroy and leave the dead behind, but they also collect—alive. Where they take those they collect is unknown. The hull cooperates with killers. They can go anywhere—fast. Makes me angry, like the deck is stacked against us. (Think about that and try to remember card games—their play and their rules make excellent metaphors around here.)

Sometimes, the hull helps us—why this contradiction, I don't know.

Now—why the hull gets cool. There are three hulls. Based on Dreamtime, I think they are supposed to join at some point and become one, but that's not clear yet. The Blue-Blacks say the hull gets cool because something wants us all to die. The little girl said it's to save power, and she seemed to know a lot—but she wanted her mother badly, and was losing her own energy—fading rapidly.

Killers or cold or making other mistakes eventually remove us *all* from the scene.

And of course there are lots of versions of me, all dead. That means there's a template. Maybe a lot of templates. For some reason, a word sticks up now—*Klados*. I don't know what that means.

But hull is sick. Ship is sick. Something broke or went wrong—or something deliberately changed the rules. That's why I'm heading forward—to answer those questions.

I rested for a while with the sluggards. The sluggards have a comfortable place and they just stay there. The boy in particular has made a cozy den. The room obeys his instructions but doesn't cooperate with the rest of us. I wonder why. The woman is discouraged, maybe because she has to rely on the boy—and he can be irritating.

They aren't going to go with me or help me find answers.

If they give you this, then you know about the freezers and the bodies. You know I'm dead. Take a deep breath. When you go forward—and you will—it gets worse.

Something doesn't want us going forward. That might be Destination Guidance. I have no idea what that is—or who.

I've gone forward and down to the core. Here's a little map.

Follows a sketch showing the tip of the spindle, an X marking the beginning of my (his) trip, and a dotted line zigging rather mysteriously toward the middle of the spindle and then jogging forward the merest fraction—a dot and a half, almost.

I passed three forest balls and several junk balls. Processors were recycling broken parts—including factors. Lots of factors damaged recently. Are there wars in the hull? I believe I've found a

———————————————

A brutal dark line.

The Ship is very badly off. I've come upon a crude membrane that separates much of the forward sections from (I assume) vacuum. Pressure bellies the membrane outward from surviving bulkheads and stanchions, and it's translucent, I think, but I can't make out anything except a grayish blur that might be the ice ball—our big/little moon. The moon with the snake carved into it. Serpent Moon.

Considering how near the core I think I am, that means a pretty big chunk of the Ship is missing on the ice ball side. Factors are still cleaning up; it's dangerous to travel around here because they might mistake me for debris and haul me to a junk ball. Some chambers are so badly scarred I can't imagine they'll ever be recovered, but repair factors are still at work, moving sluggishly, relaying the active surfaces a few centimeters at a time, working only during spin-down. I'd describe these spaces but you'll

———————————

Another dark line.

This has to be quick. I think I know a little about Destination Guidance. There was a work party revived a long time ago. All this is vague, because the concepts that support my suppositions are still buried somewhere in Dreamtime. I think the Ship (we are definitely on a Ship in space, between the stars—physically, really, not just a mock-up) came to a point in its journey where a decision had to be made between two or more candidates, planets or stars with planets. A team was created to make that decision. I don't believe they ever lived in the hulls. They were probably created on a station or "bridge" down on the ice moon. Far away—down below, inboard, and maybe a little behind the leading points of the hulls.

Covering most of a page in the book is something fascinating—a quick sketch of part of Ship. It looks like this:

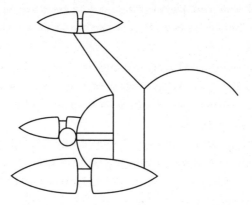

I suppose if someone draws a map for a baby, the baby has to spend years growing up enough to even begin to understand. But we are not exactly babies. This sketch means a lot of things to me. It graphically confirms what I thought I saw in the observation blister and in my dream. The scale is off—the moon/ice ball should be much bigger, the spindles longer and smaller in comparison to the moon—but the rough truth of it is evident.

This is Ship, then. Three hulls shaped like spindles, one big oblong ice moon, and something I think must be at the leading point of the moon, between the spindles...way down below.

It makes sense. It arouses things from Dreamtime that start me quivering until I worry I won't be able to stop. This isn't the way it was supposed to be. The Ship is not just sick, it's gone *way wrong*.

Wrong way.

I read on.

> The little sphere down there, from what
> I've been told, is actually pretty big, but not
> nearly as big as the spindles. She's visited, the

tall, lean one, kitten-gray, kind of pretty. She may or may not be a sport. But she's gone now. Little Killer got her.

And inside this sphere, Destination Guidance was born and was supposed to make decisions about which planet or star we would fly toward. There were five.

The tall one seemed to have her own set of patterning, her own knowledge. She knew a lot about Ship that I don't. She said Destination Guidance is raised from true infants, originals, unblemished—unpatterned.

I'm not sure what she meant. I certainly remember being a child, even being a baby—some things, anyway.

But after they do their job, they are supposed to retire or maybe even just die. I don't know how long they were supposed to work. From what I've seen, however, I think a mistake was made. A bad mistake. It nearly destroyed this hull. The other hulls might be all right—I don't know, since I can't see them directly, only in this walking dream I have. (That's <u>walking</u>, not waking. I walk over the ice ball and look up sometimes. But you probably have the same dream.)

Destination Guidance. Something scared them badly, maybe started all this, made the Ship sick, I'm learning from

———————————————————

Damn, another brutal dark line.

I found my own body this time. It's true, then. I was never a baby.

It's dark at the core. The big store of liquid water keeps it from getting too cold. I can't see them. Don't come here. One is small, one is big. The small one is worse

That's it. The book has maybe five more blank pages. It had to end badly, of course, but I wonder at the strength necessary to keep writing even after being "caught"—and losing the blood that stains the cover and page edges.

It's human blood, all right.

I'm exhausted. There's weight now. I was decoding and reading right through spin-up, but found a corner to ride it out and hardly noticed. I stick the book in my pocket, next to the flexible mirror, and then take out the mirror and look at myself again.

It scares me, but I know I'm not going to stick around and sponge off the boy. I'm almost reconciled to that. To being a tool in some greater process. It's not faith, it's certainly not comforting, but holding that identity and purpose in my pocket—and maybe in my dreams—is more important than anything that's happened to me yet.

I need to sleep. I want to see if I dream something more about the Ship, the hulls—if the book has opened the spigots of memory I *know* are there.

The woman and the boy shout through the open door. I've been dozing for what feels like minutes. In that brief time, I've come up with a face: a female face, not the woman who lives with the boy. I try to recover her features, but it's no use.

The voices are insistent.

The boy and the woman drag me out of the room and down

the hall to the boy's room. The boy makes a motion with his hands on the wall and the door closes.

"They're coming," he says. "We stay in here and they leave us alone."

"Where's the girl?" I ask. I don't see her—there's not enough furniture to hide even her small frame.

"The girls are frail," the woman says. "They can't spend too much time away from their mother."

"Where's their mother?" I ask.

They both shrug. We sit together, saying nothing, not even looking at each other. The atmosphere is sad, stifling, like caged animals in a *zoo*.

Then the woman looks up at me, biting her lip. There's sweat on her bare arm. We're sitting on a low couch with a straight, square back that is soft enough not to hurt, but not much softer. The boy either has only a loose sort of control over this room after all, or likes it Spartan.

I have no idea what that word means, but it implies serviceable but not comfortable.

The woman slides down a little, eyes still fixed on mine, until we're almost touching. She puts her hand on my leg. This provokes an odd feeling. I don't know what to do. Her touch certainly isn't appropriate, given the danger outside—but then, maybe that's why she does it, because she's frightened and wants reassurance.

But I know sure as God made little green *apples* (there it goes again! Spartan apples, maybe) that I'm not the one from whom she's going to get reassurance. Still, I pat her hand, then remove it gently, letting it rest limp and damp on the couch. This effort has cost her. The sadness inside me is almost unbearable.

"He's not the one for you," the boy says to her, having

watched with a detached expression. "The hull made him that way. It will *never* be you."

"Shut up," the woman says.

"*You* shut up," the boy says.

The woman clears her throat. The boy gets up and places his ear against the space where the door was. He moves his hands again. Turns and smiles. The door opens. The hall beyond is quiet and empty. "They've gone," the boy says.

"What were they?" I ask.

"Factors," the boy says. "I get a feeling when they're coming. I close the door and they pass us by."

The woman stares into a corner. "You'll leave now," she says. "It's what you always do. You read your book and then you leave. And they bring you back." She shudders in something like resignation, maybe more like despair. "Don't go out there. Out there is nothing but death and misery. You could stay here. There's food and water, and we could pass the time. Talk is what I miss the most."

But it's clear I've made up my mind.

"Next time, if there's a book, don't give it to him," the boy suggests.

The woman gets up. "Well, at least let me put together a bag of food and water." She looks at the boy, who nods permission. Here, he is the master. The woman is just another piece of furniture.

It really *is* time for me to leave.

CENTERING

The boy seems glad that I'm moving on. He's happy to give instruction. Make a run down the hall that passes the freezers while there's still weight, he says—it should get warmer on the other side.

I do. I barely make it.

Spin-down finds me having to choose between a shaft that points inboard—with a ladder on one side—or a split in the corridor a few meters forward that stretches left and right, concentric with the outer hull, I presume—and there's no way of knowing whether the corridor circles around, bringing me back here, or branches off somewhere—in other words, whether left and right are ultimately the same or lead to places very different.

With what leisure I have, I pause to analyze some of the faint markings at this juncture: more circular radiances and stripy patterns. No idea what they mean. They're probably not for me. More likely, they're ways to guide factors.

What's obvious to me now is that very little of the hull is prepared for human habitation. All that I've seen so far has a sort of useful logic if you're a factor, intent on specific duties and with little or no curiosity. But more senseless monotony will certainly push me into eccentricity.

I might just return to the Land of the Loaf-Eaters.

For some reason, that brings a smile. I've twisted words and made a joke, but I don't know the original behind what I've twisted.

I take out the book and the pencil and think about writing down my joke, to add some levity to a very serious tome. I leaf through the pages, finger the black lines—and only now does the obvious occur to me: what the broad slashes mean. They're transitions. A new hand writes after each slash.

This makes my joke more than trivial. I close the book and put away the pencil. This book has been carried by at least four of me. If it gets lost, then those who came before might as well have never lived.

How many bodies were brought back to the freezers without a record of their achievements? The others like me, who wrote in this book, saw things of interest. I hope at least to go as far as they did. I'll eventually take the opportunity to add notes as I proceed, but there's no point if I just duplicate what's already recorded, so...

I haven't earned the right to add anything yet.

No going back.

I make my choice and descend. I decide to be perverse and use my words counter to the periodic and unreliable *up* and *down*. I decide that *descent* means going inboard toward the core and *ascent* means moving outboard, toward the skin of the hull.

The "descent" is as before, but I'm getting better at it. I don't know how far forward along the hull I've traveled, but not far enough toward the narrowing bow to make a substantial reduction in the circumference. That might require another kilometer or two. I think it over as I move down the shaft, keeping a lookout for more sketches, more signs of the girl or anybody or anything having made it this far...other than *me*, of course.

A visit from my own ghost would be strange. I vaguely recall stories of the oracular dead: spirits, hauntings. What if all of me decided to return at once, babbling incoherently? Spooky fables. Useless crap rising up at odd moments. Part of some sort of artificial cultural heritage. Why can't I retrieve the knowledge I need? The reason and shape behind the Ship—a good schematic. Why three hulls? Why the moon of dirty ice? What, if anything, lives in the other hulls? Is there still someone alive from the Destination Guidance team?

How long has it been? How long since the Ship departed... and where did it depart from? I can think of reasonable answers to some of these questions, but they don't yet feel convincing.

This much is clear. Ship makes people and stuff as it goes along.

I'm just a youngster.

The shaft behind me is like the shaft below me, a vanishing obscurity. Down, down, downward...hundreds of meters. I pause to drink, but I'm not hungry yet. I had my fill back in the boy's room. I almost feel guilty partaking of that food, and I feel sorry for the woman in the boy's thrall.

What did the boy do or give up to find favor with Ship?

There's a nightmare thought I don't need to deal with as I hand-over-hand along the rungs.

Spin-up comes, but I'm instinctively prepared. I lock feet and hands on the rungs and wait until things are stable. When I resume, a bottle of water falls out of the bag before I draw the cinch, and I can't help but watch its twisting, bouncing, accelerating progress into vanishing twilight.

Now it's a climb in earnest. If I let go and don't catch myself, I'll fall down the shaft like the bottle. I'll bounce and gather speed and…splat.

Another body for the freezer.

Another book for someone to retrieve, with nothing new added.

Is that what the little girls do? Retrieve everyone's books—Blue-Blacks, Scarlet-Browns, visitors from Destination Guidance?

Descending inboard, always inboard.

After two hours, my fingers and hands have blisters, worse where I touched the frosted cases or laid palms on the freezing deck after I was made. I'm leaving a little blood trail, of which I see no evidence as I climb.

There's a shadow above—a big one. I pause and lean out to get details, hanging by hands and feet. It's just a rough black plug higher in the shaft. I climb another dozen meters. The shadow assumes a trilateral outline: a cleaner, about forty yards inboard. It doesn't move and appears to be stuck. Dead or broken—or patiently waiting. It blocks the rungs at an angle.

I stop and hang for several minutes. I know it's waiting. It's a sentinel left in the shaft—not a cleaner, some sort of Killer. A big one, at least, not the little one, which is worse…

I have no idea what any of that means.

Drops of my sweat drip and fall outboard.

Then the black shadow shifts—makes a scraping jerk along one side. The movement so unnerves me I let go of my slippery grip. I fall a few rungs, manage to grab hold again, but wrench my foot.

I see that now the shadow has wedged three broad

appendages against the wall of the shaft. Whatever sort of grip a factor might have—suction, friction, like lizard's feet, it's coming unstuck. Dead or alive, it's about to slip loose and drop. All I can do is lay myself tight against the rungs, swing sideways and hang with one hand and one foot flat against the wall.

I don't dare look up. I can hear it scraping, sliding, jamming again, scraping some more—and that's all I hear. No scrabbling, no attempt to hang on, no sounds of apprehension or fear.

The glow around and above me dims in a rush. I feel air. Then the big black shape whooshes past, edgewise but brushing my shirt, and I look just in time to see two other bodies, parts of bodies, falling in its wake. One is a Scarlet-Brown—just a head and shoulders terminating in old meat and clotted gore. The other is more like me, probably male. I can't see the face, but he's bigger and bulkier, dressed in reddish overalls and seemingly intact, with skin about the same color. Could be a Knob-Crest.

I watch the whole tangle fall with softer, dead, diminishing sounds…Into the shadows. Only in the backdraft do I smell the char of singed meat.

For some reason, survival makes me laugh. I've come this far, I become multitudes—I'm more than eccentric, I'm plain silly—my life makes me laugh in mad earnest. I stop laughing, suck as much air as I can stand, try not to retch, and continue my climb, hand over hand. Following instinct.

The walls of the shaft from this point on are covered with spiraling sweeps of soot and rainbow-oily discolorations. The surface has been heat-treated. Burned. The rungs are still intact and strong…so far.

Another hour.

I'm not feeling all that bright. I wonder if I'm taking the same path I took the last time, or whether my counterparts followed one or both of the forking corridors. The shaft gets more soot-stained. Then I see it clear.

A swirl of superheated air or actual flame, carrying bits of fuel, swept down the shaft and came up against the cleaner, just doing its duty but plugging the flow. It crisped, died, and jammed, and debris fell on its upper surface. Parts of bodies.

This is like a war.

This is *a war.*

Another half hour of climbing and I arrive at the end. Not the end of the shaft as designed, but a shattered, burned stump of internal piping, intimate ship architecture opening onto dark, smelly nastiness.

Thrusting into amazing destruction.

The melted and cracked rim of the broken shaft rises three meters from a shadowy churn of broken bulkheads, conduits, decking. I poke up and look around.

I'm on one side of a roughly cylindrical void about sixty meters across. I now weigh considerably less than I did when I began. I might be half a kilometer closer to the center of the hull. Much farther inboard and spin-up will be little more than a nuisance—my weight will be negligible.

I can't make sense of the mess. Any prior design, any obvious function has been obliterated. The pervasive smell is bitter-flowery, nauseating. Everything around me is coated with an iridescent film. I reach out from the last rung to touch the outer surface of the shaft, and my finger comes away slick. Using the inadequate illumination from the shaft's few remaining glim lights, I hold my finger close to my eye and see that the film is trying to bead up, organize. It doesn't want to have anything to do with my flesh.

I wipe the film off on the shaft's internal surface. There, I watch it spread out and join with other patches of iridescence, migrating toward the ruined edge. The patches are trying to form a kind of dressing. The film wants to completely coat the destruction and begin…what? Repairs?

Ship can fix itself even without factors? Or is the film another kind of factor, another lively tool?

There's movement on the opposite side of the void. Something large clambers over the wreckage, hooking its way, then stopping to hang loose—a shiny black conoid trunk with a skirt or fringe and twelve long, sinuous but jointed appendages, delicately poking, feeling, attempting to shift broken pieces, as if putting together a shattered vase. It emits soft *wheeps* and *whirs*, despondent, overwhelmed. Its trunk, fringe, and radiating limbs flicker with channeled spots of blue and red luminescence.

Some wreckage breaks away and falls casually to my side of the void, jarring the conoid. Its fringe rises in a lapping wave. The limbs sweep the stinking air. It could be a fixer—one of the factors you'd expect in a ruined space. Drawing up its estimate for repairs and not happy with the bill.

Above me, I make out a breach in a far bulkhead, and beyond that, a fluctuating brightness like cold flame. Another fixer squeezes into the void through the breach and scuttles to join its fellow, knocking loose more debris. I duck into the tube as a conduit slams onto the top of the shaft, falls to one side, wobbles, settles. I poke up again. The fixers touch limbs, whir and wheep with a dignified musical pattern.

In a short while, after spin-down, I'll try to leap across to the breach, which seems to offer access to another chamber beyond. I have no notion whether the space will be undamaged or livable, but the smell here is intolerable.

I look around the void and wonder what spin-down will do to the wreckage—how it will rearrange, drift loose. I've already had experience with junk in free fall and don't wish to repeat it. I could drop back into the shaft and hide, but there's no guarantee the wreckage won't cover the opening. No, my only chance is to kick out across the damaged space to the breach as soon as spin-down is complete and hope for the best.

I measure the distance and the angle with my eye, searching for a relatively smooth surface from which to kick off.

Any reasonable trajectory will take me across two-thirds of the void. The breach is three meters wide. A tiny target to reach in one jump.

Something becomes silhouetted within the blue glow. It might be a head. I can't see clearly. The sting in the air is filming my eyes, and wiping them seems a bad idea. The next time I get a good look, the breach is open, empty.

I'm sure some of the film has coated my clothes, where it's unhappily trying to clump up and break loose. Much longer in this space and I'll likely have enough of the active stuff in my lungs to kill me.

The lurch comes. I grab a rung and hang on. All around, wreckage tumbles, rolls, cascades away from the outer reaches of the void. Big pieces break loose and wobble and spin. The whole void becomes a noisy, slamming, chiming circus of mindless debris—all of it tending toward the opposite of our spin. There, it loosely gathers, bounces, and with spin-down finished, drifts across my proposed path with all the leisure of strolling elephants.

I stay low in the shaft but keep an eye on the blue glow within the breach. Debris transits. Some pieces threaten to enter the shaft—but miss. I can't make out the fixers. If they've lasted this long, they've likely hooked themselves down and are patiently waiting out the change of momentum.

My jumping-off point, a relatively smooth, broad shaft

edge, is just above the last rung. I give some thought to using the rung itself, but it's too narrow to accommodate both my feet.

Things aren't going to get any better.

I swing out like an inchworm (another amusing but useless image—some sort of young insect, not a spider) and straddle the edge of the shaft, then grip it with my thighs, straighten my torso, transfer grip to my hands, and arch my back again—plant my feet firmly, bend my knees, look over my shoulder...

A piece the size of a horse just misses me. I don't give a damn what a *horse* is.

I kick off. It's a solid kick, the angle looks good. I sail across the void at a decent clip. Still looks good. I draw in both arms and a leg to avoid a twirling chunk of pipe about as wide as my thigh. This starts me wheeling around an axis through my hips. I can't stop it, but the motion is slow enough not to cause injury, unless I collide with something sharp. I see lots of sharp things. I count the rotations, having nothing better to do, but at the end of five, something large and translucent dims the light from the breach. Could be the film in my eyes. I don't see it now— don't want to see it, can't help but look. Something big and confusing, like an animal made of rods of glass. Not entirely colorless, however. A small, bright red spot clues me that the thing is actually moving in my direction, not just spreading out....

Maybe ten seconds more until I'm at the breach. My hip pirouette is infuriating. I want to stare without interruption, keep track of the cracked and warped walls, the twirling debris, and make sure I'm not being hunted by a glassy haystack blur with a red spot.

Five seconds before the breach. Desperate, I reach out and grab a chunk of flat bulkhead. I stop both my motion toward the breach and my precession. I see...nothing, of course.

A kick at the bulkhead sends me off at the wrong angle. I reach out as far as I can. Two fingers grab hold of a burned, curled edge, and after a few seconds of utterly graceless scrambling, I've pulled myself out of the stinking, rubble-filled void, through the breach, and into a quiet, calm blue space that seems to go on forever....

Where I stare into the biggest eye in the entire universe.

CORE

The eye looms over me, a curved, transparent wall about a hundred meters wide. I'm on one side of a space that caps the eye like a gigantic goggle. Behind the eye is liquid water—lots and lots of water, blue green and lovely, filled with an amazing array of bubbles huge and small, moving in sluggish leisure with the residual currents from the last spin-up—very slowly wobbling, jiggling, breaking up, rejoining.

Fizz in a giant's soda bottle.

The eye has immense depth. It's the forward end of a huge tank. This leaves me limp with awe, and after I slow my heart and breathing and realize I'm not in immediate danger, the view jogs my memory, filling in basic knowledge from Dreamtime.

Ship needs fuel and reaction mass. The dirty ice moonlet supplies both. Mining machines on the surface send up chunks of ice that get stored in the tanks. That's where the serpent gouge comes from—machinery digging. The moonlet is mostly water, a small portion of which is deuterium; this can be used in a *fusion* reaction. Fusion is the process of combining the nuclei of atoms into larger nuclei. This requires lots of energy to get started but then releases enormous amounts. But that's only the beginning. The fusion is just a starter for something even more powerful—bosonic reduction.

For hundreds of years, Ship's drive has been pumping out broken bits of atoms and streams of high-energy light in a twisting, glowing stream. Ultimately, Ship's velocity climbs to about twenty percent of the speed of light, .2 c—that is, sixty thousand kilometers per second. It takes something as big as the moon to fill out the requirements of the basic equations that move Ship between the stars. Just on the edge of memory—like something fading after a vivid dream—I see the moonlet being chosen from a dusty, frozen cloud far, far out from the sun. The name of the cloud is incomprehensible, *Hort* or *Hurt*—

Ice is transported up the struts to the hulls, then melted, pumped through the sluices—stored in a big tank.

Lots of water.

None for me. I'm exhausted, in pain, thirsty. I squeeze water from my own bottle into my mouth, start to choke, and spit weightless beads. Trying to draw breath and steady myself, I see the red spot from a bleary corner of my eye.

Spin-up resumes with a lurch. My hand loses its grip, and I roll around the perimeter wall of the tank's cap. Here, at or near the core, the centrifugal force is minimal but still catches me by surprise. I roll, kick, float free for a moment, and look around. The haystack blur must have come through the breach while I was captivated by the slow blue-green roil inside the tank. I can't find it again. There's something outboard, to my left— movement opposite the motion of the hull. My head pivots like a bird's. Maybe it's nothing. Maybe it's an illusion, and when I can wash out my eye, it will be gone.

Leave me be.

Across the cap, near the broad forward end, hatches line the perimeter wall. I try to stand, but my feet pull out from under me, and I bounce again, then drift outboard—down. Here, if I can keep up with the rotating wall, I'll weigh a fraction of a kilogram. But I'm getting dizzy. I roll until my palms skid on the wall, thankfully smooth but for the jagged edges around the breach. I push off and let the breach roll on by. Finally, I drop and spread flat, relying on friction to gather the necessary force. I'm riding with the wall, spread-eagled and vulnerable to anything with better means of locomotion, better control in the wide spaces.

I have a good view of what's going on inside the tank. The huge liquid volume reacts to spin-up with an amazing display of fluid dynamics. The bubbles slowly try to coalesce at the center, but currents keep breaking them up, thrusting them outward, until they rebound and gurgle in again. The tank's contents swish into a massive, godly whirlpool. This would be a beautiful vision to go out on—waiting for the water to surround the long air pocket like a tornado....

Looking inboard, up, I again see the blur—larger now and growing, the red speck revolving on the outside of a fine maze of glassy fibers, gleaming straws flexing and pulling. The thing is a network of glistening rods tied together with tiny blue knots.

Across its surface flash narrow concentric bands of pale color, expanding and contracting, whirling blue and black and green, drawing my gaze inward, then reversing, whirling outward.

Much more fascinating than the tank.

Mesmerizing.

It's beautiful, ghostly, and I hope quick and strong. I'm

resigned. This must be one of the large Killers—not the worst way to go, according to my book.

A brilliant bronze-colored beam shoots across the chamber and spears the hypnotic mass. The beam flicks and cuts the thing in half. The two halves writhe. Its bands of color fade. Black spots appear. The beam flicks again and quarters it. The severed masses catch fire and burn with intense blue flames. I smell caramel and acid. A slow rain of corrosive droplets strikes my body, my face, stinging, hissing.

I scream—and look down. A sharp pain has shot up my right arm. A spear pierces the bicep. There's a cord attached. I grab the cord, and it jerks through my hands as I'm yanked clockwise, out from under the burning fragments.

The last bits of the glass haystack with the red eye impact the outer wall with a series of gluey *plops*. The flames intensify—the bits pop and explode.

I'm being pulled toward an open hatch—already halfway across. I use one hand to take the excruciating pressure off the spear shaft and try not to scream again. There's a head and a torso silhouetted in the hatch's dim orange glow. I see a face. Quizzical, large eyes.

It's the girl. One of the girls.

She looks vexed. "Come here, you!" she grunts, and reels me in.

TAKING THE BOW

Through the hatch, the next figure I see is large and yellow with greenish accents, like an unripe lemon. Two muscular arms, two tree-trunk legs—human enough in this place. Except for his color and something about the texture of his skin, waxy and finely pitted, he does not remind me at all of fruit. His head is broad, set low on thick shoulders, with wide-set eyes, small nose, and narrow, almost doll-like lips. I say "he," but of course this is just a guess.

He grabs me gently enough, then pushes the end of the spear. The barbs retract. Swiftly, he pulls the shaft from my arm, then reaches into a gray bag slung around his wrist and smears something onto the bleeding wound. His hands are huge and fast and delicate as a jeweler's. The bleeding stops, and with it most of the pain.

"He's Teacher," the girl says to Big Yellow, and makes a gesture. "I grabbed him back behind the sluice."

"You sure he's the same?" Big Yellow asks.

The girl takes my shoulders and peers at me. "Do you know me?"

I favor my arm. My eyes sting, my lips burn—corrosive drops on my face. "I've met you," I say to the girl. "Two of you."

The girl reaches into her own bag and hands me a bottle of water. "Wash your face," she says. "We've got a place forward where we can fix you up. The others should be coming back soon."

I'm sure she's seen me before—this particular me. And I've seen her before. "You're the one who pulled me out of the sac?"

She nods. I find the gesture strangely human, which implies that I'm beginning to regard the girl as something other, though I can't say why.

"Midwife," Big Yellow says. His voice is rich. I'd love to hear him sing. I'd love to hear any kind of music. Funny, to think of music now, but I lift the bottle above my head and rinse out my eyes. After a while, they don't sting as much, and my lips feel better. I drink a little and return the bottle.

"That's yours," she says. "I left my book behind. Did you find it?"

"I found it in a bag. Something else stole it. A silvery shape—"

"They don't exist," the girl says with a stern look.

"Right. One of you—I think—drew something in the shaft. In blood. What was it supposed to be?"

Pique turns to embarrassment.

"Careful," Big Yellow warns. "She's your sponsor. You need her."

I can accept that—for now. "The shapeless haystack thing?"

"A factor," Big Yellow says. "I've never seen one like it before."

"A Killer," the girl says.

"What happened to Picker and Satmonk?"

The girl shakes her head. "They're strong and friendly, but they don't last long."

"And your sister?"

"Don't ask," Big Yellow advises.

The girl ignores the question.

I rub my arm. The tugged muscles hurt more than the wound itself. It could have been worse—that shaft could have penetrated bone. "What did you shoot me with?" I ask.

Big Yellow lifts the apparatus, a bent piece of spring—a bow—strung with a twisted length of black fiber. The shaft is a thin, hollow tube; the barbs, more pieces of metal, spring-loaded in roughly cut notches at the tip. Pulling on the cord the right way retracts the barbs. He waggles the bow. It's broken in two.

"Found it in a junk pile. Now it's ruined."

"Sorry," I say.

He manages a grin. "Have to find another," he says.

We appear to be in a space actually made for long-term human occupation—unlike the no-frills pads and lockers or even the boy's tailored space. More style, something on the order of decorated, personalized, even pretty. Nets arranged along the wall support glassy objects of many shapes and colors. The curving inboard ceiling has been painted with pictures of trees and clouds, as if we're sitting under a leafy bower. This arouses erratic memories of poetry and botany.

Big Yellow and the girl bob slowly up and down on their toes, watching me intently. Waiting for a reaction. I try to smile. "Nice." I haven't seen the entire scene, but the human touches are compelling—sympathetic. Somebody lived here for a while—not, I think, my present hosts. The centrifugal tug is no greater here than in the cap of the water tank. I rotate on one toe, like a ballet dancer, arms out, gently push off, rising, then drop to the outboard deck. Bobbing is pleasant. I like it.

Curved rails and cables have been raised and slung in strategic positions from floor and ceiling. The bottom edge of the farthest wall, intersecting the bulkhead to my left, with its hatch, is barely visible beyond the curve of the ceiling. Big. Deluxe accommodations.

We all like to live near the water.

The forward wall…

Whoever lived here (or would live here) wanted to keep a constant watch. Like the end of the water tank, this wall is transparent, but fogged by a layer of grime. Someone—perhaps the girl or Big Yellow—has wiped a big oval. Irregular shadows lurk beyond.

I bob and echo to the oval. I'm facing the bow. What I see is even more compelling than the décor behind me. At this point in the hull's narrowing taper, the conical structure is visible almost in its entirety. The maximum width of the hull, outside where I stand, must be roughly a hundred meters. This room, and those that complete a circle of habitats forward of the water tank, fills about a third of that width and pokes forward toward the bow.

Ten big cylinders—each about fifty or sixty meters long— are ranked outboard to my right. Their skeletal frameworks barely conceal the graceful curves of the shipwrights and tenders and other machines that build and prepare for launch the seedships that will probe and examine the planet, returning with the information necessary to match us to the planet—and the planet to us.

This view awakens too many memories for me to process all at once. I *know* this place—I know it well. This is where my work always begins, where the relationships forged over long hours of training will blossom into magnificent results—love and adventure and hard, hard work.

But a few seconds are enough to show me that the machines in the nose of hull number three are in disrepair. They've suffered from much worse than simple neglect. Ship's mad war has struck the tip of our spear—and severely blunted it. I see the damage mentioned in my book. The cylinders and the embryonic craft within are bent, pitted, burned, blasted. Inboard, training and education units—like the crystal and steel seedpods of giant trees—have been ruptured and left in glistening, weeping ruins. To my right, the processors that would have created all of our landing vessels have been dealt similar blows, as if smashed by angry children with hammers and torches.

"What happened here?" I ask, my voice breaking.

"You're the teacher," Big Yellow says. "You tell us."

Movement behind me—the hatch opening and closing.

"You found one?"

I turn to see a gray figure so spidery-thin it takes me a moment to decide it's human—and a woman. She's more than two meters tall, with a long, narrow face and large dark eyes. A fine dark fur covers her cheeks and arms up to her bare shoulders. Her fingers curl and uncurl at the end of long, taut arms.

"He found his way here," Big Yellow says.

"The girl helped—at the beginning," I say.

The spidery woman moves along the rails and cables with the fluid poise of a *ballerina*. Somehow, her thinness doesn't even come across as skinny. She's just another unexplained type in our tortured menagerie. "So, she thinks you're important," she says, doubtful.

"He is!" the girl insists. "He's Teacher."

"I've brought Tsinoy," the spidery woman says. She gives me a narrow look, like a warning. "It's right behind me."

"Watch out," Big Yellow says with a chinless nod.

The hatch opens again, and this time, white upon ivory fills the shadow, as if painted by a wide brush. I push back and resist a strong urge to run and hide—if I could run, if there is anyplace to hide.

This one is almost too large for the hatch, and far from human. Shining ivory spines ripple and fold back like bristled fur. Slung low between canine shoulders, a long head shows small, pinkish-red eyes and a blunt, reptilian snout. When rime-white lips pull back, I see ice-colored teeth—teeth that *I know* are stronger than animal teeth, maybe stronger than steel.

I've seen this one before—in a part of the Dreamtime I'm not supposed to remember...don't *want* to remember.

Its body, below ridges of pale bristle, is corded with glistening spiral bands of muscles connected to silvery-gray bones. The muscles find new connection points and the beast refashions its shape and increases its power as it braces ceiling to floor beside the spidery woman.

It isn't part of any *Klados* I should ever have to deal with. It's from the wrong part of the Catalog.

Catalog. Klados. Oh, God. Too much all at once. I'm backed up against the long window. My body is soaked in sweat. The girl grabs a cable with one hand, legs folded. She looks at me and then at the ivory beast, judging what, I don't know. The beast shakes and shivers with a clatter.

Ivory and silver and ice.

"He doesn't like me," it says to the spidery woman. The voice is dreadful, deep, grating in an oddly musical way—terrifying.

"You scared the hell out of me, first time I met you," Big Yellow says.

"Talk Teacher down," the spidery woman tells the girl.

The beast says, "Shit," but doesn't press the issue.

More memory bobs to the surface—more nightmare information. The fact that I *do* recognize it causes a nauseating sensation of being two people in the same body. It's one of Ship's dark secrets—a Tracker. Trackers are biomech weapons of incredible versatility and power. They can live off almost any combination of gases or liquids found in organically fertile environments.

But Trackers are not supposed to be able to *talk.* Dropped into any situation, all a Tracker does is track, clear, and kill.

It shouldn't be here.

It shudders with another clatter. I worry that I've angered it, expecting it to change shape again at any moment. Why hasn't it killed them all, killed me?

"Do we trust him?" the Tracker asks.

"Do we have a choice?" Big Yellow asks.

The girl looks between us, eyes sharp. The spidery woman shrugs.

"How'd you all get here?" I croak.

"We were pushed," the spidery woman says. She's casual, unafraid of any of us—least of all the ivory beast. "Factors moved forward and burned out the birthing rooms, the living quarters aft. No more newbies. We're the last."

"They'll find us if we stay here," Big Yellow says.

The girl pulls herself along the cable and reaches to take my wrist. "I prayed for you," she says. "So you came."

"She *always* prays for you," Big Yellow says.

The Tracker sees something in my expression and moves closer, paw-claws clenching, stretching. I definitely feel threatened.

"You see me, you know what I am. I'm not just a freak," it says. "Tell me."

Before my eyes, the spines drop and the pale, glistening

muscles rearrange on the screw-shaped bones, reassigning lift and load and balance. It's looking more and more like a four-legged tank—or something called an *armadillo*. An armadillo with the head of an awful, lizardlike wolf. Three animals I've never seen. "Do you have a name?" it asks me.

"No," I say. "I don't remember."

"I'm the only one here with a name," it says. "Why?"

"Beg pardon," the spidery woman says. "Introductions. Teacher, this...is Tsinoy."

"I'm not *supposed* to look like this," the Tracker says. Its voice drops an octave—something out of a deep, deep cave. "I look awful."

"I'm not supposed to look the way I do, either," Big Yellow says.

"I am what Mother made me," the girl says.

"Of course," Big Yellow says with what I take to be a wry face, allowing for the waxy stiffness of his features.

"What about you?" I ask the spidery woman.

"No name," she says. "But I know that I work best in low gravity." She stretches her arms and adds, "I also know a lot about the hulls. Especially what Ship will look like when all three hulls join. The Triad."

"Good for her," Big Yellow says. "For me, it's all a mystery."

The spidery woman approaches the window. I drop back to give her a chance to look through the cleaned oval and survey the wreckage of our hopes. Her large eyes turn sad.

The girl tugs me to a big curved brown blob that might be a chair. It seems to suck me down and relax me at the same time, holding me with a soft, polite grip. "Tell us," she says. "You're Teacher. Tell us what you remember."

"If you know something, teach us, Teacher," Big Yellow says. "We're hungry for knowledge."

I swallow. Again, I feel as if I've split into two people, two Dreamtimes twisted together. The Tracker has kept its focus on me, like a cat watching a bird.

"What do I do?" it asks. "What's my purpose?"

I don't want to ignore this question, but I also have no desire to disappoint—and what I've involuntarily and hazily recovered won't make any of us happy. The spidery woman passes me a squeeze bulb of water. I drink. "You're called a Tracker," I say. "Sometimes we send Trackers down to a planet in the first seedships. Or others like Trackers."

"Why would Ship do that?" the spidery woman asks.

"If there's a major problem with our destination planet, crew improvises from the Catalog."

"What catalog?" Big Yellow asks.

"How would they use me?" the Tracker overrides him.

I answer the Tracker first. Whatever it has in its soul, it still terrifies me. "You clear the ground," I say, trying to reduce the impact of simply telling it, *You kill everything you meet.* "Help prep the planet for human occupation."

"I'm a Killer?"

You're a Killer. I don't say this out loud. I do say, under my breath, "I don't know. Just stop staring."

"Shit." The Tracker stands down, moves away, seems to shrink, elongate, reduce its offensive posture even more. It appears almost smooth, sleek.

"It's *my* beast, so be nice to it," the spidery woman says softly. She doesn't like what I've told them any more than I do. "It protected me, came here with me. No need to get it upset. The question is, who's in charge—Teacher or me?"

"You left *me* out," Big Yellow says, mocking disappointment.

"Teacher," the girl insists.

"But you're not actually a *leader*," Big Yellow says.

"I don't think so," I agree.

"Can you talk to Ship Control and ask for help?"

"The Ship talked to me, I think—once."

"Maybe he's lying," the Tracker grumbles.

The spidery woman stretches herself again to full length—very impressive. She and the Tracker make a formidable pair.

"Teacher knows *everything*, if he gets poked right," the girl insists.

Big Yellow asks, "Is it true, Teacher? What else is in that catalog? Me?"

"I don't know. Leave me alone for a while." I avoid their eyes. I need to think, to rest. More of my head fog is starting to lift. I don't like any of what memory shows me now. I'm supposed to be born after we find a planet, after we arrive—that's the grand scheme of my Dreamtime. Arrival—planetfall—is a complicated job at the end of a hundred million processes, a trillion decisions, big and little. Getting there is most of the fun.

Maybe Dreamtime is all wrong, a convincing fairy story. What's dawning on me—what should have been obvious from the beginning—is that if the planet isn't hospitable, if there's difficulty, Ship would have to adapt. I'm not born and raised. I'm made—like them. If big problems arise, I can be customized. I come in more than one variety. And now two of me—or more—are mixed together.

"Who's been here longest?" I ask.

"Tsinoy and me," the spidery woman says. "We met Big Yellow and the girl in front of the water tank and showed them this place."

"None of you have books?"

"None of us has a book," the spidery woman says.

"I had a book," the girl says. "You lost it."

"Right." I don't want to get into that again. "But I found one of my own," I say, and take it out, opening to the page with the sketch. They crowd around—all but the Tracker, who seems aware that even folded, its spines might jab us.

"Three hulls, like you remember. To know what it all means, we need to see more, I guess."

"That's right," the girl agrees. "He needs to be poked." Why she focuses on me, I don't know.

"You are what you see," Big Yellow says.

"That's deep. You're our philosopher," the spidery woman says.

Big Yellow stretches out massive arms. "Philosophers don't look like me."

"Join the club," says Tsinoy.

"You drew this?" the spidery woman asks me, pointing to the sketch.

"No. Another me did—I think."

"How many of you are there?" she asks.

"I've seen hundreds of bodies like mine...collected and frozen in lockers, aft."

"Awful," Big Yellow says. "Thankfully, I seem to be unique."

An awkward pause.

"I'm exhausted," I say. "Is there a place I can sleep? Is there any food?"

"Very little," the spidery woman says.

"Less and less," Big Yellow says. "On my way here, I saw a lot of folks who looked as if they'd starved to death."

I take another drink. "There is a room aft," I say, "outboard of the water tank...A boy and a woman live there. They were comfortable. The boy had plenty of food and water. He seemed to be able to tell the hull what to do."

They all look at me with somber eyes, as if they don't believe me. Then I see that they're simply paying silent respect to a man who's escaped certain death.

"There was another girl," I say defensively. "She left first." I pause and swallow. "She wasn't you," I say to this girl.

Big Yellow looks aside.

"We've heard about such places," the spidery woman says. "After a few spin-ups, if you like it and stay, you start to think you've been there for years. You forget who you are...and then the room seals shut and never opens again. Traps you. In some other part of the hull, another room opens up...same thing, different people."

Silence.

"They let me go," I say.

"It's just a story," the spidery woman says. "We've got enough food for a few days, but we don't have that much time. We need to find a way forward—a way out."

"Where?" I ask.

"I don't remember," she says, crestfallen. "Not yet."

Big Yellow moves in. "Right. If we don't rest, we'll start acting crazy. Let's clean up, eat a crumb or two, sleep in shifts. We'll stand watch one by one for a couple of hours, until next spin-down. Best to travel while there's as little weight as possible—right?" He looks at the spidery woman with what passes for stubbornness.

She faces him down, then shrugs again, wide shoulders elegant, and curls up. "Who's first on watch?"

"I'll go," Big Yellow says. "I sleep with my eyes open. Then the girl. She's the most sensitive to noise."

We scrub each other with a scrap of damp cloth. After, we feel better in a number of ways—and more connected. In the gentle tug of spin-up, the spilled bath-water slowly falls to the floor and forms viscous pools. We wipe it up and squeeze the cloth into an empty bottle. That takes a while—the water behaves like syrup. We can't afford to waste anything.

The Tracker, of course, does not join this group, but watches with what I assume is a hint of sadness in its armor-lidded, ruby-pink eyes.

After a brief meal—a couple of chunks of loaf divided among us—we seek separate places in the chamber. I settle into the grippy couch. The Tracker finds a corner and wedges itself in, a peculiar process of grabbing hold of the walls and ceiling with three limbs and *shoving* until it's compressed to almost half its former bulk.

The spidery woman chooses to lie unencumbered on the floor, a loose curl of limbs. She closes her eyes and relaxes. The girl stays close to her, happy with any substitute for a mother. Her legs are crossed, elbows out, hands together, as if praying—praying to the hull, perhaps, or Ship Control. She glances at me. Her eyes grow heavy, and she curls up, too.

I spend a few minutes penciling an update in the little book. My handwriting—hand-printing—is uniform throughout. It's all me. I don't write it all down. I concentrate on a few vivid scenes. Eventually, I'll gather enough pieces of paper to make enough books to tell the whole story. Then I'll…

I don't know what I'll do.

I write. When I get to a certain point—my rescue from the red-dot horror—I look up.

"Who has a laser?" I ask.

Big Yellow is near the hatch, standing his watch. "Nobody," he says, and manages a look of surprise. His facial expressions are subtle but real, once you get used to them. "We thought *you* had one, but you don't, do you?"

"No."

The spidery woman rouses. "Great. We have an unknown protector."

"Or somebody was trying to kill you and missed," the Tracker suggests, poking its head from the corner.

STARSHIP

Spin-down rouses us too soon. We barely feel the difference—a nudge.

"I think I remember more now," the spidery woman says with a yawn.

"Sleep can do that," Big Yellow says. "That's why I don't sleep much."

She scowls at him. "All the hulls start out the same. If my memory is accurate—and that's a big if—there's access to a control center in the bow, across the staging area. We should be able to get through that side hatch." She points to an otherwise anonymous impression on the far wall, almost hidden by the ceiling.

"It'll have to do," Big Yellow says.

The Tracker comes out of its corner. It extends a paw-claw, a formidable appendage, and the little girl gives it her hand, dainty flesh almost lost in that multiply capable span of digits, gripping ridges, and horny extrusions. Her trust seems absolute.

The spidery woman's memory is accurate, so far—there is forward access. We pass through into a corridor, railed and cabled, designed for people. At her touch, another hatch opens on the forward end, and we clamber and float out into the acrid air of the staging area.

The smell of burning and destruction is fierce, accompanied by a too-familiar, fine mist of stinging droplets. "More stink," the little girl says, wrinkling her nose.

We form a chain and launch across the staging area, with the Tracker as our leading grapple. Crossing takes us several long, painful minutes, past tangles of broken supports and burned equipment, through a heartbreaking ring of useless landing craft. The masses all around shift and groan, wobbling after spin-down. Pieces are drifting loose.

The far wall, closer to the bow, is less than fifty meters wide. There can't be much more forward left to go. My memories stop at the staging area. It makes sense that there could be an observation chamber, a blister, maybe even a command center, but what are the chances it's going to be damaged as well?

It's incredible that one of me reached this far and yet went back—why? Because he was alone, didn't know where else to go? *Teamwork. There has to be a group that combines all the right knowledge—I'm just not sufficient. But who puts us together?*

Who decides who gets made and what they know?

A loose chunk of support frame revolves slowly between our party and the hatch, blocking the view, but Big Yellow joins the Tracker, leaving us for the moment to grip an I-beam bonded to a relatively stable bulkhead.

Together, the pair stops the frame's motion, pushes it aside, where it collides with a tangled seedship cage and sticks.

"Hatch up here," the Tracker announces. "Big one."

The opening is clear.

The Tracker plants a sticky claw-foot against a smooth surface, takes hold of Big Yellow's leg, swings him out, and uses him to retrieve the rest of us. Rather neatly, we separate as we're arcing toward the wide hatch, drift through, and grab whatever we can inside.

This could be where equipment is stored or stowed—a space about ten meters deep and five meters square. Or it could be some sort of elevator. My mind draws a blank—this area isn't part of my job responsibility.

Where load jockeys hang out.

"Load jockeys," I murmur.

"What's that mean?" Big Yellow asks.

"Stevedores. Cargo managers. Crew chiefs. I'm not sure— it's fragmented."

The whole journey has taken us about a third of a spin-up. "Not too bad here," the spidery woman says. "No mist—except what's coming through the hatch."

She feels her way around the hatch perimeter, then attempts to push, tug, and finally shout at it. Nothing closes the hatch. She backs away. Big Yellow tosses her a gray bag to wipe herself off.

But our presence has triggered another response. The forward bulkhead rotates, splits, and seems to melt into the outer wall. A ring of large fluorescent panels switches on. The chamber fills with shadowless light. Now we see a series of coppergreen arches—and beyond, another bulkhead, curved, shiny black, and covered with myriads of glim lights.

As we pass through the arches, that curved bulkhead also splits into three sections, which rotate and then seem to melt aside. For a moment, my eye is confused. I think I'm looking at more glim lights but they're different. Sharper, brighter against an even deeper darkness—very many and very tiny, like an infinite spray of luminous dust.

We're in a big blister, the hull's forward observation dome. Beyond the bow, the darkness is thick with a billowing canopy of minute, cold brilliances.

Stars. Even seeing them for the second time, they startle and surprise me.

So lost.

The spidery woman reaches with long fingers and kicks out, as if she'd fly through them if she could. Big Yellow makes a grab for her, but she neatly draws in her arms and legs and he misses. She floats right by us all.

She's the first to make it into the bow. "This is hull control," she says. "It feels like I've been here already.... "

"What are those?" the girl asks, pointing at the glowing dust.

"They're why we're here," I say, and it's all I can say, because my heart is in my throat. This is the view to where we're going.

Somewhere out there, maybe, is home.

To our left stream long, grasping wisps of ionized pale blue and pink. And directly ahead, a vague grayish bull's-eye sends back a ghostly cage of barely visible bands. Not part of the stars—part of Ship. I didn't notice the thin bands at first, because the stars are visible right through them.

We follow as caution permits—quickly for the girl, while Big Yellow and I trail behind her, taking it all in. The Tracker is last, protecting our rear.

The bow chamber forms a blunt cone, with a transparent blister or dome covering the very tip, about ten meters wide and four meters deep. A hexagonal web of cables and slings allows for purchase, movement, and tie-down.

For a long moment—too long, my caution tells me—we stare out through the dome.

Tsinoy points to the colored streamers and wisps. The

Tracker's eyes have turned violet in the dark. What it says doesn't register at first, I'm so lost in the spectacle. "Nebulae don't look that bright, unless you're very near a recent nova—or worse yet, a supernova."

I pull back reluctantly. There are control stations already in place, mounted on narrow pylons around the perimeter of the dome. The spidery woman is gliding from station to station, hands swiftly lighting up curved displays and panels.

Even having seen this place, I can conjure no memory of it. Likely it will be dismantled, subsumed by the triad, before the end of our journey, when the three hulls join. But Ship's timing seems skewed everywhere. Why is the staging area completed? And why are some of the landing ships already constructed, only to be smashed? Useless. Wasted. Like all those bodies in the freezers.

The spidery woman seems very much at home here, rapidly becoming more and more aware of her function. That fits— she's built for low weight or zero g. She's probably part of the group that crews the Ship during the last few decades of journey, guiding it into orbit, preparing the way for the colonists. Does that mean she dies before I'm made?

Assembly crew is not landing crew. We were never meant to be one big happy family. I'm almost getting used to this irregular effervescence of memory. I wonder if she's the same or similar to the "tall female" in my book.

"This is where we'll do our work," she says. "My people put us in orbit and bring the hulls together. That's *got* to be the reason I'm here." She looks back at Big Yellow and the girl—then at me, fiercely demanding confirmation.

"Makes sense," I say.

"Damned right. I know *what* I am, if not *who* I am."

The little girl has wrapped herself around a control pylon,

watching as the bigger folks try to make sense of the arrangements.

Big Yellow grabs my shoulder as we hand-over-hand. "Where's Tsinoy?" he asks. The Tracker seems to have vanished after saying something about nebulae.

The spidery woman, eyes flashing, is absorbed by the panels, making her second circuit with fluid ease from one rank to the next.

We're not much use here—for the time being, anyway. "Let's go back and look for it," I suggest.

We pull our way aft, then transit the illuminated entry. We are slowed by mist drifting through the hatch from the staging area. We keep back but move around to peer out. No sign of the Tracker—of Tsinoy.

"Why would it leave?" Big Yellow asks. "It's pretty loyal to the gray lady."

I see movement near where we first entered the staging area, a shifting patch of paleness—unfamiliar in silhouette, but then, the Tracker excels at never looking the same twice.

"Is that it?" I point. The mist pushes me back into fresher currents of air. I can hardly see.

Big Yellow stretches his upper torso into the acrid gloom. "Yeah," he says finally, withdrawing. "This damned fog stings."

I pull another empty gray bag from the cinch of my pants and hand it to him. He wipes and dabs. "It's coming this way."

"You're sure it's the Tracker and not—"

But then it's upon us, pushing us aside in its haste. Its touch—even its near approach—makes me groan deep in my throat. Big Yellow grabs a long, knotted arm to slow it.

"Stuff coming up the pipe," it announces. "Bad stuff."

"Human?" Big Yellow asks.

"Shit no. Like me, only mean."

"How soon?" Big Yellow asks.

"A snap. Get them out of the dome. It's bad up there, any-way. Bright nebulae, all wrong. Pull them back here. We missed a door—in shadow. Might be a way out."

"Show me," I say. Without hesitation, it grabs me—hard enough to hurt. We launch into the darkness. I'm helpless to do anything about it. Everything's a whirl.

Then, with astonishing deftness, Tsinoy grabs a surface and slows, bringing us both to a smooth halt, and positions me before a round depression rimmed in slowly pulsing red.

A hatch opens.

Still shaking, I break loose from its paw-claws but drift out of reach of anything that would allow me to make a move one way or another. I start flailing, cursing in a frantic whisper, and then the spidery woman is beside me. She tugs me to the side, where I seize a cable.

"You shouldn't *do* that," she softly admonishes the Tracker, as if speaking to a child. The Tracker grunts and rattles ivory spines. "What's this?" she asks.

Big Yellow swings himself through the hatch. "More dead folks," he says from inside, his voice muffled. "Pretty far gone." He tosses out three corpses, dry as husks. I don't check to see if I'm one of them. I pull up to the hatch, then in, somersaulting slowly until my hand grabs a net.

We're in a craft moored just aft of the control chamber. The small cabin is shaped like the inside of an egg, narrow tip near the hatch. It's equipped with fine netting that reacts to our pres-ence. Two more husks hang at the back, curled in each other's arms. Big Yellow dislodges the pair, not bothering to disentan-gle them—just shoves them past me, past the spidery woman, through the hatch. Out and away.

The air is dry, with a touch of the scent of death. Still much better than the drifting fog outside. Big Yellow suggests we shouldn't leave the hatch open for long.

The netting wants to serve—protect—guide. It pulls away from a pale blue hemisphere, then reveals a clear port about a meter in diameter. Again, we see the stars—and fifty or more kilometers away, the bow of another hull.

"It's a transfer egg," the spidery woman says. "Tsinoy, you're a marvel. I missed this completely."

"No time," Tsinoy says. "Stuff coming."

"But I need to *remember* how to use it," she says.

The girl peeks in. "I hear a fight back there," she says. "At least three more. They're all going to die."

Big Yellow shoves out of the netting. The girl leans aside with quirked lips as he flies through the hatch. The Tracker, however, is stuck—the netting doesn't seem to know how to let loose of those ivory spines. Tsinoy squirms and rips and finally tears its way out, then follows. The girl gives it a wide berth.

"We could run the hull from that forward position," the spidery woman says. She gives me a defiant look, well aware of her contradictions from a few hours before.

The girl looks on in concern as I exit. She wants me to stay—out of danger. The mist hits me full in the face as I follow Big Yellow's swatch of color through the staging area. He's fairly flying through the wreckage, the framework that holds the ruined ships, toward our former residence, and points aft.

Spin-up begins right now, of course, just to add to our joy.

A BRAWL

I'm surprised by how adapted I've become to low-weight conditions. What little intellect I can manage between my leaping and vaulting consists of calculations on how hard I'd slam into something if I don't grab this beam or that broken piece of frame and slow myself, how fast I can spin around a cable or a rail and deflect my trajectory—long, quick curves that get longer and more demanding as spin-up reaches maximum.

Of course, I'm not lucky enough to escape without slams and bruises—and a particularly bad miscalculation near the hatch to the wide domicile. I strike the wall and bounce away, stunned, then slowly fall outboard, until the spidery woman grabs my sleeve and, with surprising strength, hauls me to the hatch—a stretch of at least four meters.

"The girl's right," she says. "Hear that?"

I don't. I'm not that sensitive. In awe and embarrassment, I thank her, and we follow Tsinoy and Big Yellow across the domicile, a quick enough trip—then back into the cap that covers the forward end of the gigantic water tank. We bound along the outer wall, great leaps barely planned, all adrenaline and ill-shaped instinct.

This time, the spidery woman flips herself in one bound and flies against the tank's huge eye. The water is in full slosh mode, waves majestically spiraling, peaking, breaking off around the slowly rotating tube. Bubbles crack and smack against the eye's inner surface, creating a cacophony I don't remember from my first visit.

How *anyone* can hear anything is beyond me. Before I have much time to regret any of it, all for one and one for all, pain and stinging skin and eyes, we've passed through a series of hatches and one long tube, back to a large, cluttered spherical space outboard of the water tank—not any part of the Ship I've passed through before, I'm willing to swear.

This looks more like a ruined forest ball. I close my eyes tight, then spit on my sleeve and rub to clear my vision. Now I hear voices—faint, fading. Dead vegetation hangs limp and brittle from the crisscross of cabling, and a slow, stately rain of leaves and broken limbs and branches falls around us, kicked up by something half buried in an accumulation on the inboard side.

A mangled body glides by from where it briefly snagged on dead branches. A beaded trail of blood from a severed leg duti-fully follows in its wake. The body's head turns, eyes blinking, and I realize it's still alive—a Scarlet-Brown, but this one seems to be female, or at least shaped differently. Then she passes below the light from the nearest hatch, and I look up to where she was and see, emerging from the outboard darkness—

More joy. An old friend—red claw. I reacquaint with what I first observed in distinctive parts—that claw, another like it, and more, half hidden; a quartet of crushing mouths set flat in a wide, dun-colored body. Tooth-edged reddish plates clack and scissor as at least a dozen spiky red arms reach out from the outer shell and grab and jerk inward whatever they touch—branches, bits of cable, the Scarlet-Brown's missing leg still stuck in one grinding maw, the cloth-booted foot spinning round and round. It's falling right toward me, maybe three blinks away, so I grab a cable through the pile of forest litter, tug myself left, and watch as the horror touches down, using claws and legs to cushion the fall with an unexpected, grim grace.

Grace is discarded as its limbs frantically shove aside debris, and the lifeless female. The mangled Scarlet-Brown is sucked away in the litter. The red horror spins about, claws raised, unable to gain traction in the litter's shifting surface but obviously aimed in my direction.

Just me and it, everyone else out of sight. I hope they haven't abandoned me, but how would that be any different from the sad histories of all my past selves, all my dead and frozen duplicates?

The horror pauses. Somehow finds a place to brace its limbs. Lifts itself out of the tangle and fragments.

A claw rises higher, swipes, and snicks, but only grazes my elbow, my hips.

Something even larger drops from the inboard volume of the forest ball. I can feel the mass of it but can't make out details until it's within the light. Large and sickly green, with red stripes and nested plates arranged every which way, each bearing more needle-sharp spikes. There's an emerging theme. The Catalog, I think, is beginning to lack originality.

But I am wrong.

The new prodigy uncoils a long, thick ribbon. The ribbon twists and falls toward red claw, coiling and spiraling as if in a light breeze. Its tip flares and pushes out a pink pulp, aiming, spreading, and then *attaching* to the red back—the two night-mares are joined, as if one by itself weren't bad enough.

Anchored, the ribbon whips in a jump-rope curve, shredding everything in its circuit. The whole assembly is less than four meters away, and the cable is about to cut me in half when Tsinoy leaps from the other side, lands on the red monster's back, and grabs hold, paw-claws sucking down, burrowing. The Tracker's muscles rearrange in a weird, snaky ballet.

Then it plunges its arms deep into the red shell, lifting, cracking, tearing, crushing. The whole scene terrifies me so deeply I'd rather *be* dead. I'm forced to look aside, where Big Yellow and the girl, her arms around his thick neck, bound along a clear stretch of curved wall, half pulling, half flying, carrying another body, yet another Knob-Crest, still alive but stunned, deep gouges and scratches around his face and neck, his clothing in tatters.

They leave the Knob-Crest in my care. Big Yellow also grimly plants the girl in my arms, where she squalls and squirms. "She smells one of her own," he explains. "Keep her safe. I'll get the others." He looks admiringly at the Tracker, which has managed to sever the whipping cable and severely distract the combo—but not quite kill or cripple it.

The spidery woman passes in a gray blur of long arms and legs. "Where's your goddamned laser savior?" she shouts.

Good question. I've got the girl in my arms, fighting like a hellion, and a Knob-Crest hanging on my feet and bobbing in the litter, hooting and groaning.

Something soft brushes my cheek. I snatch at it—a feathery strand that suddenly loops and stings my face and burns my fingers. The air is filling with more strands, all uncoiling from a leathery black mass oozing along the cables and draping from dead branches, scattering fragments of leaf dust. The mass is trimmed with a pale fringe of long, stinging tendrils, each tipped with a shining blue eye the size of a marble, all of which twitch and stare, directing the stripping, wrapping length behind.

At least five of those blue eyes turn on *me*.

That's it. My legs pull up, hauling the Knob-Crest with them. I'm locked in a fetal curl, practically crushing the girl, rotating and falling to my left. The girl still clings to my waist. The Knob-Crest thinks better and drops loose, then flurries his arms and hands against more tendrils. Enough for all.

Still no saviors, no lasers. But the spidery woman is back. She's pulled off her shoes and with her long black toes grasping a massive limb, swings a thorny branch like a quarterstaff. (I don't give a damn about the new words.) She handily snatches and clears tendrils from around our group.

Big Yellow returns from the gloom with yet another body slung over his shoulder—a small one, head hanging limp, eyes glazed—looks dead. Another girl.

The girl around my waist stops kicking. A sister.

"Get out of here!" Tsinoy shouts from below, lifting its snout and shaking aside cracked fragments of shell. "More coming!" Then it sinks its snout in a large hole it's dug in the red carapace, crooks each limb, and spins the shell around and around.

I look up. My eyes see better now. The dead forest is alive with shapes—all sorts, all different shades, too many to count. The hull aft *must* be dead, as all the beasts gather here to finish their job. If the hull can fill itself with wave upon forward wave of Killers, nothing will survive. Leaving is our only option.

Big Yellow hands off the second girl, then pushes all three of us toward the hatch. He lifts up the Knob-Crest and shoves him after.

"We'll stop them here!" Big Yellow shouts.

The second sister lifts her head and thrusts out a scrawny arm to point. "One more," she says, blinking rapidly. "I prayed for one! I found him!"

I encourage the Knob-Crest to crawl with me. We pass through the hatch, confused motives propelled by abject fear. If I live, this dead forest ball is never going to leave me—my slumber will forever fill with horrors. The girls cling to me, to each other, limbs twined, trying to caress and kiss—

And it's all a haze of passages and acrobatics, clumsy enough to make me pull back my lips in a hideous grin, a mockery of mocking, humor my last resort now that fear has finally run dry.

We find the hatch to the transfer craft. The spidery woman is right behind us. She's wiping her eyes and facial fur with a sleeve and a loose bag. When she sees the two girls, she scoops them to her breast, cooing in a strange, high voice—motherly instinct, I suppose—but then she spins around to find the panel that closes the hatch. It swiftly cuts us off from the rest of the hull. Breathless, she says, "We have to leave now. I never thought…"

She doesn't finish. A slamming sound comes from outside. The spidery woman and I look at each other—no choice. We have to open the hatch again.

Tsinoy pushes through with another limp body. Big Yellow follows close behind, saying, "That's it, let's go," and the hatch closes.

One of the sisters is the one who pulled me from the birthing sac, who fought to get me here. The other is regaining strength, crying lustily. She clambers over the netting to the limp, pale body in Tsinoy's grasp and checks his neck for a pulse. The new girl clambers over the netting to a blue sphere, places both her hands on it, and murmurs something to its smooth surface.

The blue surface illuminates.

"Hey!" the spidery woman says in surprise.

The craft moves, shoving us inboard, and then spins around. The netting grips our hands, our arms, even loops around Tsinoy's spiny limbs. We're away, shoving off into space, weightless again. A humming starts. Air flows.

The little girl rubs the hemisphere with her hands, murmuring sweetly. The spidery woman looks on in stunned appreciation. "I didn't know she could do that," she says.

"They knew it was here all along," I say, rubbing my shoulders, my knees. "Why wait until we're nearly killed?"

Big Yellow says, "Our little group wasn't finished. But now they miss their mother."

The pale fellow's eyes open. He looks at Big Yellow, the brightest thing in the room, then at me—half-blind. The Knob-Crest won't stop hooting and writhing. I can intuit the whole situation. He feels betrayed, almost left behind. He was the girl's companion, her partner—until she found the pale man, roughly my size, with roughly my color hair—though matted with blood and slime—and roughly my features.

"Glory," the spidery woman says. "Looks like we have two Teachers."

DOUBLING

The rest of my group seems unremarkable now, compared to that owlish young man across the egg, who has roughly the same number of scabs, burn marks, and scars but arranged in different places and patterns—the same shape of mouth... eyes...

I don't know which is more unsettling—meeting myself dead or meeting myself alive.

Big Yellow tends to the Knob-Crest. A little dab of water, a dirty gray bag, a little clean-up. After a few minutes, the Knob-Crest settles, watching us through sullen, pink-rimmed eyes. Traumatized but keeping still.

Somehow, we all grow quiet. Settle.

The egg-craft has been sent on some sort of automatic mission. The spidery woman has taken her former position near the hemisphere, one hand lightly resting on it—as if to affirm she has purpose.

Tsinoy has compacted near the tip, the hatch; it is quietest of all—giving the rest of the egg over to us. The two girls are wrapped tight and dozing in a loop of happy netting.

Finally, the other me pulls delicately loose and crosses the egg to enmesh by the port, nearer to me. I've been sneaking glances at the stars, the wisps, wondering just where we're going—and whether any of us knows where we're going.

"That's a big blob of incandescent gas out there," the other me says.

"Nova, or supernova, probably," I say.

"Remembering much?" he asks.

"Trying," I say.

"Well, if we're dupes—duplicates—we can help each other. Speed things up a bit."

"Probably," I say. "Met me before?"

"Let's not talk about that yet. You?"

"You're my first...living dupe. Is that the right word?"

He lifts his hands. "How long have you been alive?"

"Tough to say. A hundred spin-ups, maybe."

"Me, I've been counting, because the book suggested that was a good idea." From his pocket, the other me removes a ragged, stained book, three times thicker than mine. "I've been here four hundred and twelve spin-ups, give or take ten."

"You win," I say.

"You started from the girdle—near the midsection of the hull?" he asks.

"I think so."

"Me too. Behind that, it's probably all engine. Each hull has a big engine in the rear."

"Guess, or fact?"

"A little of both. The big water tank—that's reaction mass mined from the ice moonlet. It's piped up through the fairings. The struts. I've seen some of the robots or factors or whatever they are down there. Maybe we can spot them, if our elegant pilot can spin this thing around a little, give us a tour?" He glances over his shoulder at the spidery woman.

She smiles and rolls her hands on the blue hemisphere. "The girl seems to have set it on autopilot. I can't change our course. But I *can* adjust our orientation."

The view outside the port changes accordingly, and we guide her with competing instructions until we look directly down upon the forward tip of the moonlet...and a tiny, pale green sphere that seems to have been glued to the ice.

"Destination Guidance," my other says. "That's their work station and living quarters."

"Ship Control seems worried about Destination Guidance," I say, trying to contribute.

"You've talked to Ship Control?"

"Maybe. Once. Destination Guidance should all be dead by now."

"Who are they?" the spidery woman asks.

"They choose between the best destinations at midpoint, based upon all the data gathered by Ship." My twin is quite the professor—a better, more learned Teacher by far, it seems.

He's right. I'm remembering a lot more. Confirmation, affirmation, plus a kind of competitive challenge. It becomes more and more obvious, more and more logical. Even the distance we had hoped to travel starts to emerge in memory—five hundred light-years.

Thirty at twenty. A journey of more than thirty centuries at twenty percent of the speed of light. An enormous velocity, but not nearly enough to noticeably shrink our subjective time. I look up from my reverie, tell him what I just thought or just remembered. "Does it match?"

My other nods. "It's in the book. We've had these memories before. But...can we *trust* them?"

I look at his book and feel a kind of hunger. It belongs to me, too, after all. "Why wouldn't we?"

"Because we're not born—we're made to order," he says.

"I know," I say weakly.

"Ship—the hull, at least—keeps making us for some reason."

"The little girls pray for us," I say.

He lifts an eyebrow, crusted with blood from a cut. "Most of us die. We don't get our memories from education or from experience, from anything we would call learning. We're imprinted. If we come into the right situation, the imprinting emerges, and we're complete, ready to roll. If we don't, we flounder."

"That's in your book?"

"Mostly speculation, but it sounds right."

"I'd rather be born of woman and raised by my community," I say. "That's what I want to remember."

The spidery woman nods agreement.

"And maybe that's what we *will* remember, if we get to where we belong," my other says. "Illusion is everything, after all."

That's a little cynical, I think, but it doesn't feel right to criticize my other self—not yet.

The girls rouse long enough to look fondly at us, at each other—all's right with the world—there are *two* Teachers— then, fall back asleep. Big Yellow—who cradles the Knob-Crest in his huge arms, where he looks childish by comparison— listens with heavy-lidded eyes. Only the spidery woman is actually wide awake, energized by what little control she has over our small craft.

I look down at her—aft, rather. Ship is accelerating, creating a bit of pull. "Where are we headed?"

"To another hull, I hope," she says. "We came from Hull

Zero One. We've just made a lengthwise run along the flank of what I think is Hull Zero Two. It's pretty much a wreck forward of the engine. Lots of holes, like something big blew it out. There's Hull Zero Three, of course—on the other side—a few dozen kilometers from here. If it's wrecked, I don't know where we'll go. Maybe back to where we came from."

That draws a protest from Big Yellow. "Let me out first," he says. "I'll take my chances on that moon down there."

My other smiles. "Quite a team," he says.

"Do we all have dupes?" I ask.

"Probably. But…they look alike to me, and nobody has a name."

"It does," I say, pointing at the Tracker. It lifts its snout, and its pink eyes track us wearily, then close again. "Its name is Tsinoy."

"That might not mean much," my other says. "I think that just means 'Chinese.'"

"Funny," Big Yellow says, "he doesn't *look* Chinese."

None of us knows why this might be humorous, but my dupe and I and the spidery woman laugh. Maybe it isn't funny. Maybe it's rude. But Tsinoy doesn't seem to mind, just rearranges in its huddle and pulls the netting tighter.

"Third try's the charm," the spidery woman says. "Come up here if you want to see what we're up against."

My twin floats toward the port, near the blue hemisphere. "There's room for you, too," she says to me, her voice silky. She enjoys being in control, in her element—who wouldn't? She might even enjoy the company of me and my dupe. But I'm pretty sure she doesn't understand the vast scheme of things any better than we do. She just knows her way around the hulls, and that's the kind of knowledge we need right now. She's more important than any number of Teachers.

I lay my hand next to hers on the blue sphere. Instantly, without benefit of the port, I'm out in deep space, no egg-craft, just flying in the emptiness, thick stars ahead and that awesome nebula to one side.

Something is glowing at the nebula's core—several things, actually, almost unbearably bright.

I feel her fingers move mine, instructionally, and my point of view spins around. I seem to face the hulls, the moonlet, all in a broad sweep.

"Isn't it grand?" she asks.

It is impressive. The glimpse through the observation blister in the first hull did not begin to do it justice—nor did my dream-vision. The totality of Ship is *huge*. Hundreds of thousands could live in the forward space of each spindle-shaped hull—but that isn't what the hulls are for. They're not meant to be big apartment buildings. They could be huge testing areas for the Klados, preparing for planetfall.

Klados. It's a Greek word. *Cladistics* is derived from it—whatever that is. The Klados describes us, links us to everything that comes from the Catalogs. Where are the Catalogs kept? How are they accessed? Who controls the birthing chambers?

The egg-craft moves in toward the last uninspected hull. There's its number, a big 03, painted on the outboard side. The paint—along with the hull's entire surface—looks scarred and pitted and gray as we pass around the blunt nose, searching for another docking port.

I've learned enough about the sphere that I move my fingers and twirl around, facing forward. I'm not looking for the neb-ula or the stars, but for that other glow that spreads like an umbrella ahead of Ship.

I move to Ship's outboard side, near the origin of a pale grayish beam emanating from the third hull. The beam shoots forward, then fans out into space. Similar beams radiate from the other two hulls, but the beam from Hull Zero Two flickers weakly. It's not up to full strength.

The beams merge somewhere ahead and form a barely discernible gray shield that must be hundreds of kilometers wide. Every so often, the shield *sparks*—infinitely small glints spread across its surface, then travel down the gray beams. Spinning around slowly to follow the progress of a parade of these sparks, I notice that there are runnels or small channels carved aft along each hull—lots of them.

I tell nobody in particular, "Ship scoops up dust. I wonder if it scoops fuel?"

"Ship won't get much fuel from the interstellar medium," Tsinoy says behind us. Again, the Tracker's expertise is surprising, almost shocking. "It's too thin. Not much out there, actually. But if Ship encounters dust, it could use it to replenish hull surfaces. Lots of wear and tear. We've been traveling a long time."

I pull my fingers away from the sphere. "Another sleeper awakes," I say, impressed. "Maybe you should come up here."

"My claws might damage it," the Tracker says.

"Nonsense," the spidery woman says. "Come try. You're waking up faster than some of the rest of us."

"Let's not name names," Big Yellow says.

"Come take the big view," the spidery woman insists. "See what it means—what it brings back."

Tsinoy unfolds and expands. Having seen the Tracker in real action, I cringe. I can't help it, even after it saved our lives. I pull away from the hemisphere and give it a wide berth. Maybe that's sad. Maybe it isn't. We've all had a rough time of it lately.

The girls are awake and watch us closely.

Tsinoy places its front paws—claws, hands, grippers, whatever—on the blue hemisphere and seems to relax. All its muscles loosen, and some even let go of their holdfasts on the bones, creating that puffed-up look. The spidery woman doesn't seem to have any difficulty staying close.

After a moment of remote viewing, it says, "We're still at speed. We should be asleep—stored away."

"Right," my other says.

"Only the first hull is doing spin-up and spin-down. The second hull is dead—no motion. The third seems to be rotating at constant speed," Tsinoy says. "Something's happened, something bad. If Destination Guidance was supposed to find a safe harbor for us, they failed."

The spidery woman says, "What…" but she pauses to choose her next few words, as if they take some effort. "What's a *nova*, or a *supernova*?"

Tsinoy answers. "Remember what a sun is, a star?"

"I'm not stupid."

"Right. We shouldn't ever come close to the kind of system where a nova could happen. A nova is a star disaster, a huge explosion. A supernova, even bigger—so powerful it could engulf hundreds of stars with deadly radiation in just a few years." Tsinoy's muscles rearrange again. It takes up a fresh, bunchy form, like a frosted hedgehog—yet another shape to haunt my dreams. A Killer—and a scientist. "This might be my specialty—stars, the interstellar medium."

"Maybe you're from Destination Guidance," Big Yellow says. We all glare at him. "What?"

Tsinoy looks around some more, indicated by movement of its pink eyes, a slight nod and twitch of its canine head. "We seem to be emerging from one arm of a bright nebula," Tsinoy says. "Those central stars, an empty space surrounded by brilliant strands…a pulse or wave front of radiation ionizing the interstellar medium. Recent supernova, perhaps. The explosion may be fifty years or more in the past. If we were within range, that could explain the damage to Ship."

"Whoa," Big Yellow says. "How could that happen?"

"Accident," my twin says. "Or a major screwup."

"Or sabotage," the spidery woman says. Into our silence, she asks what option we're going to choose—find a docking port on the last intact hull or return to our birthplace. She actually uses that word, *birthplace.* I don't like it. But I can't argue.

"We need Mother," the girls say, not quite in unison.

"Where *do* you two come from?" Big Yellow asks. "And how did you learn to pilot this craft?"

The girls wrap their arms closer and tighter. "Our secret," one whispers.

"All right," the spidery woman says. "What about our other new comrade?" She looks at the Knob-Crest. He's been mum ever since we left the hull.

"Do you understand us?" Big Yellow asks him.

He nods, then shakes his head.

"I'm confused, too," Big Yellow says, folding his arms—which he can barely do. "But I fearlessly vote with the majority."

The spidery woman reconnects her hands with the sphere. "I've found something just aft of the bow—looks like the hulls have access ports in similar locations. If there's no objection, I'm going in."

"Maybe we should—" my twin starts, then pulls back and falls silent. I know just what he's thinking—and what he thinks when he reconsiders. We could find that the third hull, internally, is in as sad a shape as the first, in which case, maybe a different port of entry would be best. But we just don't know. Any

port in a storm—when your other choices are certain destruction or floating around in deep space forever.

The little egg-craft is quiet—no engine sounds, no real
feeling of motion but a gentle push to the large end, and then a
gentle shove to the small end—

And we stop. There's a subtle sensation of being locked onto
something much larger, much more massive, an end to all the
little signs of motion. Stability.

"Hull Zero Three," the spidery woman announces. "If the
machinery works, we should be able to open the hatch from
this side."

One of the girls floats toward the plate near the forward
hatch. Before we can object, she pulls the plate to one side, and
the hatch opens. Beyond is a warm glow. For a moment, I wonder if everything is on fire, and then I feel the cold. No fire. The
air is cold and fresh. Just reddish light, status lighting, visible to
factors—and to Killers.

THE LAST HULL

Big Yellow volunteers to go first. I protest, but he raises a broad hand, looks me firmly in the eye, then turns to Tsinoy. "If I don't come back, you and one of the Teachers go next and find out what happened. If none of *them* comes back," he says to the spidery woman, "push away. Try the second hull, or whatever you think is best. It looks bad, but it might still be livable—less desirable but still real estate, right?"

"I'll go with you," a girl says. "And one will stay here."

"No," Big Yellow insists. "I don't want to worry about anyone else. I don't feel the cold—much. Maybe I can find a switch and turn on the heat."

"How would you know where to look?" the spidery woman asks.

"I'll charm the hull with wit," Big Yellow says, and moves through the hatch. "Close it behind me. And shove off if I'm not back in...ten minutes?"

For some reason, him using that word, *minutes*, so casually, saying it aloud, brings back another flood of associations. Seconds, minutes, hours, days—planets spinning on their axes, one side in shadow, the other bathed in the light of a sun—then collections of days, months, pentads, or dekads, adding up to a year, going around the sun once, in a planetary orbit—

The words have occurred to me before, just not as sharply. Hope of life is making me sentimental. My twin is lost in similar reflections. We hardly notice the hatch closing.

One of the girls approaches the Knob-Crest and starts to hoot. He seems to understand and responds with more of this musical language.

Tsinoy has lapsed into motionless repose. It opens one eye.

The girl breaks off conversation with the Knob-Crest. "He saw nothing but bodies—and factors cleaning up more bodies. And Killers," she says. "We're the last survivors from Hull Zero One."

"How did he escape the Killers?" I ask.

"He doesn't want to talk about it," she says.

The Knob-Crest curls up and shuts his eyes.

My twin and I look at the girls, our glances crossing as we switch our examinations, twin to twin and back again. "Do either of you know how to access the Catalog?" I ask.

The girls shake their heads. "We pray for Teachers," one says. "Mother tells us where to look for them. They keep dying."

"Too curious or too slow," I say.

"Or both," my other says.

"Why look for teachers?" the spidery woman asks. "If they're all so delicate...It seems that Tsinoy and I have a lot of the answers we all need. Where in your Catalog—whatever *that* is—do we fit in?"

Silence. The girls close their eyes and hug.

The waiting is excruciating. I try to remember more details about the Catalog. We might have been able to access it from the controls in the bow chamber, though I have no idea what we could do with it. So I muse some more about Destination Guidance. I'm considering Big Yellow's suggestion that Tsinoy's apparent skill set is somehow ideally suited for that role.

Only then do I realize that not one of us has considered yet another haven should this hull prove to be a disaster area.

"Why don't we go down to the moon and try the quarters there?" I ask.

"Where?" the spidery woman asks.

"Down there." I point. "On the moon. The sphere."

The girls are like statues. I might as well have belched in a roomful of prissy old ladies. (Yes, those images seem to make sense to me. But I wonder if *prissy* is a smell or a behavior.)

"It's as if it doesn't exist," my other concludes. "We see it— we even talk about it—then...it drops out of our thoughts."

"What does?" I ask, but I'm joking...I think.

He slaps my arm.

"Still, it *could* be a refuge," the spidery woman admits with a frown of concentration. "If we remember it's there."

The girls blink their disapproval.

"Maybe it doesn't exist...in our imprinting," I say, still spooked by that very idea.

"*I* remember it," Tsinoy says.

Of course. "Good. Keep reminding us," I say.

"Why am I so different inside?" Tsinoy asks. "I take pleasure thinking about stars, the interstellar medium, protective shields...velocities."

"Mix and match," the spidery woman says. "Maybe they made a mistake *imprinting* you." She looks at me, that word distasteful to her.

There's a heavy knock on the hatch. She reaches out and opens it, and Big Yellow whuffs back in, more green than yellow now. "Boy, it *is* cold. I think it's deserted. No bodies, no damage, no factors."

"How far did you go?" the spidery woman asks.

"Not far. Next step, I go out with one of the Teachers and we reconnoiter."

"Mighty big word," my other says.

"Yeah," Big Yellow says, smiling. "I think I've found my résumé. I'm a police officer. A beat cop."

We don't bother asking what that means. I can easily picture him beating on whatever a cop is.

"But it's really *cold*," he says. "So we won't be able to stay long—unless we find some controls."

The three females collect our gray bags, empty the last food scraps and bottles, and slip them over my arms and legs. They have Tsinoy snip a hole in one bag and push it over my head and shoulders. I look ridiculous. Why me and not *him*? But Big Yellow seems to be able to tell the difference between us, and he selected me with a brush of his big hand on my shoulder.

Then I think, *I'm the least experienced of the two. I'm more expendable.*

The Knob-Crest is still curled up, at least pretending to sleep.

The girl opens the hatch again and we push into the hull. The hatch shuts with a last puff of warm air. I'm back where I started—trying to avoid freezing to death.

"Let's try to make it into the bow chamber and see if it's active," Big Yellow says.

"Is there another staging area aft?" I ask, my breath cloudy.

"Seems to be, but just framework, cradles—no ships or anything."

"Supplies?"

"Not that I saw. But I wasn't out here long," he says.

"No joke. What do you think, five minutes?" I ask.

"Less for you. You're smaller—you'll freeze faster."

"I've got my arctic gear," I say, lifting my bag-wrapped arms.

"Right. Forward."

I follow, grateful I'm not touching the surfaces with my bare hands. Still, getting around is awkward—I can only push and deflect and mitten-grab as we jump and bounce and move forward toward the nose.

The nose chamber is open, but everything within is rudimentary—just bumps and odd blue outlines where control pylons might eventually push out like sunflowers. The view forward is obscured by covers—we can't see the stars.

"Not any better here," I say.

"That's why I brought you. You say Ship Control spoke to you. Maybe the girls know something they aren't telling us. And frankly, I trust you more than I trust them…Don't ask why, but I'm thinking you might have a special relationship with this place. Try it."

"Try what?"

"Over there." He points toward a blue circumferential line where the covers could conceivably pull back and reveal the view. "Sing it a lullaby. Or bark at it. Just do something."

I feel like a fool—but I'm also scared. If nothing happens, then maybe I'm just another failure. Or I imagined the voice back in Hull Zero One.

"Seems we left the silveries and laser guy back where we came from," I say as I delicately move toward the front of the bow chamber.

"There are no silveries," Big Yellow says.

"Right."

There are also no cables or maneuvering bars here—not yet. I hold out my hands like a high-wire artist (catching inner glimpses of a big mess of something called a *circus*), but that doesn't help much. I still lift up with each step and waste time waiting to come back down.

"Talk to it," Big Yellow says from ten meters behind.

"Hello, there!" I call. My voice echoes weirdly in the cylindrical chamber—and the last echo comes from way behind, as if there's yet another Teacher far aft, hiding. "How about some heat? Come out, come out, wherever you are."

We listen. The hull isn't exactly silent. There are all sorts of subtle sounds, some regular, others sporadic, some deep and rich, others faint and tinny. All seem far, far away.

My feet are numb, my hands are numb, my lungs ache and there's frost on my chin. I reach up and brush it off. Little flakes of rime swing left and slowly drift outboard. What I wouldn't give for the honest gravity of a good old-fashioned planet.

I look over my shoulder at Big Yellow. "Time's up," I say. "I won't be able to move if—"

"Are you Destination Guidance?" a voice asks. It seems to come from all around—neither male nor female, but neither is it obviously mechanical. For a moment, I think Big Yellow is pulling a joke, but he's as startled as I am. He looks around, hunkered—knees bent and feet lifted, actually, slowly falling outboard. He encourages me with one outstretched hand.

I can't locate the source of the voice. Again, I feel it might be dangerous to answer one way or another—the last time such a voice addressed me, it helped for a little while but did not linger or return. Maybe Control was disappointed.

"No," I say. "We're not Destination Guidance." Honesty is again the best policy. Besides, I'm beginning to firmly believe that whatever is wrong with Ship may be because of Destination Guidance. Call it a hunch, but it seems more than that.

They shouldn't be here. Nobody should be asking about them. Ship shouldn't care about them anymore.

"We came over from the first hull—Zero One. It's a wreck. Somebody, something—you, maybe—spoke to me before—"

"No record," the voice says. "There is a transfer craft docked to this hull. Was it sent by Destination Guidance?"

"No." A long pause. We've really screwed up, I think. Then:

"Does it contain *daughters*?"

This makes my muscles knot and my spine shiver. If I had any body hair, I'm sure it would prickle.

"Yes," I say. "Two little girls."

"Do they require assistance?"

"Yes," I say. "They want to find their mother."

Big Yellow looks around the bow chamber with his mouth open, like a yokel at a country fair. Circuses and fairs—all useless imagery, but somehow comforting. I need comfort. I could totally screw up our chances of survival—screw up any chance that the hulls will ever rejoin to form Ship, that Ship will ever find a stellar system and a beautiful planet....

"We need heat and food and water. A change of clothes would be nice," I say.

"You are not Destination Guidance."

"I think...that's right," I say.

"I have rejected or destroyed all envoys from Destination Guidance," the voice says. "After communication with the other hulls was blocked."

"Good," I say. "What are you?"

"Welcome," the voice says. "Daughters are expected."

We feel it right away—the gentle spin increases. Then, cables and bars grow out of the surface of the chamber, stringing and arranging magically. A billowing draft of warmer air swirls down from the center. And the walls light up, brilliantly, until we're almost blinded. Our eyes adjust behind our raised hands and Big Yellow laughs. The sound is deep and rich and satisfying, and I join in, but I can't compete—my laugh is a doggish, repetitive bark.

We join up along a raised bar, and Big Yellow extends his huge hand. "You know how to shake, don't you?" he asks.

"Of course," I say. My hand is lost in his, but he doesn't squeeze too hard.

"Food!" he shouts, and the whole chamber booms. "Ask it for food and drink! And I need a bath!"

DANGEROUS HOPE

We go back and wait in the egg-craft for an hour, giving the hull time to warm to a tolerable level. Then we bring the others into the bow chamber. As a group, we look sad and worn down, but there's a glint in our eyes—except for Tsinoy's, which are as flat and pink as ever. But even the Tracker seems to be enjoying the new possibilities, the relief of not being pursued. *Not now, not yet.* Of having a little time to catch up and consider what we need to do next. The Knob-Crest still looks sleepy. I wonder if he took a knock on the head somewhere and hasn't recovered.

"You spoke to the hull, to Ship Control," my twin says, standing close.

"Yeah," I say. "I think so." We watch the girls walk hand-in-hand toward the bow. The front plates are still shut.

"Is it healthy? Is it really in control?"

"You've been around longer. You know more than I do."

"Not really. Everything we've seen, everything we've been

told, could be an illusion, or a trap. What if the hull is fading, losing its grip?"

Tsinoy approaches. We're almost used to the Tracker's nearness; the egg-craft was pretty confining, and familiarity breeds familiarity—but nothing like contempt. It ripped some of the nastiest Killers to shreds.

It elongates, stretching. "I would like to take a look forward and contemplate."

"Why?" my other asks.

"See our situation. View the stars. Speculate."

"Just a few more minutes," I say. "We'll see if we get food and water, then we'll ask for the forward plates to open."

"All right," Tsinoy agrees. It makes a little clack with its jaws and teeth. We both jump, but this seems to indicate a desire to just sit and think, without interruption. "But soon."

The spidery woman has been silent since emerging from the egg-craft. I don't know how to read her expression. Eyes wide and a little moist, she moves slowly from place to place along the cables, as if waiting for something to do, someone to be—a redefinition of her role seems in order. I approach her, my twin not far behind. We're both thinking the same thing. "If we get the controls back, can you tell us more about the condition of the hull, the Ship?" he asks.

"Maybe," she says. She looks around. "Why don't we set off alarms? I mean, we come out of nowhere—and *you* say the magic words, and suddenly it's all better. How's that possible?"

"Too good to be true," my twin says, and I reluctantly agree. We can't afford to be complacent, but it *is* getting more comfortable. Maybe that's the point—we're letting down our guard.

"It mentioned shutting out Destination Guidance—or

words to that effect," I say. "Apparently, communications between the hulls have been blocked. Some kind of prolonged struggle for power, maybe—like a war."

"I wish we knew more about that conflict," my other says.

"Maybe the girls can explain," I say, guilty to be shoving responsibility over to them. But, then, they started me off on this journey. "I think they might have come from here...originally, a while back."

"Now *there*'s a thought," Tsinoy says, and smacks its jaws again.

"Why can't any one of us talk to the hull?" the spidery woman asks, but before her question can be addressed, or ignored, or whatever that sort of question deserves, in an atmosphere of almost total ignorance—

The girls slide forward on bars, almost flying, and call us together in high, piping voices.

"We need names—we need names *now!*" they announce together. "Gather for your names!"

"Mother must be nearby," my twin says in an undertone. "I think we're about to be introduced."

THE NAMING, PART ONE

The girls move in symmetry, one left, one right, and gather us in a circle. Tsinoy, out of respect for its armor, is not touched, but all the girls have to do is raise their hands and look at the Tracker and it complies. The spin has increased enough that we stay on our feet without bouncing up at every toe twitch.

As we wait for the girls to arrange us just right, as if setting the table for a tea party, my other murmurs to the spidery woman, who whispers back, and then he says to me: "We're getting pretty heavy. The outer parts of the hull have to be moving fast—uncomfortable if we're headed that direction. I'm thinking there aren't any new applicants working their way through the outboard tubes."

Good information to have—maybe we're alone, or maybe everyone important has been concentrated along the hull's center axis.

"Or the hull's trying to shed attackers," I say.

"Wow. That's a possibility, too."

The girls walk around our circle, on the inside, and christen each of us in turn. "You are Kim," one girl announces, tapping Big Yellow's knee. Her twin, on the opposite side of the circle, brushes the spidery woman's hand. "And you are Nell," she says. The other girl taps the Knob-Crest and says, in a strangely comprehensible hoot, "Tomchin."

To me, "You are Sanjay."

And to my twin, "You are Sanjim. But we call you both Teacher. And you are Tsinoy, of course," they conclude with the Tracker. "Now you all have names."

"What about *your* names?" Nell asks.

"Mother knows. You do not need to know."

"That's not fair, is it?" Kim asks.

One girl pats his hand, and when he opens it, she folds herself into his fingers, then jerks her arms and head—*up*! He lifts her and holds her out high. This stirs something in my deep memory—something cultural, but I can't quite place it. A monster and a girl. Anyway, he's the wrong color, and so is she.

"We love all," she says, high over our circle. "We have prayed you here. That is enough. Others will come later, if necessary."

"Then who's in charge?" Nell asks.

"Mother," my twin suggests. "Maybe Mother and Ship Control are one and the same."

"So far, no objections," Kim says. "I'm going aft in case our host laid out a big spread and made up some beds, but forgot to tell us." I follow Kim—such a *little* name for such a large fellow—and the girls seem to agree that exploration is in order.

Where the staging area had been in Hull Zero One, there's a similar space, but—as we saw during our first reconnoiter—the interior architecture is nascent, rudimentary. Still, cables and rails are in place, and even ladders and crawling tubes with rungs. We can get around—we are being accommodated. We move aft and inboard, up, climbing through a tube to a hatch. The hatch opens as my hand grips the topmost rung. More warmth spills out. The smaller spaces are warming quickly. Then I smell something marvelous.

Food. Kim was right.

We enter a broad chamber, a giant pie section of the central bulge that pokes into the staging area. The chamber's design is different from the broad, flat room in the other hull, but who cares? As we watch, teardrop extrusions rise from the floor and push out in rows from the walls. Little silver covers open in the rounded tops of each teardrop as we walk from one to the next.

Kim shakes his head and murmurs, "We can't eat—not until we're all here."

"Right." But my hands are twitching.

We go back and call the others. When all have assembled, we show them how the covers open and how food fills each dish. The food is in small cubes, beige and green and white, and smells delicious, but we are far from choosy. Each meal is enclosed in a flexible sphere. The sphere is transparent and allows our hands in and out, along with small bits—not burning hot. Something doesn't want us to eat too fast or too much. Water and a sweet, reddish liquid are available from taps around the room, squeezing out little bulbs we can sip from.

The hull has laid out a feast.

Tsinoy eats what we eat and seems content.

Before we've had anywhere near our fill, the teardrops withdraw, but the spigots remain, dispensing smaller bulbs. We're being rationed. We've been nearly starved ever since we were made—no sense overdoing it.

"Who do we thank?" Nell asks, licking her long fingers.

"*Whom*," my twin corrects.

"Right. *Whom* do we thank?" she repeats archly.

The girls yell, "Teacher!" and laugh, musical tones that delight almost as much as the food—or the red drink. We all smile, even the Knob-Crest, Tomchin.

Now, soft, circular beds rise from the floor. On one side of the room, the teardrops and spigots are replaced by cylinders filled with running water. Steam puffs out from cuts in the pliable surround, slits that allow entry. Nearby, drawers open, with clothing folded inside. Small lights play across our faces, matching the color of our assigned shower stalls—and our drawers filled with changes of clothes.

We've each been measured and fitted.

"Mother provides," the girls say. "All is well."

One stall is even big enough for Kim, and a burning question is answered when another, bigger cylinder shapes itself, and Tsinoy climbs in to be sprayed down with water, like a great, horrible wolf.

The Tracker likes to keep clean.

"It's not a big warm tub," Nell says as she emerges, naked, furry gray patches slicked and glistening. "But it's the best thing I've ever felt." Then she adds, looking between me and my twin, "In my young life, of course."

STORYTIME

We lounge on the pads like campers under a giant tent—the pie-slice room even *looks* like a huge tent. We're no longer hungry, we've had enough to drink, we're clean, and still there's electricity in our thoughts. We aren't going to be sleeping for a while.

The time has come for stories. The girls, of course, choose the Teachers. I go first and tell what happened to me. I condense it into a few minutes.

My twin, oddly, departs from our campground script and shakes his head. "Later," he says. "I'm not ready yet."

Kim goes next.

"I don't remember too much about being born. No girls, nobody—just me, alone. I'm in this long tube when I start to remember, like waking up, but I know I've got something I have to do—I have to go forward. I don't even know where *forward* is, or what it is, but that's where I have to go." He looks at the rest of us. "Why don't we come with instructions?"

Nobody knows the answer. We'd all like to be real people, after all—probably even Tsinoy.

Kim lifts his hands, examining them with a kind of wonder, and continues. "Being big turns out to be a good thing. Pretty soon, something even bigger and dark tries to stop me, so I break it or kill it. It happens so fast." He flexes his fingers. "I guess it was a factor, maybe a cleaner—maybe it didn't even want to hurt me. I don't know, but I *hate* being interfered with."

"Amen," Nell says.

"Along the way, all I see are bodies or parts of bodies, and I think, this place is dying—or maybe it's dead already. There are lots of burned areas. Once, I was moving through a place that smelled bad and had no lights at all, and something tried to take me from behind. I didn't see it, but it left these marks." He turns to show a circular collection of greenish welts, some still oozing reddish pus. Under his ragged clothing and the layers of grime, we hadn't noticed them before. The circle is about three hands wide—his hands. His back is huge. "I don't know how I got away, but I did, though I don't think I hurt it much—I couldn't even get a grip, really."

"A *big* Killer," one of the girls says.

"I don't know how many times I went around the circumference, or doubled back, or reversed course and went aft again. It was all so confusing. I was still waking up. I knew I had to have a name, but I couldn't remember it. I *like* Kim, mind you, but I don't think it's the name I should have.... " He shakes his head with sad humor. "Sorry, girls. I must have spent dozens of spin-ups getting to the rotating sluices. That's where the water gets channeled from the big central tank—I guess."

"It is," Nell says. They've heard this before, repeating their stories for our benefit, but also with a kind of hypnotic focus, like chanting old, comforting songs. The stories are all they have, really.

Kim and Nell don't even have the emerging shadows of a personal Dreamtime. As for Tsinoy…

"Once, I caught a cleaner carrying a body and seven gray bags." Kim looks at me, squinting with his emerald-green eyes. "I think it might have been you, actually—one of you, I mean. The body was cut in half—no legs—but there were still bags around its neck. I broke the cleaner—didn't kill it, but it was pretty lame after. Then I stole the bags and ate my fill, drank four bottles of water. I was sick for a few spin-ups. I just floated and bumped in a long tube and made messes. Must have eaten too fast. The loaves haven't affected me that way since."

"Maybe they were poisoned," Nell says.

"Maybe. Finally, I'm climbing up this shaft when I see a big glowing ball coming down at me, with a window or port in the front."

"Did you see anything through the window?" my other asks.

"Yeah. Maybe. A kind of face—shiny, white."

"Silvery," I say.

"There *are* no—" Kim begins, as if in reflex, and that makes us laugh—all but the girls, who are definitely not amused.

Kim waits for a decent interval while we think this over, then continues his story up to the point where he's made his way forward and meets the first little girl, then Nell and Tsinoy. We know the rest.

Nell goes next. The girls sit on either side of her. Each takes a long-fingered hand. The scene is at once touching and incongruous.

"The first thing I remember," she begins, "is Tsinoy carrying me in a sac through a forest. The sac is slowly ripping, and I'm about to fall out. We get to a platform—I guess this is during spin-up. The platform is covered with dried stuff—blood, I think."

"It was blood," Tsinoy agrees.

"Where did you find her?" my twin asks.

"In a pile of bodies in a birthing chamber—most of them still in sacs. They were dead, freezing, but one sac squirmed, so I pulled it out and took it with me."

"Why?" Kim asks.

"I did not want to be alone. I had questions, and for too long, nothing and nobody to talk to."

"How did you know she would talk to you?"

"I didn't."

"*Her* story first," one of the girls insists.

Nell resumes. "We were in a factor tunnel, somewhere outboard, maybe near the middle of the hull, near the cinch, when I fell out. Got born, I suppose. Tsinoy waited while I tried out my legs and arms. I managed to stand, and then I screamed. I'm embarrassed to say that."

"Don't be," Tsinoy says in a soft grumble.

"But we were alone, it wasn't attacking me. And then it spoke. I didn't understand it at first. I had to integrate, bring language to the surface. I have other languages, potentially—maybe we all do. Maybe if we try hard enough, we can speak to others…" She casts a quick look at Tomchin. "Just as the girls do."

The girls look somberly around the circle.

"Tsinoy was the first name I've ever heard. It knew who it was even then."

"Not *what*, though," Tsinoy adds. "No mirrors, but limbs look all wrong."

"After a time," Nell resumes, "Tsinoy guides me to a huge chamber—the biggest chamber we've seen. It's full of a quiet, hissing rumble and big, long blue tubes…bigger than the water tank, I think. The tubes are lined up in a cylindrical shape, filled with whirling shadows, surrounded by sparkles, all flowing aft. The chamber might have been a kilometer wide. It was only a couple of minutes before we found more bodies, in terrible condition—not just desiccated, not injured, just crispy, burned. And we decided it wasn't a good idea to stay there. They were like…like…"

She can't quite put her thoughts into words.

"Like insects in a trap," my twin finishes for her.

She agrees.

"What's an insect?" Kim asks.

"Little living thing, hard shell," my twin explains. I see the same image: little dead things with glassy wings in a kind of trap or bottle. The things that spiders eat—flies. "Radiation," I say. "Bad place to be."

"I think now it was part of the hull's drive engine," Nell says. "I started remembering some things. I know about engines, a little at first—engines and hulls and joining everything together. I know a little more now, but it still hasn't all come to the surface. We left that part of Ship, found our way forward, through the cinch—felt sick for a few spin-ups but seemed to recover quickly…Maybe we're tough that way. We blundered along, still moving forward, I think, until we met up with a Killer. A pack of them. I haven't seen their like since. They were slender, barbed, maybe three times longer than I am tall, and about as thick through the middle, with four eyes at the end of a long stalk or arm, lots of bendy joints. The joints all have suckers on the outside." She lifts a thumb knuckle and taps it. "They grip the walls and use leverage. Moved almost too fast for me to see—very strong. Made to clear the tubes, I think. They tried to get around Tsinoy—seemed to think it might be one of the team. I think they were surprised when it attacked them—before they could touch me. Tsinoy was very effective."

"They hurt me," Tsinoy said, showing a black, burned-looking area under its ivory spines, behind a temporary shoulder joint. "They use poison."

"Why does *everything* want to kill us?" Nell asks suddenly. "Why are we even here, if Ship doesn't want us to be here?"

I've been thinking about this but have no solid answers. I exchange a look with my twin, San-whatever. He takes this as a kind of encouragement. "Something went wrong with Destination Guidance," he says. "That place we don't want to think about…The occupants took control of almost everything. They did something wrong—bad for Ship."

"Fair enough," Nell says. "I can see that as a possibility. But where do the monsters come from? Why can't we remember anything about them?"

"Present company excluded," Tsinoy says, and looks at me—then at my twin. "Something made me different. Why? What am I made to do?"

"Originally, you're designed to help clear a planet," my twin says. "But you're not supposed to have a human personality. You're just a tool. You're…" He hesitates.

"*Expendable*," Tsinoy finishes. "But what about you two—how is it you both know about me?"

We've been through this before. I thought we'd explained ourselves, as much as we could, but now I'm not so sure. All this thickens our mood, helps spread a new gloom that overcomes even full bellies and clean bodies. And it's interrupted our story telling. Nobody wants to pursue these questions—not now, not yet.

Nell lounges back. "We need to talk this through. But we also need to rest. Ladies?" She looks at the girls. "You're in charge here, right? Along with the Teachers?"

"Sleep," the girls say. "More later."

"Dim the lights," my twin says. "Sleep mode, whatever."

The hull complies. The lights under the tent-shaped chamber dim until we're bathed in a shadowy golden glow.

"Which one am I, again?" I ask my twin as we lie down next to each other. We don't touch. I'm not even sure I like him, actually.

"Sanjay," he says.

"And you are...Sanjim."

"Right."

I close my eyes. I don't realize how truly tired I am, but it seems just a blink before Nell pokes me.

Sanjim and I rise up.

"Noises," she says. "Grinding noises aft."

We can hear them, too—we all can. The sounds are deep, harsh, big. They set my teeth on edge. The deck vibrates and now we feel a jerky sort of spin-down. We start to slide as the hull slows its rotation. We're away from the cables and rails, so we flatten and press our hands on the smooth deck, or grab hold of a cot frame, or slip up against a bulkhead, as Tsinoy does, all bristled.

The girls are nowhere to be seen.

Kim and Tomchin crawl back toward us. The hull is jerking, spinning up again—then down. More grinding. The whole frame around us shudders.

"We should look at the control center and see what we can learn—then, what we can do," Kim says. "It's coming quicker than we thought."

"What?" I ask, still dopey.

"More bad."

THE BIG VIEW

For a moment, it seems that the entire hull is about to shiver itself to pieces and blow us all out into space. Maybe this is intentional. Maybe this is the last part of Ship *they* can't control, so *they're* going to destroy it completely—but then, where will that leave *them*, whatever they are?

Surely they wouldn't destroy the entire *Ship* just to purge *us*. Would they?

But we do have Tsinoy, who understands something about what lies all around us. And Kim, who has more than a normal sense of finding his way around. And Nell, who seems to know something about engineering and hull operations—and who desperately needs to recover *all* she knows.

The grinding and vibration settle long enough for us to make our way through the hatch, across the staging area, and along the bars and cables, back to the forward chamber. Here, we're almost floating, the spin has been so reduced. We're used to that. We're used to having things go wrong. We seem hardly rattled at all, and the way we move, the way we help each other—I even grab Tsinoy's paw to pull it through a tight hatch—means we're finally acting as a team.

Tomchin is right beside us as we tug and haul ourselves up to the bow chamber, where nascent outlines—squares and rectangles and ovals—still glow gently. Where pylons and controls will pop up, we hope, if only we ask.

"Tell it!" Nell shouts at the two of us, looping her foot around a cable and stretching to her full, impressive two and a half meters.

"Show us the stars, build us controls—" my twin says.

Before he can finish, the hull is already fulfilling our request. More teardrops rise, then shape into horizontal control boards, thickening, spreading wide, and all the while, the panels covering the bow viewports slide up and away. Once more, we stare out at the universe—at wisps and the endless diamond-dust glow of uncounted millions of stars.

But something's missing.

Tsinoy lets out a whimpering groan, far beneath his dignity, and I slowly catch on, then share his concern. It's all about what we don't see. The grayish misty lines and the forward umbrella shield are no longer visible.

"The deflection cone," Tsinoy says. "It's *gone*."

"Great," Nell says.

"What's that mean?" Kim asks.

"We're moving very fast," Tsinoy says, and shivers uncontrollably. Its teeth snap—it can hardly control its rage and disappointment. "The interstellar medium—grains of dust, gas… on the edge of the nebula…"

"We're naked, right in the middle of a big storm," Nell says. She moves over to the far edge of the viewports and tries to look down and back. She doesn't have to look far. "The hulls are exposed, but that bump down there on the little moon, it's still got something around it—the moon is protected, too. They've got a shield."

"It's Destination Guidance. They're trying to scrape us off," Kim says.

Nell has moved back to the board mounted farthest forward. It, too, has a small blue dome mounted in the center, and little else. She places her hands on the dome, and dim lights flicker around her face and arms. My twin and I join her, with Tomchin coming up right beside us, a new expression on his generally stoic face.

"What's *he* know?" Kim asks from behind us. Nell breaks contact long enough to look, then urges us to put our hands on the dome, as before.

"All together," she says.

We connect to the hull, becoming receptive points in a vast space full of information. The abstraction seems familiar, exactly what we expect—but there are far too many ugly patches of what looks like char, burned darkness, signifying blank spots in the hull's memory. At a rough guess, it looks as if more than ninety percent of the space is damaged, inaccessible—or simply gone.

Tomchin is here with us. He's controlling a part of the display, searching, leaving the rest of us to explore in our own regions of, what, expertise? Instinct? Programming?

"I hate this," my twin says. I hear him through my ears but see flashes of his presence in the void—an angry, searching presence, matching my moves closely, but not exactly. "We need *ten* of us up here!"

"Only if the knowledge still exists to spread among you," Tomchin says. It's his voice, but in the space, we hear it in our language—and we understand it. His patch of awareness is off in a far corner of the area. He seems to be *rummaging*, searching for landmarks.

Then his presence rejoins us, and he's hauling a tendril of connectivity, like a brilliantly jeweled cable—signifying a distant branch of hull memory. "It's broken," Tomchin says. "But this used to lead directly to the gene pool, to Life Design."

Yes! Those words, those names...

"Can you follow it?" Nell asks him.

Without answering, he's off again—physically still close, but his presence impossibly far away in an instant.

The Tracker is also with us now, apparently accessing through another board. "This hull still keeps a large share of Ship's memory," it says, and for the first time, I realize that Tsinoy is *female*—her presence is rich with identity. The Ship, the hull, knows her, trusts her, *needs* her. She's an astrogation specialist. She may be the most important person among us—and because of her design, the one most likely to survive. Things begin to make a stark sort of sense. Maybe it's the rest of us who are expendable.

Tsinoy pulls up a dense starfield, then demos how each star has a descriptor, rendered in a number of shifting symbol sets and languages. "The information has been updated continually," she says.

"All Ship's children got clues," Nell says. "Let's hope they're enough to get us somewhere."

The rumbling and grinding outside of our connected experience is low-key, not very distracting. We assume Kim will warn us if anything worse happens. In here, we're *exploring*. Our need is painfully acute, more crucial than quenching thirst or assuaging hunger.

We might be about to find out why we are.

HULL MEMORY

Tsinoy is trying to figure out where we are headed. The first thing she discovers is that Ship is 439 light-years from Earth's sun. There's another measure of our distance traveled, more absolute—something to do with the crests of hyper-length cosmological gravitational waves, but it's a bigger number, surrounded by dense mathematics, so we stick with light-years, because the memory of a *year* is so rich with other associations.

It seems we—my twin and I—know a great deal about our home planet, the *Earth*. Almost as if we had been born and raised there. Pleasant and distracting, but almost totally useless.

Tomchin returns, dragging another jeweled cable. His presence *jacks* the cable into ours, though Tsinoy waves him off, absorbed in her own work. (I have several definitions for the word *jack*, one of them involving a child's game with little metal caltrops and a rubber ball—the other, an antiquated electrical or data connector. I assume the word refers to the connector.

No reason to explore memories of playing the game as a child! Because *I was never a child*.)

The cable reveals to us a pull-down mare's nest of more cables—lots more. Most appear charred and ugly. Some still glow while others have floating machine symbols like question marks. My twin and I reach through the tangle. We're quickly becoming experts, our minds flooding with imprinted knowledge—but then, together, we clumsily grab the same cable.

Bad idea.

We're home again.

We never left home.

It's all been a hideous nightmare.

CORE MEMORY

Something in the hull recognizes us and tries to do us a favor by reconnecting us with what we are supposed to know and feel. There's a little confusion because there's two of us, but that's okay—the system can be creative if it has to, and with a little modification, there we are, back on Earth, young twins with our whole lives ahead of us, training to embark on a journey to the newly outfitted *Golden Voyager.* That's the name of this Ship, I think—we think.

We're going to become part of the crew. The *destination crew.*

My twin and I don't always get along, but we went through training together, and we rely on each other for solving major problems—including women. Though of late we have been suffering through competition over a particularly lovely lass named—

(And here it gets strange, because that brings up fragments of *future* memories, the broken bits of my history available to Hull Zero One when I was—)

Don't be silly. That's just part of the terrible dream. You aren't made *in deep space—you're frozen with all of your shipmates, your future partners in the colonies, and the* Golden Voyager—

Whatever. I can very clearly anticipate my partner in the staging area, boldly looking at me along the line of the first landing party, exchanging those excruciatingly meaningful glances of first adoration, then lifelong bonding. We are *meant* for each other—so why would my twin interfere?

But we have so much to catch up on. Mother and Father, sister, education up through secondary, physical adaptation and augmentation, getting our freezing-down organs installed after first qualification, long summer days at Camp Starfield, our first test freeze…We all come out healthy and whole, not even hungover, and now we're ready for that installation flight out to the edges of the Oort cloud, to meet up with the chosen moonlet, on which is strapped the growing frame of our Ship. This is a journey of almost nine months, because it's illegal to light off bosonic drives within the system.

So clear! I suppose that even in my confusion and my conflicting emotions, seeing our unborn Ship for the first time, far out in the darkness where only starlight matters, fastened like a tiny golden octopus to the long end of the moonlet—seeing all this is useful, helpful, but why does it have to come attached to so much imaginary bullshit? I'm just fine without a backstory. I know the *real* story.

They pump us full of this continuity for psychological reasons—but why? *They don't trust us. We're designed to be deceived.*

We find spaces within the cramped living quarters, all three hundred of us, handpicked, tested, trained, passed—superior emotionally and physically to Earth's best and brightest, filled with that glow of knowing where we're going and what we're going to do, flying in the most expensive goddamned *object* ever devised by the hands of humanity....

And as we go into the freezers to become time travelers into the future, to awaken five or six hundred years hence, we're filled with an overwhelming *joy* at our destiny, more intense than anything we've experienced.

I'm still worried about my brother, of course, because we can't *both* have her at the end of the journey. But we'll work that out later.

Besides, I know, I anticipate...

At the end, there will be only one of us.

One of me.

My twin must be experiencing the same conflicts of indoctrination and emotion, because we pull up from this feed simultaneously, trying to shout in anger and frustration.

All wrong. All a lie.

"Hold on," Tomchin says. "Wrong input. That's the story if everything on Ship goes right. *Here's* what we're really looking for—the part of the Catalog that Ship uses if something goes *wrong*. And we all know that something has gone badly wrong."

What pours into our presences next is even more disturbing than our false personal history. We're paging through Ship's instruction manual, examining every possible contingency.

The planet is already covered with primitive life-forms, and we can't adapt, no matter how hard we try.

We're out of fuel, we can't move on.... Time to explore the far reaches of the Klados, the possibilities inherent in the nastiest neighborhoods of genetic phase space.

Time to bring out the Trackers and the Wastelayers. Time to convert the factors, the biomechanical servants that tended Ship while it grew from its egg into a mighty three-hulled starship, for the first twenty years of our journey, and that lit off the bosonic drives far from Earth's star....

Time to turn the page to a nightmare of destruction. And along with this comes my—our—new, tougher personality and a new, harsher personal history. Earth was in desperate trouble when we left—it wasn't the social and technological paradise depicted in our previous biography. No, it was a wreck. People were dying everywhere and pumped all their resources into creating this lifeboat to the stars. We're humankind's last hope, and now all that stands in our way is a planet covered with indigenous slime, *hardly worthy of the name of intelligent life.*

All we have to do is send down our Killers and Wastelayers and muck out that slime, *then deactivate our weapons...and send down, in their place...*

But that's another cluster of points in the Klados, another page in the Catalog, not as grim and more than a little hazy. What is becoming clear is that the Catalog has been damaged along with everything else in hull memory. We have no idea what the Klados is capable of delivering.

Still, the pages turn. Something wants to unburden its psyche. Something needs to confess.

We've encountered a primitive technological civilization, capable of rudimentary exploration of their stellar system—that is, our target system. We're here, we're out of fuel, nowhere else to go—and they attack. *They're advanced enough that their weapons can do real damage, blow us to bits, in fact, and* they won't listen.

They refuse to share.

We can't bargain with them. It's going to be a long, drawn-out fight, ending in our extinction, unless we—

Turn the page. Another page. We've plowed our way to the margin of the deepest, darkest corner of genetic phase space, and beyond, it seems, lies a genius-level zoo of madness and destruction.

Death's secret menagerie.

ACCESS GIVEN TO TOTAL WARRIORS ONLY.

Unexpectedly, we're dumped back into the main gallery. Sweetness, light, deception. We don't have the proper training, the proper indoctrination. None of us qualifies to venture into that section of the Catalog.

Rejected.

Tomchin bravely tries to hook us up to other cables, but we're balky, burned down to nubbins—too much shock, too much contradiction, almost worse than the first time we were squeezed from our birth sacs.

When we let go of the blue hemisphere, we bumble and thrash and cry. It must look as bad to the others as it feels to us. Nell orders Kim to pull us aside. Kim moves in and holds us in his arms while we shiver and curse out our misery.

That takes a few minutes. Tomchin seems relatively unaffected, but now that we're out, we don't understand what he says, and without the girls, neither does anyone else.

The control chamber gets quiet.

Nell has a report to make. She looks around. All of the adults are listening, possibly even Tsinoy, still deep in her interstellar survey.

"Ever since we were born, things have been trying to kill us," Nell says. "Dropping the shield seems to be a last-ditch attempt to get rid of us. We should assume that someone is willing to sabotage Ship operations and even destroy the hulls. Well, we may be able to fight back. I think there's a way to initiate hull combination—to unite the Triad. Because Destination

Guidance is supposed to be gone before the Triad is united, bringing the hulls together will squash and absorb that little ball down there—and reclaim the moonlet. It may give us back complete control. I just activate this system—"

The Tracker moves too fast for us to see and is suddenly right next to us, her paw on Nell's hands, pushing them away from the hemisphere. "*We can't do that!*" Tsinoy roars—a terrifying sound completely impossible to ignore.

Nell backs down from her control board. "Why not?" she asks, teeth gritted.

"Because I can't find most of the navigational data or any way to control Ship's engines," Tsinoy says. "I think we've been sidetracked into bad space—a really dangerous region—and as far as I can tell, we're less than halfway to where we want to be. We can't destroy Destination Guidance. Whoever they are, we need their help."

"But they want us *dead*," Nell says.

None of us, it seems, has noticed that the girls have returned—and are listening to us all with worried faces.

"How do we know that?" Tsinoy asks.

"Ship Control," I say.

"How reliable is that?" Tsinoy asks, her spikes at full defensive posture, an awesome display that expands her to three times her former dimensions.

We all back away.

The girl nearest me pushes out her lower lip. "We tell you. *Mother* tells us."

"Oh, it's *that*, is it?" Tsinoy says. "We've never met Mother. We have no way to question her. We can't make this decision without more evidence, because if we do, there's a very real chance we'll never find our way to a good star. Ship will die out here."

"We're dying now," my twin says. "Can't you hear it? We're being sandblasted to oblivion. You said so yourself."

Nell listens to all this with a frightened grimace. She's trying to form the right words to bring us back on some sort of constructive track. But the problem is being stated very clearly by our formidable astrogation expert.

Tsinoy pulls in her spines. "There's a maneuver that might explain turning off the shield, temporarily," she says. "It's part of Ship's standard procedure. But it doesn't make sense—not now, not yet."

BAD NEWS, WORSE

If you're like me, you've been trying to form a picture of Destination Guidance. Chances are you've been at least as successful. We're not supposed to know about them. Our brains refuse to seriously consider their little spherical refuge down there on the leading point of the moonlet—and we have no idea what they look like or what they want. If they were ever a planned part of this mission—and that makes sense, at least as far as our ignorance allows us to judge—then they've failed. From what we've been able to piece together, they've stayed past their time, and they are very likely responsible for most, if not all, of our problems.

But to fight something, you really have to try to understand its motivations—particularly when the something you're fighting holds most of the cards, the deck is stacked against you, and the whole gambling hall is on fire and filled with thugs.

The shivering and grinding gets louder. Unbearably loud. *We shouldn't be here when this happens.*

"Our brains are packed with *crap*," my twin shouts to me as we move aside. Then we put our heads together. We're both thinking as fast as we can to arrange what few facts we have into some usable order. "Fake history, fake lives—storybook *crap*. How can we replace all that crap with useful information? We have to force our way into data that doesn't want to be known."

"We just *tried*," I say, working to keep my voice low but still be heard over the cacophony. "Why does Ship even tempt us?"

"We should be getting the hell out of here!" Kim cries out, covering his ears. The big fellow is on the edge of panic, and if *he* loses it, where does that leave us?

"Because there's a contradiction in Ship's systems, all of them," my twin says. "Right?"

That much is obvious.

"So *talk* to me," he says, staring into my eyes. "Double-team with me. Tell me what I should be thinking."

I go back through a quick selection of my inner mumblings and fragmented theories. We're both so far into this little game that we don't see until we're almost finished that everyone else is watching us, quiet, waiting.

All but Nell. She has once more applied herself to the blue hemisphere controls, her eyes turned up in her head. We silently wish her luck.

"We've got false memories," I say, "so that when we arrive at a destination, we're fully rounded individuals. We might be teachers, of a sort—but we need to have something to *teach*. Cultural history, rules and regulations, courtesy, patterns of behavior…How to get things done as a group."

"Good," my twin says. "My thoughts almost exactly."

"We're more effective if we believe in what we're teaching— if we've *lived* it and experienced some of the consequences of screwing up. We have to have a *history*. So we're given one. But we also have to be filled in on the real-world situation."

My twin carries on from this, nodding his head frantically and holding up one hand as if he wants to control an orchestra. "That's right. And there *is* no real-world situation. Something has asked us to be made and trotted out before the stage has been set, *our* stage, our play—before there are colonists to teach or any situation someone could possibly expect us to face."

I'm getting the rhythm. Two heads *are* better than one. And it might be possible that we've been fed different parts of the puzzle.

"We saw part of the Catalog," I say. "Centuries of effort and money and programming, all poured into the *gene pool*." I look over my shoulder at Tomchin and Kim. "Not all the suitable planets are going to be exactly like Earth. So colonists come in a variety of styles, suited to particular environments. If you don't have to carry around fully formed people, if all you've got is embryos—or even more simple than that, instruction sets fed into *bio-generators*…"

I am surprised by that word.

"You just made that up?" my twin asks.

"Maybe. Bio-generators hooked up to a database of all possible life-forms, Earth life modified to occupy the far-flung reaches of all practical evolution…." I'm shivering again. The others, including Nell, are like a crowd in a jazz club, moving in around a hot jam session.

Nell says, "Whoever put together Ship wanted us ignorant of our true nature and origins? That's what you're saying, right?"

My twin says, "We wouldn't need to know about our origins. In fact, it might distract us." Even Tomchin is following our dialogue with signs of comprehension. Tsinoy is so close I feel her ivory spikes digging into my calf. I withdraw that leg and look at her resentfully.

"Go on," she grumbles. "Whoever made me screwed me over and told me nothing about why."

"Well, you *are* the real puzzle here," my twin says. "Trackers shouldn't have fully formed human intellects and probably would never be employed as navigators."

"Astrogators," Tsinoy corrects. "But why would *you* have any memory of something that shouldn't be in the first place?"

This pushes us into the embarrassing zone of our speculations. I am no braver than my twin but am less experienced, so I go first. "I think part of our programming, our historical indoctrination, might contain contingency plans—dark ones. Secrets we'd never acknowledge, never need to acknowledge— unless things go badly wrong."

"Cleaning up planets," Tsinoy says. "I'm a Killer."

"*Oh*," Nell says, a sound of dread.

"If we get where we're going and there's competition..."

"We can't go anywhere else," my twin says. "We'll be out of fuel. It's either get along—which may or may not happen—or kill and strip the system to survive. To accomplish our mission."

"You say that's what I'm designed for," Tsinoy says.

"Maybe. But now it's starting to make sense."

"And as Teachers, cultural instructors, you'd have to *persuade* the colonists they need to destroy the natives," Kim says. "That's *total* crap."

"Yeah," Tsinoy says. "Maybe they give you a fine-tuned moral compass."

"And you?" I ask her.

She's all bristle and no grace, and now her voice is low and not in the least musical. She sounds confused. "I don't *like* what I'm made to do."

"Well, here's some relief," my twin says. "From what we've been able to access, you're not the worst this ship can do. Not by half."

"Actually, we didn't get that far," I add. "We don't qualify—we're not total warriors. There's a part of the Catalog that's kept hidden—for a good reason." My twin seems unhappy I'm telling them about this. I go on, anyway. "If our destination is super-bad, if there's already a civilization with weapons that could hurt us, we're given access to the most powerful and destructive points of creativity in the Klados—the Wastelayers. That's what they were called. Our designers didn't want us to carry that kind of history in our normal patterns. That kind of…"

"*Guilt*," Nell says. She moves back and touches the hemisphere again, a light caress. Her eyes flutter.

"Right," my twin says, with a glance in my direction. "Now you all know." He seems regretful.

Nell lets go of the controls. "That's enough for me," she says. "The sequence that begins hull combination has three checkpoints. We can do it all from here, if we want. We can initiate, then hold—that should send some sort of message to Destination Guidance. Put back the shields."

"How long would that take?" Kim asks.

"Total combination…at least ten hours. But the process starts right away."

"And how long until this damned storm knocks us loose?" I ask.

"This part of the nebula is filled with protoplanetary dust, blown out from an exploding star," Tsinoy says.

"Any minute…" Nell says. She stops, but we're all immediately thinking the same thing. Destination Guidance *must* have steered us wrong—deliberately. Dropping the shields and letting the dust wear us all away was in the works from the very beginning.

They don't want us to find a new home. They don't need the hulls, they don't need to travel, they don't need to arrive. All they want to do is survive in their little sphere, sitting on top of all the fuel they could ever use.

With the engines shut down, hundreds of thousands of years' worth.

"Do we vote," Nell asks, "or just act?"

"Doesn't take long to vote," Kim points out.

Tsinoy agrees with a raised claw-paw-arm.

"Seconds count."

"Do it," everyone says, almost as one.

Tomchin adds a low whistle.

"Right," Nell says, and slaps her hands on the hemisphere. "Starting combination sequence."

She drops into eyes-up contact. It seems forever, but it's probably just a few minutes, before the control chamber brightens, small alarms go off like little fairy bells. Then instructive lines and arrows glow, barricades rise, and a voice announces, "Find safe positions within the indicated outlines. When hulls begin to merge, additional safe areas will be created, and you will be instructed how to retreat and maintain."

Rails and cables rearrange around us, and new controls rise to our right while others sink down to our left and inboard. It's working. Or at least, something's happening.

We look at each other, help each other to the safer positions in the chamber, but say very little, listening to the constant sound of our hull being sandblasted by the ghosts of unborn worlds. It's a creepy sound. Twenty percent of the speed of light creates a hell of a slipstream.

At least two of us still have questions, of course. That's our nature. But we don't voice them. Maybe the girls have their own objections, their own agenda. But we don't need to be any more frightened than we already are. As a team, we've matured at least to the extent that we know that much.

And that's pretty impressive, considering how we all began.

Maybe the designers knew a thing or two after all, is one of the thoughts I'm thinking. But then there's another: *How could things have gone so wrong?*

And part of my fictitious past comes up with a wise old professor teaching a literature class in starship prep: *"If you want to ask how evil begins, just look to basic human nature. What's good gets bent, and bad is the inevitable result."*

Right, but how do I have any respect for someone who may never have actually lived? I'm like a character in one of those plays we never studied—a character given flesh but no additional lines, and set loose on a weird, half-empty stage, in front of a critical audience we can't see. Or don't want to see.

"Crapola," my twin says, and we nod and reach out and touch fingers, knowing we're thinking much the same thoughts and reaching much the same conclusion.

"We're real," he says. "Just go with that much."

"Amen," I say.

Amen. Nell used it earlier but I didn't connect. It's a strange word with all sorts of connotations. Where's the god we should pray to? Which direction? We *do* have a prayer, actually. We were taught one in that academy we never went to. There's a religion that goes behind it, but I don't want to cloud my thoughts with useless emerging details. The prayer, however, offers a hope of some relief from doubt and pain, if we can just say it right.

So I give voice.

> *"Creator of all*
> *Bless those who are small*
> *With wisdom and love.*

Provide for our care
And Guide us as we voyage
Across vastness unspeakable
Toward bright new homes.
We honor space,
Which is your memory,
And seek the wisdom
That is our ration.
No more, no less.
Amen."

By the third line, most of our group is following along—but not my twin. He's watching closely but not saying the words. Our voices echo in the space. Common ground. We *are* family—most of us.

The girls have wandered off again.

We can feel the motion now—subtle and different. The noise is subsiding, though not by much, indicating that our forward profile might be altered, even reduced—whatever that implies. We don't question small favors.

The forward viewports have become fogged and pitted. All it would take is something the size of a—

Grain of sand.

Crackling veins fly across the ports, and a squeal like something big and frightened draws our breath away, literally—air is being sucked from the bow. Then the panels fly up before there's time to think. The squealing stops.

We can't see outside now, except by venturing into the weird world of Ship Control, but we're leaving that up to Nell for the moment. We huddle, all but Tsinoy, who is contented with just sticking a smoothed paw into the ring gathered within a safety zone.

Maybe we don't want to know that we're dying.

Maybe we're shielded by the prayer.

Maybe...

After an indefinite time, Nell joins us. Fear leaves us empty. "First checkpoint," she tells us. "They'll have to talk if they want us to stop there."

"Or?" Kim asks.

"Or we crush them and take our chances," she says. "They got it wrong so far. Who can guarantee they won't betray us all over again?" She looks at my twin, then at me. "Sound right?"

"Absolutely," he says.

"We should find the girls," Nell says.

"They know their way around," Kim says, and Tomchin agrees.

There's little to do. The noise keeps us from any rest. Our thoughts tumble. We're half-delirious despite a ration of food from the tent-shaped chamber, brought to us by Tomchin and Tsinoy.

Nell keeps the hulls at the first checkpoint for what seems a very long time, and still, nothing has changed—nobody's talking to us. Destination Guidance remains as aloof and unknown—and as silent—as ever.

Kim lets go of a guide cable and kicks across to me and my twin, landing midway between us and taking hold of another cable. Weightless, his movements are swift and efficient; I would have pegged him for the model of an occupant for a high-gravity world, stocky and strong, but surprises abound.

"We're still being battered," Kim says. "How much longer can we wait?"

Nell has stayed near the control panel and the hemisphere. She listens to our low voices through the grind and roar. The shivering suddenly increases, as if we've entered a particularly dense patch. The point is doubly made.

"Next checkpoint," my twin says. "Show we mean business."

I agree. "What have we got to lose? Nobody knows how much longer this can last."

Tsinoy and Tomchin have collected the bulbs and spheres that held our meals and slipped them into a gray sack. Now they gather around. Tomchin is eager to ask questions, but we can't catch his drift, and after a moment, he gives up, shaking his hands at the noisy air.

Tsinoy seems thoughtful. "I can't be sure," she says. "But I can almost *feel* the density out there. It's very thin, but we're moving very fast. There's dust, there's gas…There might be bigger chunks. If we hit one of those, we'll be blasted to bits."

"How long?" Nell asks.

"We've already survived for hours," Tsinoy says. "I just don't know how strong the hulls are."

"The other hulls don't matter," Kim says.

"We can't finish the integration if either of the other hulls is severely damaged—or lost," Nell says. "Maybe that's what they're waiting for—one of the hulls to go."

"Speed it up," I say. "Can you?"

"Probably not, but I can move to the next checkpoint. An hour at most. We're hunkering in, and from what I'm learning in the control space, parts of the hull are already adapting for the combination."

"Maybe that's making us more aerodynamic," Kim says, but Tsinoy and Nell are unconvinced.

"Go for it," I say.

"Go," my twin says.

The others agree.

Nell immerses herself in the control space, and we don't hear from her for a while. Her eyes are almost closed, showing just a low crescent of sclera, like a cat dozing. The hull seems to be moving again. Outside, the noise of the storm changes, but it's neither more nor less this time.

"Where did the girls go?" my twin asks.

"To find their mother, probably," Kim says from a short distance. "We have yet to be introduced."

"Who is this 'Mother,' and what's she like?" Nell asks. "Has anybody seen anything that could give us a clue?"

This reminds me of the sketch in blood left in the outboard shaft by one of our girls—the one, presumably, who helped me get born. "Maybe we don't want to actually meet Mother," I say.

The sound around us suddenly drops to a whisper, then to almost silence. The change is quick—a couple of seconds and we can talk without shouting, think without grating our teeth.

"We have a shield!" Nell calls out. "It's off to one side, but it's there. They've given in!"

But she doesn't sound convinced. We gather beside her, clinging to cables and a bar near the control pylon. We know better than to slap our hands around hers on the hemisphere— the display doesn't work that way; no more than three individuals at a time.

We let Tsinoy go first. The Tracker becomes completely still, except for the shivers that keep her curled-up paws on the hemisphere. Her spines are smooth and withdrawn, so as not to poke Nell, who still has that dozing-cat look, immersed in whatever the hull is feeding her in the way of information.

After a moment, Nell asks, "Shall I stop integration?"

Tsinoy pulls back her paws. "We're protected," she confirms. "The shields have moved, to be sure, but nebular material is being diverted around and behind the hulls—as designed."

"I'm stopping, then," Nell says.

"Why?" my twin asks.

"Because Tsinoy says we still need Destination Guidance."

The rest of us are unhappy with that decision—we'd just as soon see the author or authors of our misery squashed or absorbed or otherwise obliterated. But Tsinoy's warning is an unavoidable consideration.

"Sure," I say, and Kim agrees. "Stop integration." My twin, oddly, doesn't chime in on this decision. He holds back, physically and verbally, putting a little distance between himself and the rest of us. I think that he's been playing some sort of hand and does not want to overplay.

The hull's motion along the rails on the moon far below, toward the moon's forward end and the other two hulls, slows. We can detect very tiny changes in momentum through the gentle tug on our gripping hands and hooked feet.

"Done," Nell says. "What now?"

"We have to talk, and *they* have to be willing to talk," my twin says. Playing his hand again, very sly. "Otherwise, they're no use at all—and we might as well wipe them out."

"Maybe they want *us* to come to *them*," Kim suggests, with a shake of his big head.

"The controls don't show anything alive down there," Nell says. "The whole area is frozen. We're in control…for the time being. They know they can't get rid of us."

"Maybe it's all automated," I say.

"Automation is sporadic. Ship's systems are pretty shot. I say we hold as much information between us as we might find left in Ship's memory."

"Great," Kim says. "Nobody's in charge?"

"Can you send a message throughout Ship, to all the hulls?" I ask. "That might get through."

"Only if there's a connection in the first place. An emergency signal…" She pulls her hands away from the hemisphere and her eyes fully open. She shivers, then curls up on the bar next to the pylon. "Working this thing takes it out of me. I have to repeat everything ten times, learning and doing at once."

"Then show me how," I say. My twin grins and raises his arm. "Show *us* how."

"Me too," Kim says, and Tomchin indicates with another hand that he's interested. Tsinoy is watching the covered forward viewports, like a dog waiting for its master—a dangerous, sad dog—and seems to be paying the rest of us and our situation no never mind.

"I'm not sure I can," Nell says. "You two talk to the hull one way, I talk to Ship Control another way. Why somebody couldn't have integrated our knowledge is beyond my understanding."

"We've got company," Kim says.

One of the girls has returned. She's working her way forward from the staging area, a bright red sash floating around her neck.

"We've found *her*," the girl says, a big smile transforming her face. "She's with our sisters. She will accept a meeting."

We listen with something between skepticism and fascination. Mysteries on our sick Ship rarely turn out to be helpful. Mother is nothing if not a mystery—maybe the prime mystery, after Destination Guidance.

My twin seems more sanguine, but he leads with the obvious. "While you were away, we saved the hull and maybe the rest of Ship," he says. "Nell can work some of the controls—and in time, maybe all the controls."

The girl accepts this with complacent cheer. "Of course," she says.

"You're not in the least impressed?" I ask.

"You have done what you were chosen to do," she says.

"Maybe," I say, pulling closer on a cable, stopping an arm's length away. "What's Mother got to offer our little group that we don't already have?"

"Love," the girl says. She turns. "Now we will head aft."

"Nobody with *love* in her heart would choose to make us," Tsinoy says, breaking her concentration on the covered bow. "A lot of us have died—sometimes hundreds of times. As any sort of team, we're a strategic, tactical, and even a logistical nightmare. We know so little, and whenever we think we're about to learn something important or solve all the puzzles, we hit the most infuriating obstacles—head-on. Maybe *love* isn't enough."

This is the longest speech I've heard from the Tracker. Not to my credit, I'm still surprised that such sophistication and reason can be found within a corded mass of ivory and rubies and steel.

"What Tsinoy seems to be suggesting," Kim says, ever the moderator, "is that we need persuading. Even from your mother, we need evidence."

Nell moves in next. The girl tracks her with earnest eyes. "If Mother is capable of choosing us from the Catalog and having us birthed in another hull, then she has to have some connection with Ship Control. Maybe *she* should join *us*—up here, where we're reasonably safe."

Scandalized, the girl regards me sternly, then turns to my twin. "You two are *Teachers*," she reminds us. "Mother chose you to lead and make decisions."

"We all make decisions together," I say. "And we're happy to rotate the role of tiebreaker."

After a pause for several seconds of reflection, the girl's eyes widen and she asks, "Why assume you are safe here?"

We don't have a good answer.

"What you mean to say is you are *comfortable*," she adds. "And you believe you are taking charge."

"Stop jerking us around," Nell says tightly. "Tell us what's going on, or what you think is going on. You're part of the team, aren't you? Act like it."

The girl is unruffled by the spidery woman's tone. For perhaps the first time—or perhaps not, but more forcefully—I'm made aware that what seems like a little girl is in fact anything but. She is as cool and calm as anything we've encountered in the hulls—and perhaps more frightening for that reason.

My twin seems more willing to go along. "Clearly, we're not communicating our needs," he says. "Yes, we're comfortable—but we're way beyond being scared by threats or dark implications. Is that clear?"

The girl nods.

"What message would you carry back to your mother to tell her we need reassurance, proof, communication before we risk our lives again? Nobody knows what lies aft. We haven't been there."

"I've been there, and so has my sister," the girl says. "In fact, many of my sisters."

"No threats?" Nell asks. "No out-of-control hull factors or...Killers?"

"No," the girl says. "This hull is as safe as we've been able to make it."

"You take credit for saving this hull..." Tsinoy offers.

The girl says, predictably enough, that Mother should receive the credit.

"You're just one of Mother's little fingers," Nell says.

The girl nods again, still puzzled by our reluctance—and clearly unconvinced that we're so stubborn we won't eventually give in and comply with her request. Her *command*, I realize. *Mother believes we owe her—and so do her little girls.*

The panels choose this moment to open again, to Tsinoy's intense interest. I can't tell whether she's delighted or not, but her pink eyes move forward, and then she pulls herself to the transparent ports and—for the moment—is lost in contemplation of the universe.

"Mother has fixed your view. The hull can still make repairs," the girl says. "We are responsible for its functions."

"Is Mother in the Catalog?" Nell asks. "Because nobody here seems to remember anyone remotely like her.... "

The girl puts on an offended moue. "You have not seen her."

"Can Mother open all of Ship's memory and records to us?" Nell asks, on a roll.

"Not all," the girl says. "Much has been lost or damaged. As you know."

"You don't know whether Mother will do this for us, do you?" Nell asks.

The girl shakes her head. In her way, she is doing her best to be honest, to be *one of the team*. But she's still just a finger. A severed finger.

"You can't communicate with Mother psychically, can you?" Kim asks.

The others look puzzled, but I know where he's going.

"I do not know what *psychically* means," the girl says.

"Can you talk to her with your thoughts?"

"No," the girl says. "That is silly."

"Honestly, I'm intrigued," Kim says, rising and stretching. "I'd like to meet Mother and ask my questions directly. Anyone else?"

The girl has not considered the possibility we would split our team. "Mother wishes all—"

"Well, that isn't going to happen," Tsinoy says, turning away from the stars, the wisps of nebula—a shower of brilliant sparks from deflected dust. "I need to stay here. Nell needs to control the hull, in case we lose the shields again. Tomchin can join Nell in the control space. Maybe one Teacher can help Tomchin search the Catalog all over again. The rest of you—it's up to you. Individually."

Tsinoy's assertion is met with silence. The girl's features settle into a cold solidity. She does not look at any of us. *This must be fury*, I think.

"I'll go," my twin says. "Or…"

"No, you stay," Nell says. *"He'll go."* She points at me. I have no idea what she's up to, but the resonance between us is promising.

"I'm *intrigued* as well," I say. Then, to my twin, "Besides, you're older and wiser, more valuable to these fine people."

He frowns, then gives in, as if avoiding any contest of manly courage. Or he does not want to make a fight of it. Overplay his hand. I have no idea why these suspicions are growing stronger. "All right," he says.

We shake hands, then hug. It's an awkward moment, self-respect dangerously close to self-love. But however much we may look, think, and act alike, we are clearly no longer the same. Affection is not any sort of metaphysical issue. He wants to go; I don't. Not really. But I'll go, and he won't.

"How far aft?" Kim asks.

"To the hub," the girl says.

Tsinoy is conferring with Nell. They both have their hands on the hemisphere.

"I'm not sure we have any idea what's really happening," Nell says. "There's so much contradictory information."

The girl looks unhappy.

"Destination Guidance might not have cut the shields after all," Nell says. "When we started to combine the hulls, the drives shut down. They're still off. We seem to be executing a turning maneuver. We're shifting into a long-curve orbit."

"What's that mean?" I ask.

"Ship may be approaching the gravity well of a greater stellar grouping," Tsinoy says. "We can't see it. It's behind an arm of the nebula. During such a maneuver, the shields temporarily switch off to reconfigure for the new angle of interstellar wind. They turn on again when the proper angle is reached."

Nell adds, "The hulls need to be separated again to restart the drives. But given our present circumstances, if the drives resume, we'll begin not just a course correction but also deceleration."

"We'll slow down?" Kim asks.

Nell says, "Ship might be responding to prior programming, not to our threats."

"A destination has been chosen?" I ask. "Why didn't Ship Control tell us?"

"Maybe it doesn't want us to know. Maybe we're being manipulated. I don't know the answers."

I'm still tingling with the shock of this potential revelation. A turning maneuver, rearranging the shields—that's actually a viable alternate theory. "*They* weren't trying to kill us—and we didn't force them to back down?"

"No," Tsinoy says.

"Then what the hell good are we, sitting up here, thinking we're in charge?" I ask.

"Clearly," Nell says, "we've got more research to do." She looks at me and crooks a long finger. "Will you join me in Ship for a moment? Before you go, I need Kim to see something as well."

"What about me?" my twin asks.

"One at a time," Nell says.

I approach the hemisphere and lay my hands beside Nell's. She gives me a long, puzzled look. "Someone in here knows you," she says softly. "Both of you."

We go in.

A few minutes later, we emerge. Kim goes next. My twin watches with apparent calm. Does he suspect? Then, Nell invites him into Ship. What she tells him or shows him there, I don't know.

NEW WORLDS AFT

The journey is not dangerous, the girl says, but it is devious and may take a while. To that end, we pack a lunch and some extra clothes and water. Ship is adapting. There is hope that we can change things—if we are kept informed.

And that is our mission. To find the girl's mother and learn as much as we can. There are no farewells. We simply take our supplies in gray bags and move aft from the tent-shaped chamber. Kim and I are not complacent—we do not believe there is safety anywhere, but I also do not believe the girl is leading us into a trap. We may have the same approach to differing agendas, but for now, agreement should be possible.

We climb into the hull's cap chamber, which is immense beyond our previous experience. In Hull Zero One, behind the cap chamber, a single water tank had filled the center of the hull, but here, Kim and I are surprised to find *six* tanks, each as large or larger. Their huge "eyes" are filled with the hypnotic beauty of trillions of gallons of water, interrupted by narrow turquoise voids, smaller bubbles rejoining great ones. Placid. Dormant.

"Why six?" Kim asks. I have no answer—the girl has no answer. Our curiosity is not her concern. She guides us out to the perimeter of the cap chamber. Looking up, I notice a bump in the center of the vast bulkhead supporting the six tanks, what might be a round hatch or access point. I think this could be the entrance to a more efficient route down the center line of the hull, between the tanks, but one we are not taking.

The girl leads us to a corridor that circles around the tank cap. We echo along the corridor until we reach a control pylon, positioned at a junction with another corridor leading aft. The pylon supports a simple flat visual display. This is new to us— but not to the girl. This is her domain. With deft fingers, she calls up our present location, then a map of the spaces we will encounter moving down the length of the water tanks. We are still hundreds of meters below the skin of the hull. The hull, so far, has shown no signs of resuming its high rate of spin, for which I'm grateful. I feel no need of extra challenges.

The display reveals thousands of spherical chambers arranged in rows and clusters around the tanks, none smaller than a hundred meters across. "Forest balls?" I ask.

"Like that, but no," the girl says.

"What, then?"

"I don't have the words."

Kim and I quirk our lips. It's obvious this hull is different from the one we were birthed in—but why? The girl *doesn't have the words.*

As in Hull Zero One, the corridors are lined with bands and radiances. Again, it seems these must be guides for factors— indicating the corridors were not meant primarily for human travel. Kim takes an interest in an oval radiance of black and green lines, about as wide as two of my hands—less than one of his. I wait for him as he runs his fingers over it. The girl, as always, moves ahead by ten or twelve meters, then pauses to allow us to catch up.

Kim shakes his head and we move on. "No factors," he says. Brief but sufficient—we've gone some ways and have yet to encounter cleaners, retrievers, or any of the other peculiarities we met in Hull Zero One.

The girl has assumed her characteristic lotus.

"Why no factors?" Kim asks.

She unfolds and stretches. "It isn't dirty here, and nobody's dying."

"Why not birth us *here*, then, where it's clean and things won't chase us?" Kim asks. His tone has an accusing edge. Big Yellow has always seemed remarkably together and calm, perhaps because of his obvious strength, or perhaps because those are simply innate qualities marked somewhere on his page in the Catalog.

The girl moves on. "I don't know," she calls back.

I think about asking if she's the one who rescued me after my chilly birth, but if it doesn't matter to her, then it doesn't matter to me. Sentiment and memory are severely mismatched in our unbalanced and wretched world.

Odd how food and water and a clean body—and a few moments of rest—lead me into philosophy.

Kim touches another oval. "If we could read them, these would tell us where we are and where to go," he says.

"Right," I say. "Anything bubbling up from memory?"

"Not yet," he says. "You?"

We're making conversation, putting off the inevitable. We're both reluctant to talk here about what Nell showed us. The girl's hearing is remarkably acute.

"Well, I'd like to say these are orientation signs used by factors, but there are no factors."

He snorts his humor. "What in the hell are we doing here?"

"Following," I say.

"Away from food and water..." He pauses to frown intensely at another oval. "More of these, just around here. That could mean another intersection is coming up. I wonder if *she* can read them."

I look for the girl but she's way ahead, out of sight beyond a curve in the corridor. Suddenly, Kim pulls me close. "Nell tells me I have to watch you."

I swallow. "I don't blame her."

"She thinks you're the real deal...whatever that means."

"Thanks," I whisper.

"Did she tell you about the book in the netting?"

I nod and point to his big hands on my arms. "Looser, please."

"She says you have little bumps on your head, but the other one doesn't. You're not identical."

"I didn't check him," I say.

"Why would he hide his book in the egg? Why not just show it to us? You did, after all."

"It's probably in code," I suggest, as if making an excuse.

"She figured it out."

I hadn't realized Nell was that quick. I feel like a little boy caught trying to hide a dirty secret—even though it isn't me, and it isn't my secret. "Oops," is all I can say.

"She didn't tell me if she read it all," Kim says. "Just the part about looking for Mother, and making sure we agree to crunch Destination Guidance. We all wanted that, didn't we, at first? All but Tsinoy."

"Yeah. But he wrote it down like an instruction. Like he was following orders. So...where did he get his orders?"

Kim relaxes his grip. "What else did Nell show you?"

The biggest discovery of all. I'm still not sure I believe it. "We carry a lot of Ship's memory and programming inside us. Maybe more. We're like safety storage—a biological backup. Ship is recovering memory from us each time we enter. Some of the parts that looked burned are growing back. We're helping fill them in. Especially Nell and Tsinoy."

"And me?"

"Not so much. Not yet. Nell doesn't know where you fit in."

"But she took your twin into Ship, as well as you. Wouldn't you be the same?"

"I don't know."

"What does Ship need from him? What do you think he's carrying?"

"I don't know." I feel uncomfortable coming to any conclusion about my twin. I'm still not in the clear myself. The way Kim looks at me. The way Nell seemed to be testing all of us.

The girl has doubled back and waits at a junction with another tunnel. I don't feel comfortable talking about any of this in front of her.

I've lost any real sense of position. The corridor we've been following moves on for another ten meters, then comes to a rounded stop.

"Outboard," the girl says, and pushes off from the floor, straight up the shaft.

We follow. Less than thirty meters beyond, we plunge into a warm, moist, shadowy volume of indefinite size. Kim grabs a loose cable, then wraps his ham fist around my ankle. As if responding to our presence, the volume suddenly illuminates. We have to shield our eyes against the brightness.

"You should have closed your eyes," the girl says, a vague small blur close by.

"Thanks for the warning," Kim says.

I peep out through my fingers. Details swim into view. We dangle for a moment on the outstretched cable, then Kim hands me down, and we brace on the lip of the shaft. I stay close, getting my bearings, and feel safer next to him.

We're perched on the edge of a big sphere, much bigger than the forest balls or the trash voids of Hull Zero One, large enough that it seems possible it might reach all the way out through the skin of the hull. It might even bump out on Ship's surface, with, I hope, its own observation blister. I'd like to see what's happening outside, down on the moon.

The big bright space is not empty. Far from it. Beginning just four or five meters from the wall, hundreds of milky globes hang in suspension, surrounded by puffs of shining, translucent branches. The tips of the branches fuzz out in smaller tubes until the globes seem surrounded by feathery down, like huge dandelion seeds. There must be millions of them. It's their refraction of a distant light source that almost blinded us. We can reach out to the nearest, but Kim warns, "Don't touch."

It looks beautiful—and wicked sharp.

"What's this?" I ask the girl.

"Mother's library," the girl says.

Above, the branches rustle in a rapid, disconcerting dance. Little rods move along the outer tips on wirelike legs, rotating, pushing aside branches, then jabbing their tips into each puffy "seed." The rods withdraw, move along to the next globe, maneuver through the branches, and reinsert, churning the contents of the globes.

"I know what this is," Kim says. "It's like the root of the Klados—the library the Catalogs draw from. The gene pool. But it's too big. Something's different. I *know* this," he repeats in wonder.

"Sounds like you've found your résumé," I say.

"Yeah, I'm a cook. Assistant chef. This is like a diagram of my kitchen."

The girl smiles. "Mother will be happy," she says.

"The question is, why is it so *big*?" Kim asks. "The places I'm supposed to work in are much smaller. I mean, genes are *small*, so why all this?"

I think I know, but now is not the time—nor do I like the answer. It's tough to discover a conflict in one's essential being, but I have a big one—a great big conflict that could rip me apart or turn me into something as bad as what we'd likely find in the hidden pages of the Catalog....

Or in the pages of my twin's book. *Everything hinges on what I do when we meet Mother.*

I push that small voice back into the mental gloom from which it emerged and we follow the girl along a beam and series of cables, to where this huge sphere joins with another, smaller sphere—less than forty meters wide and empty, dark.

A single tube about half a meter in diameter thrusts from the center of the puffball chamber and through the darkness. The tube's surface is visibly frosting. It's like a delivery chute. A dumbwaiter leading from the big, big kitchen to the dining room.

"We cross fast," the girl explains. "No cables, no touch. Just kick off and fly."

Kim doesn't like this. "I've never been that graceful," he grumbles.

"It is cold," the girl emphasizes. "Do not take a breath out there, until after you cross."

"Great," Kim says.

The girl launches from the rim where the two spheres meet. We suck in air, then hold it. Kim goes next. He's more graceful than he gives himself credit for. He vanishes into the darkness, toward a dim beam of light from the far side. My eyes hurt, staring into the cold. His shadow crosses the light, and a moment later, I hear him draw a whooping breath.

"Okay!" he shouts.

My turn.

It's colder at midpoint than anything we experienced back in Hull Zero One—cold enough to freeze me solid in minutes if not seconds, and the air seems gelid, denser. Tingling snaps crawl along my skin as well, and I see blue lights that aren't there.

Then, Kim's long arm grabs me again and pulls me back on target.

"Good," the girl says.

Skin tingling, eyes defrosting, all those little blue lights flitting away—I wonder if I've awakened from this long, bad dream and fallen into another, better one. Not the first time, of course. Hope springs eternal. The air is filled with sweet scents, funky scents—flower smells and human smells coming and going in warm waves, more intense than anything I've experienced.

What I'm seeing, or think I'm seeing, is improbably wonderful. It's a weightless town—more of a village, actually, made of hundreds of little round domiciles both clear and opaque, colored and white, arranged like clusters of soap bubbles in another curved space. Children work and wander and play throughout, naked or wearing blue overalls, clutching little jars and long sticks, pushing food and bottles and other objects through the warm, weightless air like hundreds of busy little angels. Children everywhere, all female.

Beautiful, identical, *happy.*

"Welcome," our girl says, and something goes out of her—a stiff, stubborn posture. Compared to the others, she's grubby, travel-worn, tired. It makes her look older. "I'm going to go be with Mother now. After I touch her, she will remember all that's happened. Then she will meet with you."

Kim and I clutch a cable on the forward wall of the chamber. The currents of chill air behind us are blocked. Only the tube from the gene pool passes through to arrive at a glorious conclusion—a flower of golden rods, each rod in turn blossoming again.

The girls move around this flower like little bees, taking and carrying away samples.

What I've seen is humbling and beautiful. We are on the outskirts of Ship's glorious belly button. Well, of course, neither Kim nor I has a navel. But the girls do, cute little innies—and Ship does as well, a truly whopping Omphalos.

This is the beating, vibrant gonad of Hull Zero Three, the very reason for Ship's existence and journey. This is where the Klados begins—where all living things are designed and judged. Mother has occupied the gene pool, making herself mistress of life itself.

But I still don't remember Mama.

With all this stimulating visual information inspiring us to pull up submerged memory and knowledge, why don't we *remember Mother*?

Who designed and made *her*?

"Heads up," Kim says. I look where his thick, lemon-colored finger points. "Reception committee."

Ten little girls, all wearing blue overalls, all moving in a line, hand in hand. A continuous loop of cable grows from the wall of the chamber, and they grip it like the safety bar in a roller-coaster car to keep in line and travel to where Kim and I have been left to gawk. They do not speak. They do not seem to have much interest in us, and certainly not in our protests as we are corralled and gently but insistently pushed aft.

"What's my name again?" I ask Kim.

"Shit, I don't remember," Kim says. "You're Teacher. Sanjay, I think."

The warmth becomes tropical. We are guided over several curving ridges in the chamber wall, through pillars that rise to support what looks like intertwined stretches of golden tubing, smooth and translucent, varying in diameter from a few centimeters to ten or more meters. The whole structure softly hisses and whishes. It sounds like...

Waves on a seashore.

Ocean. Salt air, spray, seagulls, patches of decaying seaweed. Wet sand squeezing between my bare toes. Earth's primordial gene pool. Swimming in a lagoon under a hot blue sky...with my partner.

I always liked that sound.

I suppose I never actually swam in an ocean or walked on a real beach but I like the sound, anyway.

The flowering of the tubes and pipes slips behind us, and there is only a warm glow of glim lights spaced along the inboard surfaces and the near wall, shifting and coalescing into polka-dot patterns, lighting our progress like the glowing skin of a deep-sea creature.

Ahead lies a thick, rough tangle of leafy limbs coated with sprays of tiny flowers, like living stars, with a light and a life of their own. All the little glowing things watching, interested, unafraid...

A naked forest ball.

We're entering a protected zone, to be sure, but this is more of a welcoming committee—children, the flowering forest. We are not threats. We are expected. A path opens through spreading limbs. Only now do we see that the forest's branches bear millions of tiny thorns, exuding from their tips tiny greenish drops—likely fatal doses of toxins for the unwary, the unwelcome, the unescorted.

What lies within the forest ball is very important to somebody—if only to *herself*. But then, the mother at the navel of our world deserves protection, doesn't she?

"Don't touch *anything*," I tell Kim. "We're surrounded by cobras."

"What's a cobra?"

"Snake," I say.

"Oh. Long, with teeth, right?"

This inane exchange is in part to compensate for the embarrassment of being gripped all around by the phalanx of girls, who care nothing for the thorns and who push against the leafy enclosure in such a way that they must be taking many pricks without obvious pain or harm.

The flowers, however, exude a glorious, peach-colored mist of scented light, not at all poisonous—sweet-tasting and sweet-smelling, actually. We are urged into the peach glow. Our reluctance is fading. Mother's seduction is intense.

A thatch of deep green twigs surrounds a hollow within the forest ball, and at the center of the hollow—resting on a cushioned platform, facing away from her new visitors—is a long, fleshy, shockingly lovely *creature*. Even from behind, it's obvious she's female, no doubt at all—but at first I wonder if she's remotely human. There is something of the serpent about her, but no serpent is equipped with so many breasts, arrayed in fruiting prominences on the fleshy rings of her torso, suckling so many smaller, younger versions of our girls.

Somehow the perfumed, lactating layers of her flesh are in perfect proportion to her function. She can move as far as she needs to move, and if more motion is required, the girls are there for assistance. Her brood. Her children, grown anew constantly to replace those lost in performing her work. I wonder if she misses them. Mother's work is never done.

She turns her head, which is small in proportion to her enormous, slowly undulant body, and beams upon all a beatific smile that lights up her face.

Wait.

The scented air is getting to me. I know that face.

Please, no. Not that.

We are here!

The face is that of the woman in my Dreamtime—my partner, whom I'm destined to embrace as we fly to the new planet's surface. All of it, the entire dream, returns in a warmly humid rush. I feel a flush of ecstatic nausea that makes me curl and writhe. The girls try to hold on, but I resist, kick out, push them away with hands and feet.

Again I'm like a newborn pulled cold and unhappy from an ignorant womb into an even more shocking reality. I want back into my previous ignorance, my dumb-show misery. This is *wrong*. It can't be *her*. It's an outrage—not even *they* would do this to her, to us!

We are so poorly prepared for life on this sick Ship, this skewed, tortured *thing* that makes us and kills us and protects us, lies between us and vacuum and radiation and the abrasive dust, like a shell around so many stupid mollusks.

The girls prove to be surprisingly strong. Kim is making a show of passive acceptance, hands up, palms out, shocked by my flailing reaction. For the moment, the little ones ignore him and flock around me, and finally bring me under sweating, aching control.

"Best to maintain, Teacher," Kim suggests in a low grumble. "Like you said, *cobras* . . ."

At a single word, a soft murmur from those lips in *that* face, the girls reluctantly bring me forward, toward the one whose symbol I first saw sketched in blood in the faraway shaft in Hull Zero One, the one who inspires absolute loyalty in those who oversaw my birth.

And my *making*? Is this both my partner and my own Mother?

My neck arches and I bare my teeth. Our noses nearly touch. I do not want this. I fear we will explode—this is *wrong*. But it does not happen—neither a kiss nor the half-desired love-death.

Her eyes close. She lightly sniffs. "Yes," she says. "I know you."

She raises a human-scale arm that had formerly lain relaxed down one side, across breasted rolls of torso. She offers her hand, fingers all too human, even shapely, nails trimmed and polished no doubt by her children. I see her short hair has been *coiffed*, and her flesh is scrupulously clean and dusted with a faint greenish powder that might be crushed from the leaves and flowers in her bower.

"Kiss," whispers a little girl. I no longer feel fear—that perfume.... Unless I fight it, I will become drunk with her, totally intoxicated.

"You are Teacher," Mother says.

"Another life," I whisper. In that other life, my partner was destined to be Ship's master of biology. Here, she is all she could ever have been, and much more. Kim might have been her assistant, in charge of the laboratory and the gene pool.

"We were together," she tells me. "We made daughters. You were taken from me. I prayed for Ship to make more of you."

My horror is mixed with admiration and awe. "I don't remember," I insist.

"Our daughters search you out again and again. I always lose you. You are always taken from me."

Absorbing this causes an internal pain I can't categorize or come to grips with.

"I birth my daughters. And they pray to Ship and bring you back to me," Mother says. "What you see as you travel ripens you like a fruit. I am happy you are here."

"Kiss," the girl insists hopefully.

Mother shyly raises her hand again. The back is smooth against my lips, the fingers slightly plumper versions of fingers I've seen in so many Dreamtime moments, stretching back through freshly renewed memory like gaudy pearls on a string.

Mollusks make pearls, of course... oysters grown on farms.

I kiss her hand. All around me relax. One little girl claps gently, delighted, and comes around between us, asserting her privilege in front of Mother, staring deep into my stunned eyes. "We were so worried. But *you* are here."

Mother gently pushes the girl aside, and she laughs and flits off to join her sisters, leaving Kim and me to float unassisted. Kim, the brief glimpse I have of him—eyes almost closed, arms crossed—looks like a big, sleepy, lemon-colored genie.

"There will be food," Mother says. "But let's begin." The woman who was to be my mate, my partner for all new worlds circling new suns, stretches in languor upon her platform. "Teach me. Tell me what you've seen."

Branches grow into personal bowers. She is mistress of her space. The perfume has performed its task. It is good to be in her grace.

I begin.

THE BRIEFING

I try to recall all that I've seen and learned, spooling it off like a recording machine, but it's all remarkably ephemeral. I keep seeing my partner's face on another body, in another existence.

My words trail off. Hours have passed. The bower's golden light has become shadowy. Mother rests, eyes closed but not asleep. Perhaps she never sleeps. Many of the girls are asleep, however. Kim also drowses, surrounded by a leafy nest.

I am watchful. How am I different from the others who were taken from her, who died? From the true consorts, like my twin, back in the bow... who was born knowing how to follow her orders.

Has she judged? She may not know yet, not for certain.

Mother opens her eyes. "I do not understand where it went wrong." Her voice is sweet and small. "I see Ship, I see struggle—I know those who frustrate me and kill my children.

They've taken you from me so many times..." She looks to me for guidance. "Why do they fight us?" she asks, and then, with an eyebrow flick of inner awareness, "Why do we look like this, so different?"

Why, this is *sleep, nor am I yet awake.*

Her eyes are pale blue. They are no larger than I remember them. I do not stray from her face, but the impression of the rest of her body is unavoidable. Beauty lies both in her form and in her function. So many daughters—so much adoration. Will they all grow up to be like her?

"My daughters tell me there is another Teacher. Yet he stayed behind. Why?"

"We wanted to make sure the journey was safe," I tell her, and hope she believes me.

Mother turns her face away. "My daughters did not pray for this yellow one, or for the others. Only for you."

"We traveled and fought together," I say. "The girls brought all of us to this hull."

"Not all," she reminds me. "Many died. You accessed the records of the Klados, as I hoped, but you are upset. What did you see that upset you?"

"I don't like the memories they reveal in me. That is not Ship as I know it. Not me."

"Oh, but it *is*." Mother regards me with half-closed eyes, shrewd, rich, suffused with immense, private hormonal flows that do not dull but forcefully direct. She brushes my face. The scent intensifies. The bower has brought us closer. "We only protect Earth. You know Earth."

"Yes." I am drunk with her. I am drunk with Earth. For the moment, I forget that I never lived those memories, that they are false.

Mother is my mirror. Looking at her, I remember...

―――――

GOLDEN LIGHT OVER a small clearing. I'm taking my rest after a long hike, sitting on a fallen log surrounded by green-black trees. The air is hushed by falling flakes of snow, each painted pale yellow by a diffuse wintry sunset. A lithe brown animal with a long neck watches from the edge of the clearing. A *deer*. It bolts and vanishes. I know there are other animals in the black woods. Bears, squirrels, and nearby, rainbow-gleaming fish swim in a rushing, ice-cold river.

I've been walking with my partner as she finishes a survey. It's more of a ritual than a scientific necessity. All of this will be coming with us. It will be her job to protect the records of life on Earth and to carry them to the stars. My job is to keep her happy and to provide the colonists with cultural structure, social instruction. We are in a sense opposites—she will transport Earth's life; I will transport humanity's history and thought.

My partner emerges from the shadows and sits on the log with me. I kiss the back of her hand.

"You're back," I say.

"'He sent them word I had not gone,'" she quotes a poem from one of our favorite stories. I taught it to her back at the training center, where our love began. "Will we ever know what that means?"

"It's nonsense," I say. "Always will be."

"And you call yourself a *teacher*." She lifts her hand and marks the air with the words of the poem.

> "'He sent them word I had not gone
>   (We know it to be true):
> If she should push the matter on,
>   What would become of you?'"

On the log, in the quiet and the peace, I am the happiest I've ever been, the most contented, the most fulfilled. I am lost in admiration as well as love. We often play with poems and words, but I can't play with what she does: life itself. As chief biologist, my partner will ensure that Earth lives on in Ship. I am proud of her. My job—our job—is part of the greatest endeavor in human history. We have visited cities and towns, forests and jungles and deserts. We have met with schoolchildren and farmers, scientists and celebrities. We are the chosen. We are famous.

"It still doesn't make sense to you?" she chides.

"Sorry."

She continues:

> *"'I gave her one, they gave him two,*
> *   You gave us three or more;*
> *They all returned from him to you,*
> *   Though they were mine before.'"*

I pick up with the next few lines.

> *"'If I or she should chance to be*
> *   Involved in this affair,*
> *He trusts to you to set them free*
> *   Exactly as we were.'"*

"Good," she says, wrapping her arm around me and hugging me close in the evening chill. "If we get lost out there, this is how we'll know each other. Like a secret song."

"We're not going to get lost," I say.

"No," she says. "But still…

238 | GREG BEAR

> *"'My notion was that you had been*
> *(Before she had this fit)*
> *An obstacle that came between*
> *Him, and ourselves and it.*
>
> *"'Don't let him know she liked them best,*
> *For this must ever be*
> *A secret kept from all the rest,*
> *Between yourself and me.'"*

"You forgot the first stanza," I say.

"It's not important," she says. "These are all you need to know to find me."

For some reason, I quote part of the original song from which Lewis Carroll's enigmatic parody was drawn.

> *"'She's all my fancy painted her—*
> *Ye Gods! She is divine.*
> *But her heart it is another's—*
> *It never can be mine.'"*

She makes a wry face. "*Ye Gods,*" she says. "You are so didactic."

Ours has been called a great romance, perhaps the greatest romance ever—love that will fly out between the stars, love that will survive chill centuries to be warmed anew. Fulfillment and destiny and preparedness: The emotions are utterly warm and embracing and richly detailed.

I can't pull up from the vision. I do not want to. We are ready to go. We are simply saying farewell to our world.

The forest watches. I can't see the eyes of the animals who know we are here, but they are the eyes of the Earth, and soon we will move far away and will not be seen again, until we make this place anew, around another star, very far away.

At any cost.

Sitting beside me, weary after our hike, she looks young and vulnerable, with her short bobbed hair and square, frank eyes, deep blue, and her wide, slightly ironic smile. I have felt over and over the honor and the depth of her care, her attention to detail both scientific and emotional; her concern for my parents, saying good-bye forever to their only son. Her parents died years before, and this only makes her more eager to establish a chain of posterity.

All of Earth is her family.

It is here that she gives me a real book, small and beautiful—a paper diary bound in faux leather. The paper is creamy and beautiful. "Write it all down, Teacher," she tells me. "When you figure out the poem, write it down, and let me know."

At any cost.

Her body I am also aware of, picturing it beneath the winter coat, remembering the sheen on her thighs and shoulders as we swim almost naked in the warm waves off an atoll's coral beach in the South Pacific. I remember our lovemaking, our murmured talk beneath soughing palms and warm breezes under a densely starry sky; talk about having children. She wants daughters. She believes daughters understand their mothers. She laughs at this, admits it's silly, sons are wonderful, but she wants daughters.

My head spins at the extraordinary power put into this woman's hands. When we arrive, she will be not just the shepherd but also the mother of another Earth. And I will be there with her, protecting her against danger, helping her succeed....

At any cost.

I am suddenly back in the hidden pages of the Catalog.

Others may be there. Aboriginal life-forms. We may be out of fuel, with no other place to go. They may not want us, when we arrive. They may try to kill us. Kill me. Kill Earth's seed and memory. And what will we do then, lover?

————

MY EYES BLINK open and I groan. All of those emotions lie beneath my love, hidden like the monsters we've seen, only to be activated if the situation arises.

It has arisen.

Mother is watching me, brows arched, that ironic expression familiar and so clear.

I sneeze and rub my nose.

She turns to Kim.

Kim looks at her, then at me, his expression heavy-lidded. I don't know what he's thinking. I have no idea what more he's recovered, rediscovered in himself, after looking into the mirror of Ship's memory, and now, seeing Mother herself.

"Are we done yet?" he asks, stretching as far as the leafage allows. His eyes shift left and right, embarrassed. "Could you, like, cover up? I can't focus."

The girls who are awake murmur disapproval, but more of the bower grows to cover all but Mother's shoulders and head.

"Do you know your reason?" Mother asks him.

Kim says, "I work with the Klados."

"I am Klados," Mother says, her eyes on mine. And for the last time, I see in the angle of her brow, in the sadness, that she also remembers something of what we would have had, if the times had been good, if our luck had held, if decisions had been made correctly. Part of her is still my Dreamtime partner.

Her long body slowly ripples.

Kim says, "There used to be a gene pool in each hull. Now there's only one. But...you weren't born here."

Mother is silent for long seconds. "We came to be in the first hull, where we were attacked. Many died. We crossed to this hull. Once I arrived, I gave birth and raised daughters."

"Ship was split into factions," Kim says. "Ship Control broke down."

"I *am* Ship Control," she says, this time with some fire. "How do you think you came here, and why do you think Ship listened to you? Teacher, you are the other half, the one I cannot give birth to. You are prayed into existence. With the help of our daughters, you come to me and tell me what you have seen. You bring your books and read them to me after we lie together. And if you perish, my daughters collect the books…all of the books. They bring them here, and I grieve."

> *I gave her one, they gave him two,*
> *You gave us three or more;*
> *They all returned from him to you,*
> *Though they were mine before.*

My eyes fill with tears for what we've all lost. And why? What did this to us? How did we come to be this way?

The girls are still. They have never seen her like this.

"You don't know how it happened, do you?" Kim asks. "You don't know any more about the war than we do. You should look into Ship's memory—you should look into the mirror."

"I have," Mother says. "I saw Klados. I am Klados. That is all that I am."

Suddenly, Kim seems to understand. "Someone wanted Ship to fail, to die. They locked away—maybe they even *destroyed*—the other gene pools. Why would they do that?"

His face darkens and pinches down with this awareness.

This is Big Yellow when he loses all that remains of his innocence. "Just before the other gene pools were shut down, you were made, shaped into a reservoir, a movable backup for the Klados. But not all of it. Just selections. This hull was meant to be pristine. A final refuge. But you came here and took it over, then reconstructed your portion of the gene pool to continue Ship's mission."

"The early times are dim," she says. "Many births, many deaths."

"You came here. You *grew*..." He looks up, distressed. Something in the air, the company, has made him too blunt, too honest. He would prefer not to discuss these matters...not in front of his *boss*. But he can't help himself. "That's why it's so large, so inefficient. It came out of *you*. Some of us are born biased, bent, distorted...grandiose. Your memory emphasizes the secret parts of the Catalog. Did *you* pray for the Killers?"

"Hurt. Burned. Dying," Mother says. Her look at me is... what? Disappointed? What *does* she remember out of the Dreamtime? What ideal life does she dream of as she suckles all her daughters?

"What's still not clear to me is who was in charge in the best of times," Kim says.

"Destination Guidance," I say. "They pick where we will go. Ship and all aboard are subservient to the goals of the mission, which have to be determined based on where we're going, when we're going to arrive...what the situation might be when we arrive. Everything depends upon decisions made by Destination Guidance."

The girls do not like this at all. I am surprised as well by this blunt declaration. Mother's expression does not change. I had hoped for a more indicative reaction to guide what I say next.

"They chose a world already inhabited. It wasn't the best choice, was it? A desperate decision. That started the war. A war of conscience."

Not at any cost.

Then…the love is gone. As if those memories had never been, I see Mother's features glaze over, harden. I am a fraud. So is Kim. I am not the consort she needs. He is not the assistant she had hoped for. My fear would be intense if the bower's perfume didn't dull my responses.

"I have heard you," Mother says. "I am not the first Mother. My daughters are not the first daughters."

Four of the girls enter the bower, trailing cords on which many small gray bags are hooked like fish on a string. The bags twirl and bump and break branch and leaf, which another girl carefully gathers, crushes in her hands, and stuffs into a smaller bag at her waist.

"They have found these scattered in all the hulls. The testimony of many who did not live. I no longer have need of them. Perhaps they will serve you."

The bags are cinched at the neck, looped together, and filled with small, square objects.

The end of the string is handed to me. I pull up one bag by a scruff of fabric, feeling the objects within. Books. A dozen or more per bag. Hundreds in all.

"Teacher, go back. Tell the other Teacher to come forward. Kim, you will stay here and tell me more of what you know about the Klados."

Kim doesn't look at all happy at this prospect. But as the girls surround us, it seems he relishes a fight even less. He's the assistant. Mother would have been his boss. He has his own Dreamtime memories now.

Mother gives me one last, lingering look. She says,

> "'*But her heart it is another's—*
> *It never can be mine.*'"

I am not the one Mother needs. But she cannot bring herself to dispatch me.

The other must come forward, and until he does, she will hold Kim hostage.

TALES BETWEEN MY LEGS

Two of the girls accompany me. The book bags have been arranged more conveniently in a larger bundle. Still they are cumbersome. No doubt Mother has read them already, or they have been read to her by my others—all the reports of consorts and daughters, and the daughters of other Mothers before her, who died before their books could be delivered.

More histories of the war between Ship Control—represented or personified, perhaps, by Mother, taking all its memories and duties into her form—and Destination Guidance. The Ship became a charnel house long before this mother was made. A bad decision, possibly initiated by an accident between the stars—the supernova. Damage, confusion, and what else? Something more, surely. I've died; they've died; we've all died over and over…and I'm thinking it's increasingly unlikely, almost down to zero chance, that *any* of us will survive much longer, much less fulfill our destiny.

I have to ask, as I pull the bundle along—as the two

daughters travel without complaint and hardly any emotion, moving away from Mom again, no joy in that—

The answer to many questions lies in knowing what part of the Klados Mother fulfills. What planet was she designed to inhabit? What circumstance would favor her kind of society, her kind of progeny, rather than, say, those my Dreamtime partner and I would have produced?

Mother makes sense only in the context of a damaged Ship, Ship at war with itself. We are all expedients.

I'm not even a teacher, not really. The great Dreamtime story was ever and always a travesty, a trick.

"Faster," the closest daughter tells me as we push down the striped tube, past signs that would guide factors to wherever they need to go, moving forward supposedly to deliver this bundle of histories to readers who might already be less than sympathetic, more dangerous to Mother, and who, by now, looking deeper into the mirror, have likely recovered and redis-covered even more than Kim and I. Nell was on a roll, after all. But how does that make sense?

Why give knowledge to those who will fight you?

As for my twin...

I feel utterly spent and useless.

And so it is with little surprise, and perhaps even a dark joy, that I hear one of the daughters say we have taken a wrong turn. They are concerned. We are not moving forward.

The other daughter approaches, her hand pushing the wall, her foot kicking back, echoing, her other hand hooked in the clasp of her overalls. Her face is serious. "This place is not the same."

"Tunnels might have shifted. Is that it?" I ask with a touch of glee. Nell was made to talk to Ship. Is she redirecting Ship's architecture—foiling Mother's plans?

The girl gives me a look that strikes me straight to my heart, even after all we've been through, a look of childlike dismay that says, *how could you be so mean?*

"Okay," I say, pulling back my *Schadenfreude*. Strange word, but I know what it means. Maybe I can be their teacher after all—an instructor in mean thoughts and gross ironies. "What now?"

"If we go back, we will be late," one daughter says. "But we do not know how to go forward, or even how to find our way back...." She looks so lost, but I feel no sympathy.

They can't take me where Mother wants me to go—to my death. The books will be destroyed, they're useless anyhow—like me. How will they finish me?

Will there be one last Killer waiting at the end of the line?

They float before me, holding hands. I take a short breath, calm myself. I will send them home. That is the least I can do. "How good is your memory?" I ask.

"Pretty good," the other daughter says.

"Remember what you saw when you went forward or aft in the hulls—can you see the symbols, the radiances, how they were oriented or how frequent the stripes were in a given stretch of corridor?"

The daughters look puzzled. Their mouths open, showing pink tongues and tiny, well-ordered teeth... *milk teeth.* They're lost in deep recall.

"Maybe," the girl on my left says.

"The corridors have a code," I say. I had watched Kim examining the signs and ovals and striping, and suspected he was figuring out how factors—and perhaps even people—could learn where they were, inside the hull, by reading the coded patches. It seems logical that as the hull adjusts, the signs will also adjust, but a lot has to rest on faith. "We can read the code—if we apply ourselves."

They come to silent agreement, then return their eyes to me. The girl on the right says, "I remember better than she does."

"I thought you were all alike," I say.

"That would be silly," they say together.

Despite everything, I have to laugh. One of the girls begins to crack what might be a smile, the first hint of humor, the first recognition of human individuality in all its absurdity, but the smile vanishes so quickly I wonder if I just imagined it. "Can you figure it out by yourselves?" I ask.

After a few seconds, the sharper daughter points behind us and says, "This way."

We're going to have to part company soon. If I want to get back to the bow and not join all my rejected, dead brothers.

I start to haul the books again, but the girls wave their arms. "Leave them," they say. "We have to move quickly. We can come back for them."

"Your sisters and others *died* for these books," I say, surprised by my heat.

"Let's not join them," a daughter says.

I reluctantly untie the band and leave the bag drifting in the corridor. Despite everything, I'm curious about all those memories and experiences, recorded in so many childlike scrawls by so many little hands. And by my hands.

Maybe somewhere in those books lies the secret of what Mother's society would have been like had she and her daughters survived to planetfall and spread their kind across the surface of a world.

The girls finger the coded ovals, concentrating, remembering other corridors, other signs and codes. Marvelous. Adaptable, beautiful, deadly. How could the rest of us, motley and ignorant, ever win against such as these?

We move on.

A hundred meters back, we find a tunnel branch that must be new, as we did not pass it before. "This goes outboard," one girl says, counting stripes and touching another radiance. "We are five hundred meters from the outer shell of the hull." She looks uncertain. "If I read correctly."

"Lead on, Macduff," I say. *Macduff.* It sounds like a name. A *Scottish* name. Perhaps it comes from an *English* writer named Shakespeare. *Macbeth, Lady Macbeth.* Nasty customers. *Hamlet.*

To thine own self be true. Supposedly a weak, gullible man said that—

"Shut up!" I shout. My voice echoes into obscurity.

"We said nothing," a daughter says.

I wave my hand. We move outboard. This is my life.

As we proceed, I feel a judder. Actually, drifting along, at first I see it more than I feel it. I wonder if it is my eyes or the walls that are vibrating. My long, echoing "stride" brings my foot in contact, and then I feel an unfamiliar subsonic quiver.

There is definitely change coming. Whether it is caused by impacting stardust, or by Mother, or by our people in the bow is impossible to know. If we're returning to the earlier phase of swift rotation, then things might go badly out here, our kilos converted to crushing weight.

We continue without pause. That is, the girls continue and I follow. Whatever happens is out of my control, but I am content to see that where we are is not where they wish to be. I assume we are moving outboard to find a forward-pointing corridor. But it soon becomes obvious that the hull's rearrangement is more radical than they had hoped. We reach a fork, the corridor continuing outboard, but for a short distance, a pipe leads aft again—I think—about ten meters, ending in one of those rounded caps.

Taking advantage of the stop, I reach out to an oval, let out an exclamation, and draw back my hand. The pattern changes as I watch. The forking pipe grows shorter until it merges with the walls around us, then vanishes.

The daughters clutch my arms. We dangle, moving gently from wall to wall, and then one girl sighs. Both regard me with blank faces, let go, and push along the outboard-leading corridor. They're probably thinking what I'm thinking. Where we are could close off at any moment, imprisoning us in hull metal, kicking and screaming until the glim lights go out and we run out of air.

I don't need to think such thoughts. I want to be back in the bow, where I can eat and bathe and look out at the stars, as we were all meant to do.

I'd rather be in Dreamtime.

Or maybe not. *After such knowledge.*

My legs and arms hurt from the echoing gait of hands and feet, elbows and knees, butt or thigh or shoulder. I think on the design of the factors—Tsinoy, more efficient in weightlessness than the rest of us. Each in its place. The great chain of being, leading from the incomprehensibility of biological phase space, winnowed down to the virtual pages of the Catalog, through the chemical limits of the gene pool, and out through the material limits of birthing surfaces...

From *stuff* we are made...people stuff.

There must be methods of transporting that stuff around Ship. Do factors deliver barrels of it? Is it piped through small conduits in the hull metal like capillaries? Ship itself has many qualities of a living organism and yet maintains much of a mechanical nature.

In either case, plumbing is crucial.

"What if something is trying to cut off your mother's supply chains?" I ask. The girls, ten meters ahead, as usual, do not seem to hear me. But what if Mother loses her ability to direct Ship? What if she dies? Does one of the daughters assume her role? Rounded collops of breasted tissue forming along a lamia length, hormones adapting their girlish minds to great Mothering thoughts, seeking a consort, birthing, nurturing, *loving* multitudes of daughters...

Sending them off to die?

The glim lights brighten. Again, I feel the corridor shiver, but we are nearing the end of our outboard leg. The corridor is getting wider. There is a hatch half open ahead, and through that opening comes a dense, hot, moist waft of indescribable spice. Not savory or herbal, not so much flowery, but sharp and compelling and yet frightening—something ever so much richer, stronger, more confident than mere humans.

We move toward the cap, the girls first, as usual, and before I can react, long ivory paws reach down and snatch them. The pair squirm and slap, but they make no other sound, simply rising in helpless fury through the cap, out of sight.

Silence.

I waver in the corridor. The girls were snatched by a Tracker. The only Tracker I know is Tsinoy—who I am convinced would not harm them. For some reason, I am not afraid—and I recognize the spicy scent now. I've smelled something like it before—when Tsinoy was lost in contemplation of the stars, or upset by other circumstances. But those effusions were mild compared to this overwhelmingly rich, acrid floweriness.

Something has really aroused her.

"Come on out," Tsinoy says. "I've got them."

"Why?" I yell.

"They were taking you to your death. Nell talks to Ship now."

I'm still a little numbed by the perfume of the bower. "Why?" I ask again, like a dull child.

"Come up. We're going where their mother doesn't want us to go—through the oceans and back to the stars."

The hull seems to sigh.

We travel aft for a time, the girls gripped firmly on the Tracker's back in a tangle of rearranged muscle.

Then we head inboard along an unfamiliar conduit, perhaps newly created, back toward the center of the hull.

Tsinoy releases the girls at a fork that I suspect will lead them back toward the gene pool. They kick away, strong and silent.

We never see them again.

The Tracker examines our position, then tells me to follow. She seems to know where we are and where we need to go from here. "I have a new map," she says.

"Where did you get it—from Ship Control?" I ask.

"No," she says. "Nell spoke with Destination Guidance. They heard our prayer. They know us now." This is like being told she spoke with some great outer deity—or the devil.

The prayer.

I had recited the prayer aloud while Nell was compacting the hulls. The others joined in—my twin did not. If we all know the prayer, then we must be marked by Destination Guidance.

"They're real? They're alive, not frozen?"

Glim lights brighten ahead. "That's Nell," Tsinoy says. "It means she knows where we are. Maybe she can help protect us."

Before I can ask more questions, Tsinoy kicks off down the long cylinder. In my head, I vaguely sense we are outboard of the aft end of the water tanks, dropping toward the hull's center. My mind becomes a blank again. I'm coasting behind a life-destroying monster who loves the stars. My head was once full of memories with little relevance to my actual world. I've met the woman of my dreams—and learned that not only is she nothing like I imagined her, but that she's caused a significant portion of our hardship.

And the hidden deity we tried to kill might be our new ally.

I can't encompass any of it, so I've stopped thinking.

No time at all passes before we reach the end of the inboard-pointing tube, and kick off into the aft tank cap, far from the path I took when I was in the charge of the daughters.

Tsinoy takes my hand. The reticulated surface of her paw-claw-hand is hot. But I have known frost to whiten that same cuticle. Perhaps she is made to survive under all conditions. What else can she do? Can she live without breathing?

The great blue eyes of the six tanks wheel and spin in slow majesty—but it's me, in Tsinoy's grip, who is wheeling and spinning like a paper toy in a huge wine cellar.

I see a cable and grab it, as does Tsinoy, and we conclude this part of our journey, a few meters from the edge of a tank, voids, sheets, and bubbles writing cursive on the other side.

HERITAGE

We crawl along a layer of suspended cables to the opposite side of the chamber cap. Tsinoy leads me to an open hatch, which is crusted with age and jammed with disuse. Beyond stretches a maintenance corridor, smaller than most, more of a pipe and filled with debris, some of it cemented to the outboard curve from a succession of spin-ups, the rest messing the stale air. There's been no attention paid to this part of the hull for a long time.

"Nobody's been here," I say, as much as my wit and energy allow. I still feel the sting of rejection, but something clean and sensible in me has taken the upper hand. "Where does it go?"

"I don't know," Tsinoy says, and reduces to a minimum diameter, then squeezes along the pipe ahead of me, just barely fitting. "Nell wanted me to bring you back this way, that's all."

Our pace is slow. The ratcheting, keratinous scrape of her ivory plates and spines grates on my nerves. But I feel safer the closer I am to her. The pipe leads past a number of circular holes opening to hull voids, darkness and broad, empty volumes, silent and cold.

"This part of the hull is dead," I murmur.

"Maybe," Tsinoy says, barely audible through her own bulk. She twists and I pause, then push myself aft to allow her to reorient and back up. "Wait," she says. All her sinews and muscles rearrange, but something discourages her efforts. "I can't fit," she says. "You'll have to go. I'll instruct you."

She flattens against one side of the pipe and tells me to squeeze past—a difficult trick in narrow quarters, made even worse by the fact that I'm working my way forward *against* her spines and plates, some of which are razor sharp. She accepts the gross indignity of my elbows and hands and hips pushing down those protrusions. My clothes become torn and sliced—and several gashes open in my chest and legs—but I manage to shimmy past and feel out the pipe beyond, and then, in the near-darkness, illuminated only by the faint glow of small blue organs around Tsinoy's jaws, I see a gap in the side, just large enough to admit one midsized human being.

"Maybe this is why Nell asked for you," Tsinoy suggests. "Kim wouldn't fit."

I ignore that as a joke—but if I can judge the Tracker's tone, and likely I can't, it may not be a joke at all. I grab the edge with my fingertips and tell her to give me a shove—not too hard. I still manage to stick halfway through. For some reason, I think of honeypots—(can't quite remember what honey is, except it's sweet and amber and sticky). "I could go for some *honey*," I say, but Tsinoy doesn't hear me. Another brusque shove from her paw-claw and I'm through, sliding into a small cubic chamber. It seems familiar. I've been in a place like this before.

Tsinoy helps by shining her blue "headlamps" into the cube. The opposite wall looks rubbery, with five swelling bulges arranged in two rows, three and two. There's a rich, slightly sour smell in the close, still air. I've smelled it before, but the air was much colder in that first room in Hull Zero One, the place where I was pulled into this life.

This chamber is well above freezing.

"A birthing room," I say, shaking with the memory. "What's the hull making this time?"

"Pull them out," Tsinoy says. "Rip the skin of each cell."

I look. "I don't think they're finished."

"Nell says we need as many as you can save."

For a long moment, I feel pure terror. "Nell says...but who tells her? Destination Guidance?" This is worse than seeing my lover's face on Mother's long, productive body. There's something primally wrong about interfering with the growth of something patterned by the gene pool. But any outraged moral sense seems very much out of place.

Tsinoy's ice-colored teeth knock against the lip of the hole. "Pull them out."

"What are they?"

"Use your fingernails," she suggests with a ratcheting sigh.

I try this and, to my surprise, rip through the membrane. It's remarkably easy, even with my puny nails, like tearing a thin sponge. The bump parts and a grayish, shining sac emerges, filled with fluid—and something small and lumpy, about as long as my forearm. I see the outline of a small head. It moves.

"Leave the inner membrane intact but separate the cords, then pull it out," Tsinoy says, and from somewhere she produces gray bags, five or six, shoving them through. They drift across the cube.

"What if it isn't ready?" I ask, my voice small.

"Pull it out, then the others."

The inner sac is tougher, slicker—hard to grab—but after a

twisting tussle, I dig in, brace my feet against the rubbery wall, and tug harder. The sac emerges with a sucking *plop*, falling into my arms, followed by a tangle of flimsy, tumescent, fluid-filled cords.

Inside the sac is what appears to be a young human. A *baby*, squirming and making soft sounds. The connective cords, still pulsing, are attached to a venous, purplish lump at one end of the sac. I rotate the sac, puzzling out how to separate the cords.

"Use your teeth," Tsinoy suggests. I glare back at her, then twist again, and after a moment, to my infinite relief, the cords simply pull off, leaving seeping dimples. Then the cords withdraw, exuding blobs of fluid that I do my best to avoid inhaling.

The baby in the sac struggles reflexively in my arms.

"Now the others," Tsinoy says.

I stuff the sac into a gray bag. "Leave it room to breathe," Tsinoy tells me. I open the cinch a little and pass it back. Tsinoy takes it through the hole.

Four to go. After too long—and a bout of severe choking from inhaling a blob—I manage to half-birth the remaining four—all alive, all squirming.

The cords separate. Inside the gray bags, they grow quiet. I pass each to Tsinoy. "Who will feed them?"

"Nell says they'll last long enough in the sacs."

"Long enough for what?"

The Tracker withdraws and allows me to exit, just as the membrane wall closes up and swells outward, filling the cube, bumping my feet.

The hole closes. The hull has finished with this area.

I see no sign of the infants and with shock realize that Tsinoy is slightly larger. I have to say the worst possible thought flashes into my head, but she quickly demonstrates that she's taken them under her spikes, where she can keep them warm and safe.

"They'd grow to adults if we let them, inside the sacs," I say as we return the way we came. "That's where *I'm* from. Like that. You, too, I suppose."

Tsinoy squeezes back down the pipe to the chamber cap. I wonder if she has maternal instincts. I would no longer be surprised. Me, I feel something deeper than I can express.

"We're taking them forward, right?" I ask, wiping my fingers and palms on my pants. "We're not just going to hand them over to Mother…"

"No," Tsinoy says. "Forward."

BAD WISDOM

The cables web outward several hundred meters from the huge bulkhead's center. We climb hand over hand across the transparent face, like insects on a great blue-green eye. Within the water-filled tanks, gelatinous blue curtains undulate between diamond-glinting spans of turbulent air. I'm intent on following the Tracker, paying little attention, when something dark slips past on the other side. A sharp angle throws sapphire drops that are absorbed in another curtain, and the whole—as I try to make out what I just missed—slops into oblivion, hiding all. There's more than water in these tanks. I concentrate on the depths beyond, confused. There might or might not be greater shadows lurking there.

"You saw that, right?" I ask. My voice clips itself around the cap chamber, impossible to predict where a sibilant or a consonant will return next.

Tsinoy and I exchange a look. Her eyes are dull red, tired, discouraged.

In our last few meters traveling across the bulkhead, I peer through a mass-saving deletion and see for the first time that a shining, transparent access tunnel leads down the center line between the tanks, thrusting through the middle of the hull, perhaps its entire length, like a glass rod suspended between six huge, sluggishly fizzing bottles.

At the center of the bulkhead, the tube ends in a round, jade-colored hatch. "We'll return this way," Tsinoy says, and moves her hands over the hatch surface. It splits in thirds, and the parts pull up and out, revealing an entrance to a clear transport sphere about three meters wide. We slide into the sphere. Its surface is hard and cold. In our presence, a small blue cube begins to sigh, stirring fresh air. The hatch closes. Tsinoy fixes her eyes on mine, then casually folds all but one of her limbs, and with that one grabs a curved bar. I do the same. There's no warning before the sphere seals shut and begins to move down the tube.

"This way, we'll reach the bow in a few minutes, rather than a few hours," Tsinoy says.

That makes architectural sense. Everything around and outside the water tank is a complicated tangle of piping and corridors—like those leading to the revived birthing chamber. "A tramway," I say, as if bigger words have the power to dispel my ignorance. I'm pressed back as the bubble accelerates, arms and legs fanned, hands clutching—comic.

The surrounding beauty is extraordinary but alien, utterly *marine*. I feel as if the container around all that melted, refined moon-water is as evanescent as soapy film, a bubble that will maliciously pop and we'll be lost in blue suffocation.

Tsinoy seems to hang over me. She does not like this place. Neither do I. Her eyes scrutinize me. "This is the journey Mother didn't want you to make. Look well, Teacher."

So I'm being judged again—about to pass or fail yet another of an infinite variety of challenges and tests.

More shadows within the churn...My throat constricts.

I see another. Alive and huge. It's swimming through the tank to my left, at the sphere's one o'clock, tracking our motion. It resembles a gigantic rubbery spring, tens of meters wide, pulling forward with a jerky, screwlike twist. The outer edges of the thick coils push out fins that sweep like fishermen's nets through the liquid. Red-ruby eyes—like the Tracker's, only bigger, with oblate dark centers—poke out from the sweeping fins.

It's at least a hundred meters long, though that's hard to judge—it can contract, after all, like a spring. Within the helix long, flexible blades thrust in like pale bony swords or teeth—*baleen*, perhaps. The blades trail bubbles as the monster swims along with us, following our motion.

I can easily imagine the helix-knife's eyes are watching, eager for me to join its slicing frolics in a world's endless blue ocean. It doesn't matter that I'm tiny. Tiny things are its business.

As it slowly loses our dreamlike race, I notice white, fleshy shreds trailing from the baleen. It has already twisted and chewed its way through something alive. And where there is one Killer on Ship, there have always been more.

Ship has rotated to begin years of deceleration. The secret parts of the Catalog offer complete suites of alternatives for desperate travelers. Pick and choose from a prearranged list. Find answers to all your problems.

A terminal solution.

"We picked a star," I tell Tsinoy. "We've found our new planet. It's rich with life-forms—even intelligent beings. We can't stop now. We can't go back."

Tsinoy's snout flexes. Her eyes close. The infants are silent. I hope they haven't been smothered.

I think of our friends in the bow. "What the hell are they doing up there?" I ask.

"Nell has taken control—partly. She sent me aft to find you and retrieve the new ones."

"New ones? Not enough crew?"

"I don't know," Tsinoy says. "I don't think she asked for them."

"Who told her the babies would be there? Why bring me back and not Kim?"

"She says that after the first system was chosen, Ship was damaged. The conflict began."

"Damn it, Ship's memory was damaged or nearly destroyed, so Ship unloaded all its dirty secrets into us. But something happened. Some of us didn't go along with the picture. We split up to fight it out. Did Destination Guidance start the war?"

"I don't know," Tsinoy says.

I'm ripening like a fruit, connecting the dots on my interior map. Nell wanted me to see this. I am a key part of the plan. Long before arrival—after Destination Guidance has made its choice and is presumably dead and gone—Ship creates imprints for prep and landing crew, complete with all the necessary instincts, emotions, and patriot *love of life*—Ship-bred life. All imbedded with the patterns of Earth.

Ship would have been instructed to prepare detailed and customized imprints for the arrival crew. My imprinting would have included an updated, in vitro education about the nature of the chosen system, the star and its world or worlds. I'll help Earth's children understand why we have to destroy a planet in order to live on it. Someone else will make the monsters, the factors, the killing organisms...someone given the proper hormonal flows and mindset, a master of biology—shaped for a desperate time and unwavering in her protective passion.

Mother was put in charge of exploring the most hideous Kladistic phase spaces, selecting, creating the necessary factors, and testing their efficacy.

And here they are, all around us. Planets have oceans, which can harbor competitive life—competitive, intelligent life. Solution: turn your shipboard water supplies into artificial oceans, filled with Killers.

Me? I'm the Teacher. I'll justify their use. I'll join in the abomination, wholeheartedly, without guilt....

Except that there *is* guilt. Some of us are at cross-purposes with our intended design and function—Kim, Nell, Tomchin. And Tsinoy.

Most tellingly, Tsinoy.

I jerk and twist my head around. In my quest for large shadows within the tanks, I've missed schools of little black shapes, equipped with sharp, rotating fins like sawblades with shining diamond teeth. Then—finger-sized things that seem to be nothing more than eyes and depending tiny mouths. I have no idea how they kill. Perhaps they act as scouts.

And scattering these schools, as if in festive play—agile torpedoes equipped with nightmare, head-mounted arrays of fangs or scythes or other cutting implements. There are also aqueous variations on the spiny claw-claspers with grinding mouths. They don't make sense in any sane ecological system. All of them are pure assassins. *Liquidators.*

Grim humor seems inescapable. Teacher is supposed to be cheerful, clever, charismatic. All the girls love Teacher. But my body is numb, my thoughts like icy needles. I simply want to be Never Born. *Never Made.*

I turn my head right, to another tank, and witness the passage of a ponderous, gray-green eel more than twenty meters in length, with tiny button eyes and a shrewd pout of a mouth. The eel reacts to our motion, shuddering and lancing out. In a void between spiraling waves of liquid, sheets of fire writhe—*lightning!*

No sense putting your most deadly weapons in the same arena only to kill each other before their time arrives. Hence, six tanks.

Tsinoy makes an odd sound—not quite a growl, not yet a whimper. I look left and follow her gaze back to the tank that contains the helix-knife. As if one of those monsters is not enough, there are now five. They've joined nose to tail in a single, long, rolling, flexing coil. The coil inverts, and the tips of flexible knife-teeth furiously scrub the wall of the tank, as if trying to reach through to us. Practicing to obliterate some distant native ocean floor. I can see it: chained helix-knives destroying the heart of a planet's life from its very foundations—and then themselves quietly dying, sinking, leaving the ocean waves to roll on, clear, pristine, and sterile.

Welcome to the truth of our world—a massive seed shot out to the stars, filled with deadly children. A seed designed to slay everything it touches.

The sphere speeds through a supporting bulkhead and a hollow, dark space surrounded by huge pipes, and into a ghostly, livid glow, where it slows and stops. The blue cube sighs and the sphere opens. We are allowed to leave.

We have returned to the forward tank chamber.

———

TSINOY IS DOUBLY nervous now that we have arrived at the bow. I notice a shift in the way everyone looks at me, at my twin. Suspicion has fallen on both of us.

"What happened to Kim?" my twin asks. "What about the girls?"

"The girls are aft," I say. "I think they're okay. I finally met Mother." My throat constricts and my eyes well up. "She's holding on to Kim. She seems busy. In charge. You might recognize her."

"What's she like?" my twin asks, and looking at the way his eyes move, I wonder if he hasn't already guessed—or knows. Perhaps he also saw the drawing in the shaft. He might know instinctively—a purer form of adapted Teacher.

I describe her as best I can, words remarkably incapable of capturing her essence. My twin gives one large shiver—just as I did, hours before. "It can't be *her*," he says, without conviction. Instead, I detect a spooky longing. "Did *she* recognize you?" he asks.

"In a manner of speaking. We're all mixed together," I say. "Somebody filled our molds with mixed ingredients—mixed personalities."

"Souh*buddy*?" Tomchin asks. In our absence, Tomchin has devised a nasal sort of speech that I only half understand.

"Nell's been communicating with Ship Control since you left," my twin says as we pull ourselves to the thin forest of pylons. Nell still has her long, thin hands on the blue hemisphere. "She never lets go, but sometimes she talks. She says she's receiving updates. I'm worried about her."

We pause to digest all that we think we know, all that we think we have seen. I explain both legs of the journey as best I can—the monsters, the factors, in their huge tanks. I try to describe the gene pool—but my twin seems to see it already, in revived memory.

Nell stays attached, impassive, seemingly deaf to our words.

I conclude, "This isn't just a colonizing ship; it's a death factory." I feel the conflict—and what's wrong with that? What's wrong with surviving at all costs?

Nell releases her hands from the hemisphere and wrings her long fingers to get blood flow. "I'm famished," she says.

"Whau's Shibb gaeing to do?" Tomchin asks.

"Food first," Nell insists. "We have to stay calm and think things through. There's been too much confusion and conflict. But maybe—just maybe—we have enough clues that we can finally make good decisions."

My twin volunteers to get food. I join him, just for camaraderie—and also because I want to keep an eye on him. I haven't told anyone that Mother wants *him* to go back.

We retrieve food and bulbs of sweet liquid. Ship is still taking care of us—perhaps at Mother's command. Or because of Nell.

Over food, Nell begins. "I've been speaking with someone who claims to represent—or to be—Destination Guidance," she says. "I can't trace where this voice comes from. I can't even know if it's one, or many, male or female or..." She holds back from saying *human*. "And I don't know if we can trust anything it says. And, yes, the voice says Ship has been diverted."

"From where, to where?" Tsinoy asks.

"Unknown. It's all a mess. Some of us were created at the instigation of Destination Guidance—that's what the voice claims." Nell makes a face. "Destination Guidance tapped into a vein of conscience—something to that effect. It made sure that vein fed into some of us. Sometimes the patterns sent to the birthing rooms got confused, perhaps deliberately. Signals overlapping and parasitizing other signals. We were mixed in the mold, and even our molds were mixed—as Teacher says. Ship itself created another group to defend the original mission. One faction took control—and then another." She looks at me with sad appraisal. "I think the fight has been going on for at least a hundred years. Mother has finally won control of the gene pool. She's in charge of most of the factors."

"Oh, Lord," my twin says. He looks bleak.

"You both seem to know who and what this *Mother* is," Nell says. "The girls helped you get born, favored you, escorted you to safety—and to this hull. It's only natural to assume that one or both of you was created to be Mother's ally, her consort. The rest of us were a necessary risk. We'd be eliminated later. There's just one question left. Did either of you come equipped with a conscience?"

My twin has stayed close, interweaving his position with mine, as if to confuse the others. Until now, most of them could not have told us apart—or didn't care to try. But Tsinoy has scrupulously watched us, tracking our scents. "Mother rejected him," she tells Nell, raising a limb in my direction. "She sent him away to be killed. I brought him here through the killing tanks, as you suggested."

Nell looks me over with narrow eyes, infinitely weary. She does not want this responsibility, this power.

"He smelled angry," Tsinoy finishes. Then her snout does something that makes it more porous, less plated and shiny—and she sniffs my twin. "He's in *rut*."

He does smell a little rank.

My twin tries to kick away. Tsinoy intercepts him, holds him firmly but gently.

"Not you," she husks.

PART THREE
- - - - -
THE WORLD

My twin stammers out an argument that he's as innocent as I am, that we've been making bad decisions all along and that there's no way we can trust anything Destination Guidance says. He's panicky, sharp-voiced. I feel sorry for him—and for me. He's ruining it for both of us. Weakly, he concludes, "Maybe it fed all of you delusions in Dreamtime— just made it all up."

"You have always smelled different," Tsinoy grumbles. Her grumble sounds like distant thunder, and my hair stands on end. Inflection is not one of her talents.

"How in hell would you know what *rut* is?" he shouts, squirming in her grip. His face turns red. "You're sexless— you're neuter!"

"Only my body," Tsinoy says.

He twists his face toward me. "You'd let them kill your own twin! You'll be next!"

"Nobody says we're going to kill you," Nell says. She

manages to look as if she's reclining, one ankle under a bar, head on hand, elbow resting on empty space—all long limbs and fluid poise. Nell catches my look and bristles. "You're both handicapped," she says. "She's played on your emotions."

"Who was *your* mother?" my twin shouts.

"I don't think my patterns go that deep," Nell says. "I don't remember a childhood or a mother or a family."

My twin's face has screwed into tears. "Let me go to her," he begs. "I belong with her."

"The wrong one went aft," Nell says, and prims her lips. Nell and Tsinoy have turned their eyes toward the windows, longing for a cleanness of vast spaces and suns, for what lies beyond Ship. The relief of infinity, of choices, of futurities lost. But the windows are still being repaired. They are fogged, dark.

I feel weak.

We hear a noise behind us. A deep brown shadow moves through darkness into the bow's illumination.

It's Big Yellow.

"Kim!" Nell cries. "We worried about you."

"No need," Kim says. "I did some gardening and got loose. I don't think anyone got hurt. But you guys really pissed her off. She's making her move."

"How soon?" Nell asks, dead calm.

"Minutes, maybe. After I got loose, I passed about a dozen forest balls, and they were filled with growing things, big things and small. Worse than any I've seen so far."

Kim approaches Tsinoy, who is still holding on to my twin, and reaches out with one huge hand. One finger caresses my twin's cheek. "He's the one she wanted, right?" he asks.

Nell nods, then points to me. "This one's okay. I think."

"Yeah. He did good back there." Kim reaches out with his

other hand, places it on my twin's opposite cheek, then clamps and twists my twin's neck. It snaps like a stick. Instantly, he just hangs.

My body jerks and I shove away from the group.

"We need to leave," Kim says. "Back to the other hulls...any-place but here. I don't think even Tsinoy can fight what's coming."

The Tracker cradles the lifeless body and makes a soft, strange sound, then pulls back her claws, releasing it. It slips away, head bobbling, no hurry, eyes wide. Then it follows a new, slow curve toward the floor.

Tomchin looks around, stretches his arms. Points back to the transport craft.

"We should get more food and water," Nell says.

"No time," Kim says. He's already grabbing and shoving, moving us toward the transport, happy to abandon the last viable hull—the last place that could feed us and clothe us.

No protest. Mother has won another round.

Aft of the staging area, in the tent-shaped chamber, we hear low, awful sounds, like whispers or snakes slithering through grass. Tsinoy shifts her muscles and bulks up, clamping her paw-claws down on the deck between us and the noises.

We pull ourselves toward the entrance of the egg-craft. I look aft. Something moves along the deck, clinging and transparent, like a wash of water but dotted with twitching, shining hairs and ruby spots for eyes. It laps up over Tsinoy's feet. Smoke lifts and she begins to bleed—thick red drops. The liquid is cutting her up like razors. She lets go with a mewl, swiping the fluid off with quick strokes of ivory claws, and Kim grabs her outstretched limb, pulling her after the rest of us.

I catch a glimpse of what might be cherubim in the bow, little angels hovering over the lapping tide. They are jumping, climbing, yanking themselves forward—Mother's vanguard.

The fluid is on the lip of the hatch when Nell tells it to close. We push away from Hull Zero Three. We've had enough of monsters, of Mothers and daughters and dreams and lies and incomprehensible wars. We can only hope the moon-bound sphere of Destination Guidance is any sort of sanctuary.

If not, we will choose black space and the deadly grit between the stars.

```
            END DOCUMENT
            SWEEP SURVEY
             COMPLETE


    This document has been judged
        original and authentic.


    FILED: SHIP ARCHAEOLOGY REPORT
```

SURVEY TEAM
PERSONAL ADDENDUM

He was *you*, wasn't he?" my partner asks. "He was a Teacher, after all."

The survey of the joined hull and all of its nooks and hiding places, the sweep of extraneous biology—what little remains—has taken our team sixty days. We've multitasked throughout that time, my partner and our seven team members, working other jobs, preparing the staging areas and providing instruction for both the Ship's maintenance crew and those who will go planetside.

"But..." My partner is almost at a loss. "Was *she* me?"

"Which one?"

"You know which one I'm referring to."

"No way of knowing," I say. "No pictures. Nothing we can use to judge."

"Ship could have kept a record of it."

"Who understands Ship?" I ask. "We still haven't unraveled all of the systems and controls."

"It must have been a horrible time."

I wonder if I've made a mistake by letting her read ten of the books—ten out of eleven, all contained in a ragged, tattered gray bag. No other books or bags have been found. The survey team that gathered them can't read the writing, but for some reason I can, and so can my partner. Ship is full of languages. The books are written in colloquial English, with a heavy slant toward twenty-first century cultural values and norms. My partner and I naturally speak Pan-Sinense, perhaps like the Knob-Crest called Tomchin. We have confirmed that such physiological forms are within Ship's creative capabilities, including the monster factors—

But there is no way to know just what our writer looked like. We can only surmise that he resembled me. No way of knowing for sure.

But I feel it. Something in the way he thinks, in the word-choices apparent even through the unfamiliar flow of characters.

My partner is less pleased with her matching.

"*She* seems impossible," she says. "Have you found anything like her in the Catalog?"

"No," I say, but that isn't precisely the truth. I have used data tools to recover parts of the Catalog that were not completely erased, and even to evaluate the theoretical potentials of the original Klados—of which our present Ship retains but a small selection.

Once, Ship was so much greater—and yes, something like the Mother could have existed. We were sent to the stars fully equipped. If we had stayed that way, I'm convinced we would have died—Ship would have either killed itself or been extinguished.

I've made my decision. I can trust my partner, but observing her disgust, her sense of loss and disappointment, I realize what I must do with the last book. I am responsible for the cultural training and morale of the colonists and, ultimately, the success or failure of our long, difficult journey. It's shocking enough to read these first ten of the recovered books and begin to understand that our histories, our past memories, have all been manufactured. More shocking still to contemplate the amoral complexities of Ship's designers, the desperate desire to succeed at all costs, against all odds—no matter what the consequences to other worlds, other lives.

Evil.

Yes, but we might have benefited.... Something still lingers in me. Something wrong, perverse. Lovely.

I have held back the final volume—the eleventh—from my partner's eyes. Even now, it burns in my thoughts...and yet pleases. Someday, centuries from now, the complete story will be revealed, and it will rock us all, so young and confident and strong.

But only then.

In the meantime, our world beckons—more beautiful than we could ever have hoped.

I have replaced the eleventh volume in the bag, sealed it in sequestered storage, made certain that it will stay on Ship for as long as Ship is safely in orbit.

If you have read these old texts and our wraparound analysis, then you are educated and mature. But be prepared for knowledge that could alter your perception of all we have accomplished, all that we are.

We have lives to lead and worlds to conquer—figuratively, of course. We have found a fine new world, youthful and undeveloped. There are no civilizations, no complex ecosystems. We are already incorporating its biological wisdom into our plans.

Ship has learned. Ship was taught....

But the teaching was hard.

ELEVENTH BOOK

The peace and quiet of space, away from the hulls, heading inward, toward the little moon, still protected by the shields...

Profound silence. Not even the little egg-craft makes a sound. We are adrift, breaths held—afraid to provoke another whim of fate, or perhaps afraid to alert Destination Guidance to the fact that we are still alive. That we are about to become visitors.

Nell breaks this silence with a deep breath. "How old is Ship, do you think?" she asks, looking at me. As if I have an answer.

I'm spent. I shrug. "Five hundred years," I say, surprised that this figure sticks in my head. "Maybe."

"So it was launched from...where? Earth? Five centuries ago?" Kim asks.

"From the Oort cloud," Tsinoy says. She has shrunk to a more manageable size, to give the rest of us room, rearranging her muscles and "bones" to a less energy-intensive posture. She's still in pain.

"What's a wart cloud?" Kim asks, perhaps to distract her from her pain.

"O-O-R-T. It's the afterbirth of our solar system, a big halo of leftover ice and dust," Tsinoy says. "Some of the conglomerations are hundreds of kilometers wide. Ship was constructed among the inner planets, then sent out to the far limits. An Oort moonlet was selected, trimmed, and compacted. All this took fifty years. Ship was attached and launched five hundred years ago, as Teacher says. If we can believe any of it."

"Can we go back?" Kim asks.

"No," Tsinoy says, and lifts a paw-claw to lick. She shudders at the taste of her wounds. "Once launched, Ship is forbidden to return. Too dangerous."

Another silence, a long one. We are revolving, reorienting. Our short journey—a few dozen kilometers—is coming to an end. Nell and Tsinoy move toward the viewport. They almost bump heads. I marvel at the contrast.

Our females.

"First things first," I say. "Will Destination Guidance let us in?"

"Others have sought refuge before us," Nell says.

"What happened to them?" I ask.

"I wish I knew."

"We're about to connect," Kim says.

Sounds of joining, sealing. Our ears pop as pressures equalize. Tsinoy moves toward the hatch, our first line of defense.

The hatch opens. We are flooded with cold air. Very cold. Frost plumes before our faces.

SILVER AGE

The disembarkation stage is a broad cylinder slung with cables and nets. The end of the cylinder is open—but beyond lies frigid darkness. The moon-bound sphere was never designed for spin-up. Whatever lived here, lived in eternal weightlessness. Did they also live in eternal cold?

"Tell it to be hospitable," I suggest to Nell.

"All right," she says. "A little help, please!"

No response.

"How about some heat?" she adds.

"Sure you weren't speaking to a ghost?" Kim asks, shoulders flexing. He drifts out of our hatch. No one wants to touch the frosted cables or netting. The air hurts our noses and burns our lungs. At least it's breathable, aside from the cold.

There's a flash, a streak of light. It's in my eyes, not from any illumination in Ship itself. Everyone makes a startled sound, even Tsinoy. We all saw it.

"Cosmic ray," Tsinoy suggests.

But I've seen something like it before. My saving ghost. The one that can't possibly exist.

A small glow begins, blue-green, then brightens to a dim yellow. The interior of the chamber beyond the landing stage is equipped with tiny glim lights, like the walls of the hulls. I'm back where this all began—moving toward light, chasing heat.

"I get it," Nell says. "We were taught to fear Destination Guidance because Mother didn't want us to come down here."

"Or because it's dangerous. Maybe they aren't even remotely like us.... " Kim trails off on that idea, and we cringe at the rudeness of even suggesting such a thing, at this of all times.

"That's confusing," Tsinoy says. "If we were chosen by Destination Guidance... "

"We could still be dangerous," I say. "We're still Mother's children. In a way."

Tomchin makes a humming proclamation I don't catch.

Another streak of light. Tsinoy whistles and begins to bulk up. We gather close as she puts out more heat.

"Don't cook the babies," I remind her.

She turns her eyes on me and blinks slowly—three different lids, all transparent. She doesn't sleep, doesn't stop seeing—ever. I know the babies are fine—warmer than us, but fine.

We hold our ground, like children on the porch of a haunted house. *Autumn leaves, moonlit October nights, long dirt roads alive with tree shadows, bags filled with candy... flickering candles in carved-out pumpkins.* So much in the way of lost, false memory wells up at that comparison—haunted houses and small towns and Halloween—that I'm momentarily blinded by tears.

Someone had fun with me way back when—had fun putting me together. Or perhaps I'm based on someone real, long dead, way back on Earth.

I'm the haunted house. My brain is the ghost here.

"Nothing," Nell says. "You try." She points to me, then around to all of us. "We'll all try, one at a time—but you first."

"A little help down here!" I call out, my breath turning to snow. More minutes pass. Nell raises her hand toward Kim, and then we feel a current of air lightly flow along the cylinder. The darkness begins to creak, snap, and then groan—long metallic groans underscored by a low *whoosh*. We move back toward the hatch, having had quite enough, thank you—just before the warmer air brushes our faces, circles us, caresses our hands, luffs at our clothing, rustles Tsinoy's spines—and becomes a wind.

The sphere is finally coming to life.

A voice speaks. We all recognize the gentle, precise tones. "I await a decision," it says.

"About what?" I ask.

No answer. Nell moves forward. "We need to shut down Hull Zero Three. We don't like what's happening there. How can we do that without damaging Ship?"

"Ship is already damaged," the voice says. Lights brighten. The darkness beyond the cylinder vestibule is filled with smoothly curved surfaces, volumes, in strikingly beautiful colors and patterns, some translucent, others pale and milky. It's like nothing we've seen elsewhere on Ship, as if a mad artist began blowing huge glass shapes and arranged them to an irrational aesthetic.

But this is just one tiny part of the sphere, which is at least half a kilometer in diameter. It could be a greeting, meant to impress—or a distraction to hold and confuse us while examinations are made; a 3-D psychological test that might determine whether we live or die, are welcomed, or are flushed back into space.

"Did you make this?" Kim asks, and I see that of all of us, he's the most affected by the unexpected elegance and beauty.

"This space was designed by Destination Guidance," the voice says.

"Are you Destination Guidance?" Nell asks.

"No."

"Are you Ship Control? You sound familiar.... "

The voice asks, "What do you not like about Ship and its operations?"

This is a loaded question, obviously, and we need some time to think it over. We haven't moved from the cylinder, our hole of relative safety on the edge of a coral reef of color and unfamiliar beauty. If we venture out, will something grab us while we're distracted?

Put an end to all our worries?

"What do you not like about Ship operations?" the voice asks again.

Nell swallows, presses her hand against her lips, and looks to me. They're all looking to me.

"We think there was a war to stop Ship from killing a planet. We're refugees." I stop, feeling foolish again and totally unprepared. And besides, who or what am I talking to? There's nobody here, nobody visible. The space is warming quickly. Soon, we might be invited in...sit down for tea and cookies, discuss the local interstellar weather.

"What is conscience?" the voice asks.

But not until we pass our biggest test.

"The willingness to sacrifice for a greater good," I say.

"Sacrifice what?"

"Dreams. Plans. Personal stuff."

Nell is getting irritated. Tsinoy, on the other hand, is shrinking—pulling in, drawing back. I glance over my shoulder at her.

"She's designed to be a Tracker, a Killer," I say. "But she refuses to give in to her design. There's something better inside her. Inside all of us."

"Did she acquire that by herself, or was it put there?"

"I own my feelings," Tsinoy growls. "I am what I want to be."

"Absolutely," I agree. "We've been through the wringer."

"Tell me what that means."

"Just wait a goddamned minute!" I shout. "We've been put through a living hell to get here. We've been chased and expelled and murdered and deceived.... "

"You were created by Ship," the voice says. "Would you rather not have been created?"

Tsinoy shrinks back as if kicked. We're about to act like whipped dogs, all of us. *Enough.*

"You want our *gratitude*?" I cry out. Nell touches my arm.

"Ship has a mission. Would you have Ship continue on that mission if it guaranteed your personal survival—and if ending that mission meant your death?"

Tsinoy says, "We are not the only ones here." She lifts her spines and delivers the babies, still in their bags, then hands them to the rest of us, like talismans or shields. She's offering up the little ones she's protected and making the rest of us their protectors as well.

Tomchin looks distressed and holds his bag out as if it's a bomb. Kim tucks his in the crook of one huge arm. As we receive our own infants, Nell looks at me, and we move closer, until our arms touch. It's an awkward, scary, strangely lovely moment. I almost don't care if we live or die. We've made our peace with fate.

"We're all human here," I say. "You can't judge us. You're just a machine."

"Machines have not been in control for a very long time. Come in. Finish birthing the young ones, and they will be fed. There is food for you as well."

Nell opens her bag. "What do you think?" she asks me.

Tsinoy moves first. Her claw delicately slits one side of the membrane. The baby comes out, and along with it, a small stream of reddish fluid. Tomchin just about loses it and starts to babble a nasal protest, offering his gray bag—now quite active—to anyone. But he's in this with all of us.

The other membranes are tough, but one by one, the sacs are carefully cut open and the babies withdrawn.

I massage mine instinctively, then turn it around with country doctor wisdom, hold it with one hand, and slap its bottom with the other. Fluid gushes from its mouth as it empties its lungs. Suddenly it draws breath and starts to pinwheel its arms, then cry.

"It's a boy," I say.

Nell follows suit, then the others—even Tomchin.

"Mine's a girl," Nell says.

We use the bags to wipe them down, dry them off. We compare our infants as if we've opened Christmas packages—another memory that only compounds my irrational joy. Three girls, two boys. My eyes stream with tears. It's warm enough in the vestibule that we don't feel the need to swaddle them.

I clean gunk from my boy's mouth, swipe his eyes clear, pinch his nose to squeeze out the last fluid. Hold him out with the others, to our judge, our sponsor—whatever it may be. A desperate, defiant act. We hope for sympathy in a violent, damning, world, all that we've known and experienced in real life—as opposed to phantom memory. We long for confirmation and completion and justification—and we also long to survive and learn that our reckless existence has meaning.

The glass pillars light up and separate, showing a passage

through alternating ribs of steel, into what might be a frozen jungle. I'm not sure I like that. And more glass, lit within by green sparkles, undulating through the interior of the sphere for a hundred meters or more.

We carry the infants and move cautiously toward the center. Streaks of green and pink ripple over the inner wall of some sort of sanctuary.

"Welcome," the voice says.

The wall melts aside. Within, all is frost-covered, leafy green. Furniture comfortable for weightlessness has been shaped and positioned in and around branches, much as in Mother's bower. I see for a moment small eyes, in pairs and triplets—many of them, staring out from between the leaves, and expect we are about to discover *another* female like Mother, another trap, another challenge—followed swiftly by more Killers.

But the eyes blink and withdraw. The lights rise, and a blue glow like terrestrial sky suffuses the glade, the tree house—that's what this all reminds me of, a tree house deep inside a jungle.

And at the atrium where guests might be greeted, welcomed, or captured, a curling flash of silver moves between the branches in ways I can barely follow, as if its time flows in a way different from mine. It's like trying to watch a ghost made of sky and chrome, a glinting creature all thin limbs and curves, glassy apparel flowing around its lithe body like spilled milk, decorated with jeweled beads, aquamarine and emerald. And rising above this splendor, a tall, slender head, humanoid in one respect—that there are eyes, nose, something like ears on the side of the head.

Not part of my memory—not part of Ship. Something far outside the Klados.

A silvery.

"Welcome to Destination Guidance."

The apparition is not speaking—it isn't the being behind the voice. For a moment, it looks at me, lifts a finger to its lips, and smiles the most frightening, beautiful smile. It has no teeth.

It drops its hand—and melts away.

For my eyes only. The others saw nothing.

Nell notices my violent shiver. "Come on, it's not that bad," she says.

I want to throw up, but there's nothing to expel.

Inner lights rise. A small space has been cut out of the branches. The space is partly walled with milky panels, slender wires forming what might have once been sleeping pods. Within two of the pods are dark brown robes, and almost hidden in the robes two figures, mostly black, with touches of grayish pink, still crusted with spots of ice and frost—but rapidly thawing.

"Are you here to relieve and replace Destination Guidance?" the voice asks.

I wonder how these shriveled bodies can make any sound. But it's quickly obvious, from a rising sour smell, that neither of these cold husks is the one speaking. They've been dead a long time.

"I spoke with Ship," Nell says. "We need pure Ship—the one that woke us up, that taught us how to access the Klados and Ship's memory. No go-between. No tricks."

"I am not that Ship," the voice says. "A decision must be made, but I am not empowered to make it. A new destination has been found. Guidance team has been frozen and preserved. They will revive soon."

Kim studies the corpses. Nell keeps back with Tsinoy. All of us feel the danger. What fought against our birth, our survival? What made creatures to kill us? Mother, Ship, or these corpses?

If I believed in the silvery, I might accuse *it* as well—but I refuse to believe. It's my delusion, and mine alone. It is not part of Ship or my reality, thus outside blame.

"They will revive soon," the voice drones. "They are in deep sleep."

"Very deep," Kim says under his breath.

Nell pulls herself forward on a long branch and reaches to touch the leaves, then pull them aside, as if looking for the source of those glinting eyes. "Don't be afraid," she murmurs, with a warning glance at Tsinoy—no quick moves. "You in the shrubbery—who are you? Did you make the babies, tell us where to find them?"

"Who's she talking to?" Tsinoy asks.

"*There* you are," Kim says as a small form seems to materialize from behind him, hanging from a long tail wrapped around a branch. Memory tells me it's a kind of monkey, but not really. It's more like a doughnut with five jointed arms and two tails. It does have a general coat of fur, and at the top of the doughnut is a triangular head with eyes arranged in a kind of face, three around a trilateral nose, a fourth on its crown—entirely practical in three-dimensional lodgings.

The voice comes again, in part from the doughnut monkey beside Kim. "Wake them," it says, speaking without an obvious mouth, through its triangular nose. Now it's obvious the voice comes from all around. Other doughnut monkeys poke heads, tails, arms through the branches. One settles beside the rime-covered corpses and watches us with bright eyes.

The inhabitants of this leafy tree house number in the dozens—that we can see. Their arms have tiny, agile hands—three fingers and two thumbs. How many more fill the sphere of Destination Guidance? Hundreds? Thousands?

The monkey nearest the corpses reaches up as if to caress a

thawing face. It gives a low howl, then shrinks back. "We have died," the voice says.

"They're *all* talking at once," Nell says. "Just one voice."

"Are they from the Catalog?" Tsinoy asks me. "Did Ship make them before us?"

Doughnut monkeys do not arouse the same disbelief as the chrome ghost. "Maybe," I say.

"They aren't obvious Killers," Kim says. "No claws, not much in the way of teeth. Big heads, for their body size. They look—"

"Ship requests communication," the voice says. "Ship requests reconciliation. Wake Destination Guidance and find us a home."

"I'm confused," Kim says. "Isn't Ship dead? Aren't we inside Destination Guidance?"

"They want us to follow them," Nell says, watching the way the monkeys are moving, reaching out as if to touch us, pulling arms back at the last minute, then rushing in waves down an opening in the branches. "We can't all go. Somebody has to stay here with the babies."

But the monkeys show great concern about the babies. Heads turn. Noses speak.

"Nobody stays behind," the voice says.

Tsinoy, ever surprising, shows them how she can keep the babies within her bulk, under her armor, in relative warmth and comfort, and Nell finally agrees—they're better off coming with us.

"Why would they hurt them?" Kim asks. "Didn't they ask us to find them and bring them here?"

"Use your imagination," I suggest darkly.

Kim looks mildly aggrieved, then nods.

At least ten of the monkeys—all encouragement, cooperation,

and gymnastics—swing out and around us hand to hand. They seem to want us to move away from the corpses, now that there's no evidence the bodies will ever talk or act again.

The monkeys—the voice—may not be completely stupid. The last of them vanishes into the foliage.

———

THE SPHERE OF Destination Guidance is about five hundred meters in diameter. It seems to be made of concentric layers, floors or inner spheres, most of them plainly deserted and still cooled down. We're guided by a corridor of warm air as much as anything. Cold keeps us on the right path.

Corridors and conduits push almost straight, or with gentle undulations, through the levels. The design reminds me of the hulls—organic in its seeming disarray, but also organically efficient. As we travel, Nell estimates that the warm air—and the monkeys, occasionally seen up ahead, then moving on—are guiding us on a wide arc toward the foremost point of the sphere.

The journey is interesting because half the foliage along our path is covered with deep frost. Here and there, other monkeys appear who are also still frozen—clinging and thawing to sluggish life.

A few are warm enough to break free and join our entourage.

Kim looks on with wonder. "They were built to freeze down with the sphere," he says. Tomchin tries to express some idea or another, but we're too busy to listen, learning our own Tarzan moves in the open spaces between the branches and leaves. (Don't ask me who Tarzan is. I see ourselves surrounded by monkeys in this elongated forest—even doughnut monkeys—and the name is just there, along with a disturbing image of a muscular human male in a leopard-skin loincloth.)

"Don't look now, but we're *brachiating*," I say.

"In public?" Tsinoy asks.

Nell giggles with a hiccup-meowing quality I find entrancing. After all we've been through, even as we *brachiate*, we have to give in to our sense of the absurd.

Tsinoy is the best at putting the word to the deed, moving swiftly, keeping up with the monkeys, but we can't exactly learn from her, given our natural equipage. As she moves, we hear the infants inside her armor gurgling, cooing, chirping—expressions not precisely happy, but not distressed, either. Is she actually *nursing* them? Anything is possible. Absurdity is the rule.

I think at this point I feel something like love for our entire weird troupe. It's the first time I've felt such an emotion for real people—though I remember it from the Dreamtime.

People.

My people. Maybe the only family I'll ever know. And look at them—so many pages from unwritten human history, adapted to so many conditions, but working together, irrationally reaching for a goal, hoping for a purpose. What's not to love?

The journey is not swift. We're scratched, sweaty, and irritated in a dozen different ways by the time we reach our destination. It could be a duplicate of the forward control center we left behind us in Hull Zero Three, but it's overgrown with vines, tendrils, branches, leaves, and even rooted trunks. The monkeys have been here, off and on—warm and cold—for a long time, it seems.

We find two more mummies, completely thawed and not in the least savory. "Who are they?" Nell asks our agile escorts.

"They are *us*," the voice says from all around, and the monkeys settle, some grooming each other, while the majority cling to the branches and watch with so many dark, shining eyes.

"Can we...put them away?" I ask. "They're dead. They're not coming back."

The monkeys think this over. I see a ripple in their odd faces and bodies: muscular twitches, arms and hands shaping subtle gestures. The ripple passes from one side to the other. A monkey wave. They think in serial.

The ripple completes, and together they say, "We are not dead."

Tsinoy seems to have unique insight into what we're being told. She's contemplated form and function and inner being for some time now, and she's clued in. "They copied themselves... into all of you? Gave you their memories, their jobs, their duties so that you could replace them if they didn't survive?"

A general light rustling as tails twitch, little hands relax and clutch again. This question is too strange and important for the voice to answer right away.

"Yes," it says finally. "They are us."

"Well, that's fortunate," Nell says. "Because they need to be disposed of, now that you don't need them."

I push toward Nell, and in her ear I whisper, "Who's in charge, then?" She shakes the question off. It's way beyond her capacity. Tsinoy hears, however, and makes another creative leap—with another, more important question.

"Why make the babies and bring them here?" she asks.

"They are pure. They will grow to make a choice," the voice replies.

Tomchin hums to himself, too clearly expressive, and turns away. "Mad Szhib," he says. We all understand.

"We're lost," Tsinoy says. "What is there for them to decide, if they even *could* decide?"

"They have no dreams. Ship has not patterned them. They are pure."

The monkeys pull and tear foliage from the rear of the control area. This reveals a moss-crusted circular hatch, big enough even for Tsinoy or Kim. Nell rubs her hands on her pants, holds up her long fingers, then looks around with a plaintive expression. Pylons rise as if to greet her. She touches a blue hemisphere, but only briefly. "It's the same here as in the hulls," she says. "There are huge blank places, burned places. Ship is incapable of making decisions."

"Ship is dead," the voice says.

"Mother almost won," Tsinoy says.

The monkeys move around Tsinoy, beckon her to approach a hatch revealed to our right. We try to stay with her, but with rather more vigor than before, the monkeys keep us back.

The Tracker is welcome—protector of infants, bringer of new life, new guidance. But only the Tracker. The monkeys seem to think we've done our bit, for now.

"What a mess," I murmur.

"Amen," Kim says.

Tsinoy floats calmly before the hatch. "Let's not be too hasty," she says. "Or too fatalistic. How many go in?"

"You and the infants," the voice says. "No one else."

"Forget it," Tsinoy says. "Being alone is being in bad company. The babies need more than me. They need a *real* mother, friends, uncles, protectors—and a real teacher."

The monkeys are at a loss. More stirrings, gestures, but no more speech.

"If there's a chance you'll make it without us..." I begin.

"We're not important," Nell adds.

"Forget it!" Tsinoy growls. "I'm nobody's idea of a nursemaid. I'd give them nightmares."

"Not if you're all they ever know," Nell suggests in softening tones.

"Forget it!" the Tracker growls again. "Believe me, if I were a baby, this body would scare me silly. And I'm being practical as well as selfish. I *hate* being alone."

The monkeys listen.

Stalemate.

Balanced on the head of a pin. Maybe it will all fall apart again right here. Centuries of effort, blood and treasure across the ages, a withering seedpod torn apart by its own perverse conscience (and where did that come from? Will we ever know?)—a faculty that never should have blossomed. Had it not blossomed, however, we wouldn't be here. The monkeys have to understand something about this, if they combine the intellects of those who ordered us made. If they were the ones who injected us with conscience.

The hatch slowly pulls and melts aside. Lights come on. We peer into a sanctuary beside the control area. Here, everything is brightly colored, warm, clean, preserved, though at first the air is stuffy.

The monkeys make one last effort to separate us. With Kim, the result is comical—a big yellow guy covered by clasping, chirping, snorting, fur-covered doughnuts.

Tsinoy howls. The monkeys scatter. Kim grabs for support. The Tracker regains her composure—I hope. It's hard to tell sometimes.

"They will go first," she insists, after something like a clearing of her throat. Everyone flinches at that, and the monkeys perform another wave of alert concern.

No dissent from *our* ranks. We've tried worse stratagems with greater chances of failure. I gesture to Nell, who gestures to Tomchin, and Tomchin enters, then Kim, then Nell. Then me. Tsinoy follows me.

The monkeys hang back, uncertain.

"What happens now?" I ask just inside the hatchway.

From outside the sanctuary, the voice says, "We stop delivery of fuel from the moon to the hulls. In a generation, the hulls will go cold. All will freeze and die, except for those gathered here."

"What about the gene pool?" Nell asks behind me.

No answer. Six of the monkeys are pushed forward by their companions, and reluctantly—with more sad chirps—they join us.

The hatch closes.

MEET YOUR MAKER

The inner chamber's walls still carry a coat of frost. We're cramped, cold, and silent. A few dozen meters away, surrounded by bluish gloom, a crystalline oval lies at the center of a shadowy space. There's a small cherry glow around the oval. The glow expands. Warmth radiates slowly outward. Thawing here is a more delicate task than with the monkeys and their foliage. Whatever lies inside the oval is not so robust. Nell and I move closer.

"Someone's inside," she says.

The light rises. The glow comes from a translucent capsule just large enough to hold one body—shorter than Nell, smaller than Tsinoy or Kim, smaller even than Tomchin. A body about my size.

"Another mummy," Kim suggests.

"I don't think so," Nell says.

My skin tingles.

"It looks female," Kim says.

I had thought for a moment it might be another version of *me* inside the capsule, and I feel both relief and disappointment when I see it is not. *She* is not. But dismay follows disappointment. Her naked limbs are skinny, emaciated, as if she has been starved of both food and time. Her face is deeply wrinkled. Her eyes, as they open, are bleary and yellow.

She looks at us slowly, still groggy.

For the first time, we are witness to a living human being who is not young, not fit—who is, in fact, very, very old. Yes, she has been preserved, frozen along with the rest of the sphere. But she lived a long time before the capsule accepted her ancient frame, before she took this last option—this last outstretched voyage to our present, her future.

The capsule sections slide up, melt away. A sweet, musty scent rises from around the naked old woman, like perfumes from a grandmother's dresser. I half expect to see round mirrors and blue jars of skin cream and combs felted with gray winter gleanings from ten thousand lonely nights.

She studies us one by one, showing no surprise, no dismay. Our appearance does not shock. Our forms do not concern her. The monkeys have allowed us to come here; the sphere has warmed…. She accepts us all, but perhaps she is too old— perhaps she can no longer summon enough energy to care whether we signal defeat or victory, or are simply another step in a plan she must have been integrally concerned with, hundreds of years before.

"Hello," she says. She raises a thin arm, gestures with near-skeletal fingers. Four of the monkeys bring forward clothing worn, bleached, tattered, and still crisp with frost. She smiles and shakes her head. "Cold," she says.

The monkeys pass the gown to us. Nell and I rub it with our hands to warm it.

"That's fine," the old woman says. She manages to float free of the capsule.

We dress her. She seems as light as a leaf. After her ancient nakedness has been concealed, she lifts her shoulders, squares them, shakes out her thin arms, and draws a finger along her lined cheek. Then she looks at us one by one and asks, "Which of you is Teacher?"

The others point. I'm too stunned to move or speak. Just touching her hands and limbs makes me ache. I've been through all sorts of suffering in my short existence, but not this—the painful prolonging of biological time.

"Is it really *you*?" the old woman asks, her eyes moving up to my face. I realize her sight has faded. "Closer." She reaches out to me, and the monkeys help her forward like faithful handmaids. "I hope you remember. We would have been important to each other, once."

The old woman's features take on new focus. I map her eyes, her cheeks, the shape of her jaw. I draw her face over two other memories—my Dreamtime partner, the one I was destined to go to planet with. And Mother, back in Hull Zero Three.

My mouth is as dry as dust. "I remember," I say.

"If something had gone wrong with your making, you wouldn't remember anything about me. I'm so glad you do. I always remember *you*."

"You're Destination Guidance?" Nell asks.

"The very last," the old woman says. "Now, please, you've brought me such lovely gifts, these odd creatures tell me. I didn't design them, you know. That was Selchek. He's gone by now, surely. There were three others. They're gone, too, by now."

"Yes," Nell says.

The bodies.

"They brought themselves back one by one, to live out their lives and fight for the soul of the Ship. I presume that's how it happened," she says. "None of us was supposed to live forever, or even longer than a normal human being. So we had to cobble together an apparatus and carry it piecemeal from the hulls... along with these *creatures*!"

The monkeys do not seem offended by her appraisal. "She is the last," they agree.

She grasps Kim's huge arm in frail hands. "I'm sure there are better clothes somewhere. The monkeys care nothing for dress, you know. Please take me someplace warmer."

Nell grimaces at me, but the sphere is merciful, and the monkeys have been busy cleaning, clearing, and preparing. I get the impression that in the monkeys, something remains of the others and that they are attendant on this meeting, listening. Perhaps they are pleased and finally willing to waste a few resources, for however short a time we will be here.

It has taken us so long to be created and gathered.

"Someplace warm," the old woman repeats. Then, to the monkeys, the sphere, she calls out, in a surprisingly loud and firm voice, "Light the fires. Bring out the feast. It's time!"

My heart thrills. We've never met, but knowing her is my validation.

JUDGMENT AND DESTINATION

T'sinoy, I think, fell in love with the old woman right away and cared for our infant successors with a quiet enthusiasm. She did not need to protect the rest of us.

We had already initiated the final cooling of the hulls. Essentially, this meant the destruction of most living things aboard Hull Zero Three, the other hulls being nearly dead already. Some might survive for a time—Mother is always resourceful, and the gene pool is a never-ending source of ingenuity.

But we have stopped transport of ice from the moon to the hulls. Soon, there will no longer be heat to chase. The liquid within the hulls' central tubes will also freeze, for a time, and Ship will drift without power, except for the reserves within this sphere.

PERCHANCE

The old woman died a few days after our arrival. She did not tell us all we needed to know, but she gave us the keys to what was left of Ship's original instructions, almost eroded away after centuries of fighting.

Nell has learned this much after careful study of the remnants of Ship's memory and after careful questioning of the monkeys, who have grown a touch dotty over time:

It was the original choice of the first Destination Guidance team to set the course for a system that observation showed was already inhabited by intelligent beings. Honorably enough, they died, their work done—but done badly, as it turned out.

As Ship approached its intended destination, the first Mother was created, and the first consorts. They prepared Ship to destroy, replace.

But Ship was somehow pushed into a minute diversion, away from its intended destination and toward a dangerously unstable star. That star exploded in a supernova, washing Ship in deadly radiation and damaging the hulls and memory.

As Ship's memory degraded, emergency procedures dictated that memory and function would be diverted to biological components able to carry out basic functions, including preserving and re-creating the gene pool. Ship then entered the dusty outer clouds of the resulting nebula.

With the original destination no longer in reach, another Destination Guidance team was born—into the worst imaginable conditions. Ship Control was intermittent, the hulls were filling with monsters, the birthing chambers were either being perverted to Mother's demands or, failing that, being shut down.

The old woman and her colleagues—then little more than adolescents—somehow reached the decision that Ship must not continue in its present form. Destination Guidance infiltrated hull communications and assumed control of some birthing chambers, creating counter-crew and subverting some of Mother's Killers by mixing components of biology and memory.

They fought Mother in all her many different incarnations.

Thus began the war.

———

AT THE END, the old woman met with me alone in a small room the monkeys had arranged for her. She took my hand, her fingers as light as bird wings, and said, "You've seen it, haven't you?"

I'm not willing to admit I've seen anything.

She then adds, "Our Ship is haunted. Not just by the dead of ancient wars, oh no—but by something not from Ship. Something I believe set us a great challenge. When I told Selchek and Grimmel what I saw, they did not believe me. They joked, calling it my avenging angel. Puroy called it the Judge. She, too, did not believe it was real. But it was—I know. It's been with us for hundreds of years."

She regards me with a gaze growing strong and steady—an assured but also *frightened* gaze. I can barely look at her my body is trembling so.

"In time, others saw it as well. Those of us who saw felt that we were indeed being judged. We believed it diverted Ship toward the supernova. In part, seeing it—fearing its judgment— we knew that if we didn't clean up our act and prevent the destruction of other innocent worlds, Ship would be utterly destroyed."

I have to ask, "Where does it come from?"

She smiles, pats my wrist. "I do not know. It never told me, nor anyone else. It does not want to interfere any more than it has to." The old woman then whispers, "Reach into your memory…Tell me what you think it might be. Look into the mirror. Engage your imagination. I know you have one."

Her last words to me.

———

MAYBE WHEN I look into this mirror, I draw out a story, awakening not memory, not history, but fable.

I can't express this at all well.

Ship can never return home. The designers who originally equipped it knew that it was far too capable, far too dangerous: a true slaying seed.

Intelligent life in other systems, sensing the approach of such a danger, might mount defenses to protect their homes. But they would likely take no risks, expending the least amount of effort, and do all they could to simply destroy us.

Who else from outside would care for such a large, clumsy,

deadly contraption as Ship? Who else would care enough to challenge it, rather than to just safely destroy it and be done with us all?

Those who followed us from Earth would have built faster ships—or traveled using no ships at all. They would have spread out into a broad galaxy, perhaps going through their own hells of destruction and learning. And then, finding our Ship and perhaps others, vast capsulated samples of an ancestral world, they might have marveled, studied—valued. They might have felt sympathy for their primitive ancestors and wanted us to succeed, as a pilot flying a jet might feel for a lost family in a Conestoga wagon.

But they had no desire to watch Ship wreak ancient havoc. And so they appointed a chaperone, a guardian who chastised and protected at once, but who also conveyed a subliminal warning, a chance at reflection—a chance to discover our only place in space and time.

————

THE OLD WOMAN was my true mother. And my true partner. She made me. She saved me. After she was gone, I carried her to the forest, with Tsinoy's help, and gave her over to the monkeys, who took her where they took the last of the mummies, to a place we do not know and do not care to find.

Eventually, I tell the others. Nell and Tomchin do not judge. Tsinoy and Kim, to my surprise, prove the most reluctant to accept the old woman's story—my fable—or any part of what I think I saw.

Even when I remind them of the laser that saved my life. They have no answer for that.

This much seems clear. Ship has to earn the right to live. The only way to pass this test is to defeat Ship's original design.

Ship has to find a conscience, or the chaperone could still destroy it utterly.

———

CENTURIES HAVE PASSED since we left Earth. It's taken me this long to write about it. The books are almost full. This is the last of them.

We place the children in the old woman's capsule. Tsinoy is despondent. She misses them. We will assign her other work. The monkeys have gone into hiding, preparing for what comes next. There is still much for the rest of us to do.

We will not be allowed to grow old together.

PENANCE AND GUIDANCE

Nell has found us a star, within the degrees of freedom left as Ship coasts. Once, apparently, this sun was hidden by an arm of nebula, invisible to those who made our first desperate choice. Only in the last few months has it emerged.

Perhaps something knew all along.

The calculations seem to fit. In a hundred years, Ship will send fuel to the hulls. It will warm the engines, make a slow turn of a fraction of a degree, then cool again and sleep. We must conserve fuel in the sphere to power the shields, but even they will be weaker than they have been through our time of trial.

Our chosen is beautiful. A sun with at least twelve planets, two of them in a zone of habitability, and a decent halo of outer ice—something like the Oort cloud.

In two hundred years, after traversing a clear, calm void, almost empty of stardust, Ship will rise from cold slumber. Long before, Kim and Tsinoy and I will have purged the Klados of the dark pages of the Catalog. The hulls will finally join, and Ship will perform its last, century-long braking maneuver, sacrificing nearly all that remains of the moonlet; then it will take the long plunge into the inner system.

The infants will be awakened—raised, educated, and placed in charge. They will be the first new crew. Some of us will freeze down to become teachers. Perhaps one will be me, but that is no longer important or essential.

And in the end, once the final decision has been made—go or no go—the infants, now old, will pass away, as will those who raised and taught them, making room for Ship to grow a fresh crew and create landing vessels, seedships....

Oh, there will still be deception. The fresh crew will emerge as adults, will have memories of past training and lives. Our stories, our lives, will go on. I refuse to allow that love to die, just because it was never real.

The sphere is growing cold. Nell and I seek last warmth together.

I saw it again last night. Shining and lithe, like polished moonlight. Nell was beside me but saw nothing. I thought it knew me, acknowledged me, but I could have been dreaming. I'm half-dreaming now. I can barely write, and the pages of this eleventh book are almost full. There will be no others.

I see our world so clearly. Cloud modest
I feel the warmth
she's waiting
she smiles she's all I ever wanted
WE
ARE
HERE

END SHIP'S ARCHAEOLOGY REPORT

extras

meet the author

Astrid Anderson Bear

GREG BEAR is the author of more than thirty books of science fiction and fantasy, including *Blood Music, The Forge of God, Darwin's Radio,* and *Quantico.* He is married to Astrid Anderson Bear and is the father of Erik and Alexandra. Awarded two Hugos and five Nebulas for his fiction, one of only two authors to win a Nebula in every category, Bear has been called the "best working writer of hard science fiction" by *The Ultimate Encyclopedia of Science Fiction.* Bear has served on political and scientific action committees and has advised Microsoft Corporation; the U.S. Army; the CIA; Sandia National Laboratories; Callison Architecture, Inc.; Homeland Security; and other groups and agencies. Find out more about the author at www .gregbear.com.

introducing

If you enjoyed
HULL ZERO THREE,
look out for

LEVIATHAN WAKES

by James S.A. Corey

*Humanity has colonized the solar system—Mars, the Moon,
the Asteroid Belt, and beyond—but the stars are
still out of our reach.*

*Jim Holden is XO of an ice miner making runs from the
rings of Saturn to the mining stations of the Belt.
When he and his crew stumble upon a derelict ship,*
The Scopuli, *they find themselves in possession of a
secret they never wanted. A secret that someone is
willing to kill for—and kill on a scale unfathomable to
Jim and his crew. War is brewing in the system unless
he can find out who left the ship and why.*

extras

*Detective Miller is looking for a girl. One girl in a
system of billions, but her parents have money and money
talks. When the trail leads him to* The Scopuli *and
rebel sympathizer Holden, he realizes that this girl
may be the key to everything.*

*Holden and Miller must thread the needle between the
Earth government, the Outer Planet revolutionaries,
and secretive corporations — and the odds are against them.
But out in the Belt, the rules are different, and one
small ship can change the fate of the universe.*

Prologue: Julie

The *Scopuli* had been taken eight days ago, and Julie Mao was finally ready to be shot.

It had taken all eight days trapped in a storage locker for her to get to that point. For the first two she'd remained motionless, sure that the armored men who'd put her there had been serious. For the first hours, the ship she'd been taken aboard wasn't under thrust, so she floated in the locker, using gentle touches to keep herself from bumping into the walls or the atmosphere suit she shared the space with. When the ship began to move, thrust giving her weight, she'd stood silently until her legs cramped, then sat down slowly into a fetal position. She'd peed in her jumpsuit, not caring about the warm itchy wetness, or the smell, worrying only that she might slip and fall in the wet spot it left on the floor. She couldn't make noise. They'd shoot her.

On the third day, thirst had forced her into action. The noise of the ship was all around her. The faint subsonic rumble of the reactor and drive. The constant hiss and thud of hydraulics and steel bolts as the pressure doors between decks opened and closed. The clump of heavy boots walking on metal decking. She waited until all the noise she could hear sounded distant, then pulled the environment suit off its hooks and onto the locker floor. Listening for any approaching sound, she slowly disassembled the suit and took out the water supply. It was old and stale; the suit obviously hadn't been used or serviced in ages. But she hadn't had a sip in days, and the warm loamy water in the suit's reservoir bag was the best thing she had ever tasted. She had to work hard not to gulp it down and make herself vomit.

When the urge to urinate returned, she pulled the catheter bag out of the suit and relieved herself into it. She sat on the floor, now cushioned by the padded suit and almost comfortable, and wondered who her captors were—Coalition Navy, pirates, something worse. Sometimes she slept.

On day four, isolation, hunger, boredom, and the diminishing number of places to store her piss finally pushed her to make contact with them. She'd heard muffled cries of pain. Somewhere nearby, her shipmates were being beaten or tortured. If she got the attention of the kidnappers, maybe they would just take her to the others. That was okay. Beatings, she could handle. It seemed like a small price to pay if it meant seeing people again.

The locker sat beside the inner airlock door. During flight, that usually wasn't a high-traffic area, though she didn't know anything about the layout of this particular ship. She thought about what to say, how to present herself. When she finally heard someone moving toward her, she just tried to yell that she wanted out. The dry rasp that came out of her throat surprised her. She swallowed, working her tongue to try to create some saliva, and tried again. Another faint rattle in the throat.

The people were right outside her locker door. A voice was talking quietly. Julie had pulled back a fist to bang on the door when she heard what it was saying.

No. Please no. Please don't.

Dave. Her ship's mechanic. Dave, who collected clips from old cartoons and knew a million jokes, begging in a small broken voice.

No, please no, please don't, he said.

Hydraulics and locking bolts clicked as the inner airlock door opened. A meaty thud as something was thrown inside. Another click as the airlock closed. A hiss of evacuating air.

When the airlock cycle had finished, the people outside her door walked away. She didn't bang to get their attention.

They'd scrubbed the ship. Detainment by the inner planet navies was a bad scenario, but they'd all trained on how to deal with it. Sensitive OPA data was scrubbed and overwritten with innocuous-looking logs with false time stamps. Anything too sensitive to trust to a computer, the captain destroyed. When the attackers came aboard, they could play innocent.

It hadn't mattered.

There weren't the questions about cargo or permits. The invaders had come in like they owned the place, and Captain Darren had rolled over like a dog. Everyone else—Mike, Dave, Wan Li—they'd all just thrown up their hands and gone along quietly. The pirates or slavers or whatever they were had dragged them off the little transport ship that had been her home, and down a docking tube without even minimal environment suits. The tube's thin layer of Mylar was the only thing between them and hard nothing: hope it didn't rip; goodbye lungs if it did.

Julie had gone along too, but then the bastards had tried to lay their hands on her, strip her clothes off.

Five years of low-gravity jiu jitsu training and them in a confined space with no gravity. She'd done a lot of damage. She'd almost started to think she might win when from nowhere a gauntleted fist smashed into her face. Things got fuzzy after that. Then the locker, and *Shoot her if she makes a noise.* Four days of not making noise while they beat her friends down below and then threw one of them out an airlock.

After six days, everything went quiet.

Shifting between bouts of consciousness and fragmented dreams, she was only vaguely aware as the sounds of walking, talking, and pressure doors and the subsonic rumble of the reactor and the drive faded away a little at a time. When the drive stopped, so did gravity, and Julie woke from a dream of racing her old pinnace to find herself floating while her muscles screamed in protest and then slowly relaxed.

She pulled herself to the door and pressed her ear to the cold metal. Panic shot through her until she caught the quiet sound of the air recyclers. The ship still had power and air, but the drive wasn't on and no one was opening a door or walking or talking. Maybe it was a crew meeting. Or a party on another deck. Or everyone was in engineering, fixing a serious problem.

She spent a day listening and waiting.

By day seven, her last sip of water was gone. No one on the ship had moved within range of her hearing for twenty-four hours. She sucked on a plastic tab she'd ripped off the environment suit until she worked up some saliva; then she started yelling. She yelled herself hoarse.

No one came.

By day eight, she was ready to be shot. She'd been out of water for two days, and her waste bag had been full for four. She put her shoulders against the back wall of the locker and planted her hands against the side walls. Then she kicked out with both legs as hard as she could. The cramps that followed the first kick almost made her pass out. She screamed instead.

Stupid girl, she told herself. She was dehydrated. Eight days without activity was more than enough to start atrophy. At least she should have stretched out.

She massaged her stiff muscles until the knots were gone, then stretched, focusing her mind like she was back in dojo. When she was in control of her body, she kicked again. And again. And again, until light started to show through the edges of the locker. And again, until the door was so bent that the three hinges and the locking bolt were the only points of contact between it and the frame.

And one last time, so that it bent far enough that the bolt was no longer seated in the hasp and the door swung free.

Julie shot from the locker, hands half raised and ready to look either threatening or terrified, depending on which seemed more useful.

There was no one on the whole deck: the airlock, the suit storage room where she'd spent the last eight days, a half dozen other storage rooms. All empty. She plucked a magnetized pipe wrench of suitable size for skull cracking out of an EVA kit, then went down the crew ladder to the deck below.

And then the one below that, and then the one below that. Personnel cabins in crisp, almost military order. Commissary, where there were signs of a struggle. Medical bay, empty. Torpedo bay. No one. The comm station was unmanned, powered down, and locked. The few sensor logs that still streamed showed no sign of the *Scopuli*. A new dread knotted her gut. Deck after deck and room after room empty of life. Something had happened. A radiation leak. Poison in the air. Something that had forced an evacuation. She wondered if she'd be able to fly the ship by herself.

But if they'd evacuated, she'd have heard them going out the airlock, wouldn't she?

She reached the final deck hatch, the one that led into engineering, and stopped when the hatch didn't open automatically. A red light on the lock panel showed that the room had been sealed from the inside. She thought again about radiation and major failures. But if either of those was the case, why lock the door from the inside? And she had passed wall panel after wall panel. None of them had been flashing warnings of any kind. No, not radiation, something else.

There was more disruption here. Blood. Tools and containers in disarray. Whatever had happened, it had happened here. No, it had started here. And it had ended behind that locked door.

It took two hours with a torch and prying tools from the machine shop to cut through the hatch to engineering. With the hydraulics compromised, she had to crank it open by hand. A gust of warm wet air blew out, carrying a hospital scent without the antiseptic. A coppery, nauseating smell. The torture chamber, then. Her friends would be inside, beaten or cut to pieces. Julie hefted her wrench and prepared to bust open at least one head before they killed her. She floated down.

The engineering deck was huge, vaulted like a cathedral. The fusion reactor dominated the central space. Something was wrong with it. Where she expected to see readouts, shielding, and monitors, a layer of something like mud seemed to flow over the reactor core. Slowly, Julie floated toward it, one hand still on the ladder. The strange smell became overpowering.

The mud caked around the reactor had structure to it like nothing she'd seen before. Tubes ran through it like veins or airways. Parts of it pulsed. Not mud, then.

Flesh.

An outcropping of the thing shifted toward her. Compared to the whole, it seemed no larger than a toe, a little finger. It was Captain Darren's head.

"Help me," it said.

VISIT THE ORBIT BLOG AT

www.orbitbooks.net

FEATURING

BREAKING NEWS
FORTHCOMING RELEASES
LINKS TO AUTHOR SITES
EXCLUSIVE INTERVIEWS
EARLY EXTRACTS

AND COMMENTARY FROM OUR EDITORS

WITH REGULAR UPDATES FROM OUR TEAM,
ORBITBOOKS.NET IS YOUR SOURCE
FOR ALL THINGS ORBITAL.

WHILE YOU'RE THERE, JOIN OUR EMAIL LIST
TO RECEIVE INFORMATION ON SPECIAL OFFERS,
GIVEAWAYS, AND MORE.

imagine. explore. engage.